Artania II: The Kidnapped Smile

Artania II

The Kidnapped Smile

Laurie Woodward

Copyright (C) 2017 Laurie Woodward
Layout design and Copyright (C) 2019 by Next Chapter
Published 2019 by Peculiar Possum – A Next Chapter Imprint
Cover art by Bukovero
This book is a work of fiction. Names, characters, places, and incidents are the product of the author's imagination or are used fictitiously. Any resemblance to actual events, locales, or persons, living or dead, is purely coincidental.
All rights reserved. No part of this book may be reproduced or transmitted in any form or by any means, electronic or mechanical, including photocopying, recording, or by any information storage and retrieval system, without the author's permission.

To my mother, whose smile continues to warm my heart.

Chapter 1

"I'm perfectly fine. Now stop being so silly." Placing a painted hand on The Thinker's bronze arm, Mona Lisa patted it.

"But child. The attempts."

"Failed. And now you and Father have me tucked away in this fortress. Worry not." Without giving him a chance to argue more, Mona Lisa turned and glided down the stone steps of the castle.

Artania's leader leaned over the parapet of the castle gazing at the renaissance city below. Florence. Red tile roofs topped sunflower yellow or misty white walls. Crushed granite alleyways and cobblestone side streets zig-zagged from one end of the town to the other. The Arno River snaked through this muted palette as gently as dear Mona Lisa's smile.

Mona Lisa. Ever since the attempted kidnapping, she had stayed within these castle walls. Making the sweet child restless. Today was the first time he'd agreed to let her stroll along the river. Accompanied by soldiers in striped bloomers and metal helmets of course.

"Nicolo, you must be ever vigilant. You know what will happen if the Shadow Swine capture the Smiling One," he had ordered the guardsman earlier.

"Yes, as do all citizens, whether they be painting, sculpture or sketch," Nicolo said.

"Keep her close. Keep her safe."

"I do swear," the guardsman said, bowing with one hand across his chest.

Nicolo's presence should have calmed The Thinker's fears, but for some reason he still felt uneasy. All around, soldiers patrolled the parapet wall or stood guard behind the notched battlements in the rectangular towers.

The iron grating of the portcullis was down leaving only doors vulnerable. And after the last kidnapper had made his way inside, The Thinker had ordered them locked at all times. Even so he knew that in these terrible times anything could happen.

His bronze gaze rested on the river and the short docks built beside the walkway. The Smiling One emerged from the doorway below and gave him a short wave before turning toward the cobblestone path skirting the river. All was as it should be.

He thought.

He had just relaxed his shoulders when a flash caught his eye. *He shouldn't be there!*

A man dressed in rags leapt out of one of the rowboats tied to the dock and began running toward Mona Lisa. But with her back to him, she didn't notice.

"Lisa!" The Thinker cried.

When she turned, the snarling man grabbed her by the arm and began pulling her toward his boat.

"Let me go!" Mona Lisa screamed.

Soldiers appeared and rushed down the embankment, Guardsman Nicolo in the lead.

Mona Lisa strained against the beggar's grip. But it was no good. He was half a head taller and probably outweighed her by fifty pounds. He dragged her ever closer to the rowboat. A few more feet and they'd be on the river.

"No!" Mona Lisa cried, clutching her veil in a milk white grasp.

"Halt," Nicolo cried, booted feet flying toward the dock. "Halt, I say!" He sprung over the cobblestone path and drew his sword.

The ragged man dragged her closer to the water. The Smiling One's feet skidded over wood.

"Hurry," The Thinker whispered.

As soon as they reached the dock's edge, the beggar shoved Mona Lisa behind him. And turned.

With a snaggle-toothed grin, he bent forward and unleashed a tremendous kick. Crying out, the painted girl hurled upwards. She shot over pilings arcing toward the river below.

The Thinker's bronze heart froze. He gripped the coping stone tighter.

Mona Lisa splashed and disappeared beneath the murmuring waters.

All eyes turned toward the river. Every Artanian from castle keep to the guard tower and down the stony walls held a breath. Waiting in silence.

But the waters remained calm.

"Find her!" the bronze man cried.

With a desperate leap, Nicolo dove into the River Arno. The Thinker scanned east and west for a veiled head but only the guardsman surfaced.

Nicolo submerged again, his booted feet kicking deeper. Only to break the surface for quick gulp of air before diving down. Twice. Three times. Seven.

When the exhausted soldier floated up after the twenty-fifth descent, he turned to the gathered crowd with a sad shake of his head. "She is gone."

The Thinker fell back against the wall and sunk to the ground. "All is lost."

Chapter 2

Bartholomew Borax III woke with a start. Was that a girl screaming? He blinked and for a few terrifying moments thought it might be Mother.

Seeing things that weren't there.

Even though they were tucked deeply under the covers, Bartholomew's hands turned to ice. Opening and closing his stiff fingers, the twelve-year-old sat up and cocked an ear.

Quiet.

Then he remembered the joyful dream.

He folded back the covers and slipped into his monogrammed robe before padding over to and opening the wooden screens that separated his room into two sections. The other half of his bedroom suite had a fireplace painted so brilliantly white you'd think it had never been used. Ignoring both the cold hearth and the leather loveseat in front of it, he headed straight for his writing desk, yanked open the drawer, and felt around for the latch to his secret compartment. He pulled out five pencils and laid them in a neat row.

Closing his eyes, he started to recall the dream. But the images were already fading replaced by the memory of school the previous day. Eyes narrowed, he tried to return to a place where three generations painted side by side. He had just sketched an outline of Grandfather holding his brush aloft next to Father when the memories made him drop his pencil.

He couldn't create this morning.

Trudging into the adjoining bathroom he took a moment to glare at his reflection in the mirrored wall before he stepped into the glass-enclosed shower.

"Another F!" He turned the chrome shower handles on full blast and thrust his head under the spout. Trying to wash yesterday away.

"I see wealth and brains don't always go together." His algebra teacher, Ms. Buttsfert had smirked as she handed Bartholomew back his latest test. "Bring it back signed tomorrow," she ordered, her double chin waggling with each word.

He hated math. He hated numbers. You couldn't be friends with a number. You couldn't talk to them or learn about life from them. They just stood in neat little rows, like his mother, waiting for you to mess up so you'd have to wipe them away, make the paper all white and pretty, and start all over again.

When he'd opened his mouth to argue, Ms. Buttsfert gave him detention. Another thing to hide from Mother.

Bartholomew was good at forging signatures, but he couldn't hide these grades for much longer. Mother had warned if he wasn't Borax-excellent by the end of the month, it was homeschooling.

And he couldn't face that loneliness again. Most of his life he'd been trapped in an antiseptic mansion with servants and Mr. White, his uptight British tutor as his only company. He'd only had real friends for a year.

Finally, in sixth grade Mother had allowed him to go to school. Instead of clear plexiglass desks in a room for one, he'd entered a brightly colored classroom filled with a jumble of scratched furniture. There were real kids smiling and chattering away, not just the soap sculptures or sketches from his imagination.

That's when he befriended fellow artist, Alex.

From the moment he bumped into Alexander Devinci and caught glimpses of another world, he realized that something amazing was about to happen. He was on the cusp of adventures as compelling as any in his fantasy novels.

And would do just about anything to continue having them.

Chapter 3

Below the surface of an art-created world, the screams pierced the air. Howls echoed down the mountainous stalagmite, over the sulfuric River of Lies, and throughout the cavernous Subterranea. Every Shadow Swine throughout Lord Sickhert's domain froze, cringing at the sound.

"Noo! Stop! I can't take it anymore."

"Fool! You let them defeat you!"

"But they- Noo!"

"Shut-up, Captain!" the snaking voice hissed. "You deserve worse."

The hunchbacked creature jerked, straining against the manacles that chained him to the cubicle walls. There Lord Sickhert punished any who displeased him. Many a Shadow Swine had felt these burning waters over the millennia, but this was Captain Sludge's first time under the boiling steam.

He lurched toward the opening, but the chains recoiled like a bowstring. Twitching, Sludge tried to lean toward cooler air, but the guards shoved him back under the scalding spray and his spiked hair wilted in the steam.

When the handcuffs seared his slime-covered wrists, he writhed in pain. The boiling shower paused. Hot droplets dripped from the obsidian pipe above singeing his shoulders.

Sludge shuddered. His yellow eyes looked up imploringly at his leader. But he knew there'd be no mercy there.

I have failed. All because of those idiot boys. Those whose dreams I so easily twist. He started to roar his rage but then another blast from the shower above silenced all sound and thought. Except pain, anger, revenge.

His naked back started to blister, gelatinous hide cracking and peeling like layers of bark in a forest fire. Long sheets of charred skin slid down his soaked black slacks into the drain.

Captain Sludge looked down at his large feet. Each claw on his toes had gone from glorious point to short stub.

"They completed the first task. You weren't supposed to let that happen."

"I was tricked... The boy Deliverer..."

"I made you captain to avoid such stealth." Lord Sickhert narrowed his bone white eyes and pressed a crystalline button on the stalactite hanging down from the ceiling. Another scalding stream licked at Sludge's head.

"Ahh! Please! My Lord, no! I'll invade their dreams!"

"Fool! The Deliverers are too powerful now. Their Painted Knights never sleep." Sickhert reached up to push the button again.

"But I captured..."

Lord Sickhert stopped just before his ashy gray finger reached the stalactite. "Abducted? Who?"

"The Smiling One."

"Is this true?"

"Yes, Lord."

Sickhert nodded. His tall form stood as straight as a razor's edge as he turned to address the two hunch-backed guards on either side of the Correction Chamber. "Release him."

The henchmen unlocked the shackles on Sludge's wrists and the burned creature collapsed into a heap on the floor. But he knew Sickhert was watching. Looking for weakness. Waiting for him to make another mistake. The one error that would cost him his life. Sludge would not make that mistake. He crawled to Sickhert's feet.

"Thank you for sparing me, my Lord." He opened his mouth to release the honorific spittle.

"Save your platitudes. Night falls soon in the West. Ready yourself to invade."

I am spared! Sludge thought, yellow eyes brightening.

"I must consult The Lava Pool Gramarye," Muttering to himself, Sickhert kicked Sludge out of the way. He strode from the room, long dark cape scraping the torture chamber's floor like claws on skin.

Chapter 4

Alexander Devinci stood at his mother's bedside watching her sleep. Her dark curls framed her face like a halo. He thought about reaching out to touch them but didn't. She needed her rest. Even after a year, her heart was still weak, but the color was returning to her cheeks.

Searching her face for every nuance, Alex took one more mind photo before tiptoeing out of the bedroom. With his fluffy-eared Australian Shepherd, Rembrandt, trailing behind, he headed straight for his art center in the garage.

It wasn't as nice as the one back in Boulder, but Dad had managed to set up one corner with an easel, some crates full of palettes, and his paints. And if the side door was open, the light coming in was pretty cool.

He walked over to the wooden shelves on the wall and grabbed a piece of canvas before settling onto a paint splattered stool with Rembrandt at his feet.

"True art," he said, remembering what the Artanians had told him the year before.

Alex had always loved to create but didn't know that each painting had powers until sixth grade when he and Bartholomew had ventured into a magical world. There he discovered an amazing secret. All art was alive. Every time someone painted, sketched, or sculpted, a living creature was born in Artania.

But his and Bartholomew's art did more than just give birth to a new Artanian. Theirs was special, very special.

Their creations guarded sleeping people everywhere from an evil race of beings. These dream-invaders, the Shadow Swine, tried to turn humans away from creating. So, Alex was always careful to make every painting both strong and beautiful.

Alex closed his eyes, and saw Mom's face; that small nose, dark lashes and brilliant smile as white as moonlight. Her olive skin was flawless. Even after the heart attack not a single blemish in sight.

There were lines around her eyes. Calling them laugh lines, Dad said, "Those are from all the giggling Mom did when she finally got the baby she wanted."

"What baby Dad?" Alex would ask on cue.

"Why you, curly top," Dad always replied, tousling his hair.

As he dipped the paintbrush in the palette, Alex smiled at the memory. Slowly his hand moved over the page. The eyebrows. The nose. Oval face. The brush started to move faster. He outlined curls, soft lips, and joyful lines radiating from both eyes.

His hand flew over the page like a skater racing down El Viento Hill. He painted 180's, kickflips, an ollie or two. And it was done.

He paused. Almost there. After trimming a bit from the chin, he carefully filled in the background. Alex's dog blinked up at him with silver blue eyes.

"Hey Rembrandt," he said grinning at the black and grey striped face. "Whadya think, will Mom love it?"

"Love what kiddo?"

Alex started. Almost falling out of his chair, he glanced up. Dad stood there both hands in the pockets of his slacks.

"I'm painting Mom."

Charlie Devinci crossed the room and rested a hand on Alex's shoulder. He was silent for long moments then cleared his throat.

"That's amazing, Alex. It looks just like her. More, even."

"Thanks. When I'm done I'm gonna frame it and give it to her."

"Your right. She'll love it." Dad's voice cracked.

Alex looked up at his father. He'd changed this last year. There were dark circles under his eyes and his crooked mouth was pinched and drawn. He didn't look as strong as he used to before that terrible day. Going on runs wasn't such a priority any more. And was Alex wrong or had his hairline receded in the last couple of months?

"Mom's sleeping."

"I know. I checked on her as soon as I got in." Mr. Devinci rubbed Rembrandt's ears but didn't look at Alex.

"She looks better lately."

"That she does."

"Maybe soon she'll be her old self again, huh?"

"I certainly hope so."

Alex wondered if there was something Dad wasn't telling him. Had there been some new test the doctors had done? He didn't ask though. He'd rather think she was healing. Like magic. Like one of his creations in Artania. He imagined that creating true art would somehow fix her heart for good.

"Well, I'm going to attempt to fix dinner. How does spaghetti sound?"

"Umm... fine," Alex replied doubtfully.

"I know. I'm not the gourmet cook like Mom, but we can't eat take-out every night. Dr. Bock says that the perfect parent provides nutritious–"

"Need any help?" Alex cut Dad off before he could launch into a full-blown Dr. Bock lecture.

Alex's dad had two passions: numbers and quoting from the latest edition of *Dr. Bock's How to Be a Perfect Parent*. As a math professor at UCSB, he could work equations to his heart's content. But did he ever get enough of the book? Alex had heard enough Bockisms in his twelve years to write his own parent guide. Luckily though, Dad was easy to distract.

"Umm..." Dad tapped his chin. "I do have midterms to grade. And the equations... But no, your doing that sketch is all the help I need." He tousled Alex's hair and left the room.

Alex shook his curls back out. One of these days he was going to have to tell Dad that he was too old to get his hair ruffled.

Rembrandt nuzzled Alex's knee, but Alex was staring at his painting. It still needed something. The dog nosed Alex's leg again.

"Okay boy," Alex, bent down burying his face in soft fur. Then he felt cool metal against his chest and reached for the necklace inside his t-shirt.

When the Artanians gave him the ankh the year before, the goddess Isis explained how it was a symbol of everlasting life. Trying to remember her words, Alex hung it in on a corner of the canvas and traced the necklace's outline with one finger.

"We are part of the eternal life force when art is true," she had said.

Alex studied the necklace. To create the loop at the top of the "T" just right, he added the tiny links of the chain first. Then, careful not to change the lines on her neck, he painted the ankh. The gold draped towards the left and her heart.

Alex slipped the necklace back over his head, placed the brushes in a can of water, and stood back. The ankh hung gently on her long neck.

It was Mom and a little more. And she was surrounded by a glow. Odd. He hadn't remembered putting that in.

Of course, there are some things that happen when we create that we have no knowledge of. They just come. From the stars. Or the sky. Or sometimes from a dimension far away. Another world.

Chapter 5

Gwendolyn Obranovich glanced around the skate park. Where was everybody? They said they'd meet at three thirty. It had to be close to that now.

"Well I'm not waiting," she said.

Gwen hopped onto the sugar maple deck of her skateboard and kicked off to practice something she'd been working on lately; a stance with her right leg forward. She liked goofy foot because it gave her a different view of the hills and ramps and helped her to see all the angles and places she might trip. Picking up speed, she carved a long arc on the concrete course.

"Just a little faster. Bend and you'll have it," she told herself.

Gwen scraped both axles on the curb. Score!

A few kids stopped and nodded appreciatively. She rolled around the course one more time her arms raised in celebration before stopping to get a drink.

"Hey, saw the grind. Goofyfoot. Cool," Alex said as he walked up to her, skateboard tucked under one arm.

"Thanks." Trying to look humble, Gwen glanced down at her purple high tops marked up with peace signs and skater logos. Although they didn't look as cool now as when she'd drawn them, anything was better than brand new tennies.

"Seen Jose or Zach?" Alex asked.

"Naw. Reaching into her backpack on the grass she pulled out a water bottle and squirted a long stream into her mouth. She swished the water around her cheeks, letting the liquid cool that place in her cheek that kept getting scraped by her braces.

As if on cue. Jose Hamlin and Zachary Van Gromin strolled up. Gwen noticed how Jose's long ponytail blew behind him gently in the ocean breeze. No matter what was going on he always had this peaceful hippie air about him. She had no idea how. Maybe it was all that yoga he did.

He was a stark contrast to Zach. Mr. Entertainment was always going for the flashy stunts before looking around to see if anyone was checking him out. Zach was a little older than them, thirteen from being held back in first grade. Not that he'd talk about it. He'd tell you someone mixed up his records. He did know how to dress though. That dude wore the most awesome board shorts and Vans of anyone. But he could afford it. His dad was some Hollywood producer or something.

"Where you guys been?" Alex asked.

"Mr. Fashion here had to stop at home and change," Jose explained.

"Yeah, but you gotta admit," Zach said crossing his arms as if posing for a magazine. "I do look good."

All three kids groaned. Alex and Gwen exchanged a glance and rolled their eyes while Jose shrugged and pulled out a bamboo mat from his backpack. He unrolled it and placed it on the grass before doing his usual warm-up of lying on his stomach with his back arched high and neck stretched toward the sky in a yoga pose.

"Let's do it." Gwen grabbed her skateboard and headed back onto the course.

Alex and Zach quickly followed behind. Soon all four of them were laughing and challenging each other to more and more daring stunts. Alex practiced his ollies while Jose worked on

360's. Zach, of course, went for the flash, doing jumps and grinds whenever he thought people were watching.

That night Gwen smiled at the memory as she readied herself for bed. She'd been in her element, dancing to the skate park song, sometimes getting just enough air to be able to see over the railing. Then the blue Pacific and the sky had melded with her body and they all became one.

Cool.

Gwen undid her tight red pigtails and brushed her hair just enough to satisfy Dad before threading the dental floss in and out of her braces. Her orthodontist tried to make braces fun. He let kids pick out all kinds of colors and change them every time they went in. This month in honor of Halloween she'd chose orange and black, so her smile'd look like a jack-o-lantern's.

"Gwen?" a deep voice called from the other side of the bathroom door.

"Yeah?" she mumbled through a mouthful of toothpaste.

"T-minus seven minutes."

"'kay!"

Gwen's dad was a bit of a freak about time. He timed everything; from her morning jog on the treadmill in the exercise room to how long it took her to brush her teeth. She guessed it was because he had to rush around so much, managing all those gyms and everything. Now he owned four *California Dreamin'* gyms with the slogan, "*Where the dreams of that California body come true.*" Gwen's Mom had helped come up with the phrase back when she and Dad were still married; before she took off to Europe to go back to modeling.

But it's all right. Gwen told herself. *Even if Mom hasn't called since last year, I do have Dad. Sort of. When he isn't working.*

Gwen wiped the toothpaste off her mouth, splashed a little water on her freckled face, and dashed down the hall to Dad's office.

"You beat your record by one minute twenty seconds," he said looking up from his cell phone.

Gwen beamed. She jogged in place a few times, her big white feet slapping against the marble floor.

"Okay, ready?" she called out picking up the pace.

"You know it." Dad stood up and nodded.

"Arms strong?"

Dad flexed his biceps.

"Legs strong?"

"I don't know." Mr. Obranovich did a few squats then said with a grin, "I only bench pressed 220 today."

"Oh Dad!" Gwen giggled.

"On your mark"

She crouched down like a runner getting ready for a race.

"Get set? Go!"

Gwen ran full speed toward the bear-like body of her father. When she reached him, he grabbed her under the arms and lifted her up over his head. He started to spin like a carousel; faster and faster while Gwen shrieked with laughter.

"Heads up!" Dad cried as he tossed her into the air.

Gwen slapped the ceiling in high five celebration and fell into his comforting strong arms.

"Time for bed, Tinker Bell."

"Night Dad." She nuzzled against his broad neck and gave him a kiss on the cheek.

As she snuggled under the surfboard-printed sheets, Gwen felt perfectly safe.

* * *

The girl's breathing was soft and even as the creature snaked its way through the window. His yellow eyes scanned the floor and walls. With just a few posters of skateboarders and no art anywhere she'd be perfect for dream draining.

"No Knights in sight. Come." the slime-covered invader hissed.

Two more slimy wisps twisted their way in to rest silently on the hardwood floor. Each took shape revealing hunched backs, piggish nostrils, and jagged teeth. Pairs of bony hands crowned with claw-like nails opened and closed in bone crunching pops.

The two Shadow Swine bowed before their leader who pointed a talon toward the sleeping child.

"Ahh the sweet smell of the innocent," Captain Sludge took a deep breath through rattling nostrils. "Her dreams will be easy to turn."

His two minions nodded.

"I will invade first. When the connection is complete, you two follow. This one must be turned. She is a friend of the Deliverers."

"Yes sir," Stench and Slurry grunted in unison.

Sludge glared at them, doubting their abilities. As captain of Subterranea, he knew that intelligence was a rare gift among Shadow Swine. His kind was good at following orders, but most lacked his unique ability to dream drain. And only a handful could come up with the truly terrifying nightmares that were his specialty.

Captain Sludge opened his cavernous mouth to release what looked like a swarm of locusts. Then he let out a gurgling breath and they buzzed straight for Gwen's left ear. His dream connection strengthened, causing the child to stir.

"No... no..." she mumbled.

"I see her dream. Now minions."

Two more slimy mouths opened as dual strips of dark mist joined Sludge's cloud entering Gwen's earhole.

Sludge ran a hand over his bony forehead spreading slime over the short spikes of hair atop his head. "Yes... An easy one to twist."

Inside Gwen's dream he saw a happy family picnicking on the beach. It was a sunny day; with water a sickeningly bright blue, and they were laughing. Well, he'd change that. Sludge raised his arms and the dream sky grew dark.

The mother started walking toward the water. But now it wasn't just a sea. Sludge had made it a swirling bay filled with paint-can shaped sharks that thrashed and circled the mother.

"Rochelle!" the father cried leaping into the choppy waves. He waded out several yards reaching out those ridiculously muscular arms to save her.

"Shrink...shrink," Sludge chanted.

The father's arms immediately withered as a shark's fin sliced through the water toward him.

"Dad, no!" the dream Gwen screamed.

"It is the art," Sludge said, making his voice blare from the sky. "You must get rid of it." With a snap of his fingers, a lightning bolt cracked in the nightmare sky.

The child started throwing the paintbrushes that now littered the shore into the sea.

Captain Sludge chuckled. Then he felt a tap on his real shoulder. He almost turned to brush away one of his dumb minions when Stench's cry stopped him.

"Turn away from that child or be destroyed," a deep voice ordered.

"Knight of Painted Light!" Slurry shrieked.

Sludge blinked to remove his gaze from the dream and see the child's room. There at the window stood a painting of an African warrior wielding a glowing sword.

"One against three! Ha!" Sludge pulled his own blade out from under his cloak.

Light saber raised, the Knight lunged. He swung twice, and Stench fell with a thud. As the Shadow Swine rolled over, he clamped his mouth shut, severing his dream connection. Now only two wisps of smoke remained.

Captain Sludge quickly added more terror to Gwen's dream. The paint can-sharks turned to circle the father as dozens more snapped at Gwen's screaming mother.

The girl whimpered in her sleep.

Feeding on the fear, the brazened Sludge returned his focus to the Knight. Eyes narrowing, he raised his razor-sharp sword to draw a figure eight in air. When the Knight's eyes locked on the blade, Sludge struck. The clank of metal meeting metal filled his bat-like ears.

Without hesitation, the captain swung again forcing the painted one up against the wall. When the knight jabbed, Sludge sidestepped it with an easy guffaw.

He signaled Stench to his side while ordering Slurry to stay put and continue dream draining. Stench pulled a dagger from the top of his combat boot and they both bore down on the painted soldier.

The Knight swung wildly; his saber met only air.

Sludge took a step back. He wasn't sure, but he thought he saw fear in those eyes. That was odd. Even when the odds were stacked against them, these creations were usually brave to a fault.

Then he noticed that its legs were missing.

The Deliverer had never finished this painting! Captain Sludge tried to hide the smirk that threatened to split his slimy face. His enemy would never know what hit him.

"Prepare for your doom, Cre-a-tion." Sludge sneered. With a single slice, he drew a long scrape across the Knight's stomach.

"Nooo!" The warrior clutched his side as his light saber darkened. Then the spark in his eyes dimmed. He began to fade and shrink from view.

When he disappeared with a slight pop, Sludge held up a triumphant sword.

His underlings nodded appreciatively, their hunched backs heaving up and down like a mudslide destroying a mountain of homes.

"Goo' job Captain," the taller Slurry said.

"I know." He puffed out his barrel-shaped chest.

He glanced back into Gwen's dream. Only a few paintbrushes remained on the beach. The sobbing child kept picking them up and tossing them out to sea. To Sludge, her tear-stained cheeks were a wondrous sight.

"Lord Sickhert will be most pleased," he said rubbing his claw-tipped hands together.

As dream Gwen threw the last brush into the waves, every shark disappeared, and her parents embraced her on shore.

"Keep art away." Sludge's grisly voice reminded her as the smoky wisps exited her ear. "Only then will your family be safe."

The child rolled over and her breathing returned to normal.

Sludge's work was done.

Chapter 6

After school, Bartholomew was horrified to see the meanest kids in school, Conrad Fugate and Tybold Kilgore, in detention. Not that he was surprised. Con and Ty were always in trouble for cussing, bullying or torturing any kid that was little or weak. Bartholomew had had his own run-ins with them so tried not to look their way as he signed in.

Ms. Buttsfert jowls wobbled as she barked, "You're one minute late."

"I-uh…"

"You think because you're rich, the rules don't apply to you?" She didn't wait for an answer to add, "Double detention."

"What? But–"

Ms. Buttsfert's glare cut his words short. The math teacher adjusted the frizzy hair piled high atop her head. But it did about as much good as trying to straighten the Leaning Tower of Pisa. And it only drew more attention to one of the spandex dresses she always wore. They were too tight for a woman her size and the bright belt only made her weight more noticeable.

Bartholomew mumbled an apology as a few kids in the back of the room snickered. Bartholomew tried not to look at them as he made his way to an empty seat. But he couldn't help it. No way! Not Jose and Zach! He thought they were starting to like him. The red started to creep up in his cheeks.

While the grumbling Ms. Buttsfert wrote problems for the detention students to solve, Bartholomew noticed Ty raised his eyebrows knowingly.

Ty looked like a strange breed of chicken as he bobbed his purple fringed mop of hair at Con. He pointed at her book, as this thick-necked cohort gave him a thumbs-up making Bartholomew wonder what wicked plan they were hatching now.

Until he saw the book's cover. *Math Assessments Answer Key.* And suddenly realized why the bullies were smiling.

Because here was the solution to all his problems.

Yep, with that book he could handle it all. Boring math. The hours with Mr. White filing his fingernails every other minute. Even Mother crying filth each time she saw the slightest speck would be okay.

Because he'd get to stay in school.

In that moment, he was an uncaged sparrow.

But one question remained. How the bleach bottle was he going to get that answer key away from Ms. Buttsfert?

Chapter 7

Wanting to get an early start on the painting while the folks were still asleep, Alex scampered out to the garage, Rembrandt padding behind. He pulled the sheet off the easel and gasped.

"What the frick?" he muttered.

His knight had a gaping hole in its stomach and the painted light saber was gone. Both hands were empty, and they'd changed, clenched fists raised in anger now replacing the heroic pose Alex had painted the day before. Even the noble African face was different. Today it was all twisted as if in agony.

"Did someone repaint it?" Alex asked Rembrandt.

The dog flipped up one ear and then the other as if to say, "Beats me." Hands on hips, Alex walked around examining all his supplies.

The brushes lay on the counter right where he'd left them the night before. Every paint bottle was shut tight. Reaching out a shaking hand, Alex touched the canvas. It was nearly dry. If anyone had painted over his work, it would still be wet.

"Could Shadow Swine have done this?" Alex whispered, thinking back to the god Apollo's explanation of how the Shadow Swine came to be.

"Long ago one man destroyed art and unleashed dark forces that still lie in wait. Kandart gave birth to an evil race of creatures." Apollo had said with a shudder. *"The Shadow Swine who live below*

Artania are bent on destroying us. Whenever humans curse art or spoil its beauty, their army gains power and one of us dies."

Alex shook his head remembering the prophecy on the Soothsayer Stone.

The Shadow Swine will make you live in fear.
Bringing death to those you hold dear.

Alex stared at that tormented face that had been so noble the day before. *Was he dead?* He peered closer at the painting and shook his head.

"Not if I have anything to do with it! Come on Rembrandt, let's fix this warrior."

With a quick tail wag Rembrandt pranced over to the cabinet and snatched a few brushes up in his muzzle. When he trotted back and dropped them at his feet, Alex patted his head and set to mixing colors.

Dipping a brush in light sable, Alex dabbed at the painting like a nurse swabbing a feverish patient's face. He filled in the stomach's gaping hole, softened the anguished lines on the ebony face, and loosened the clenched fists. Then he stood back to examine his progress.

"Better. But I want to make sure no Shadow Swine can defeat him."

He enlarged arm and leg muscles and then added a shield in one corner; a golden shield that would deflect every blow those monsters could throw.

Alex imagined the strength of a million suns as he repainted the light saber with Transparent Yellow and Titanium White. This sword would be greater than before. This would glow with the power of creation.

Hours later, just as father was rising, Alex stood back to admire the painting.

He is Zulu warrior and Egyptian god. He is Roman gladiator and American boxer. He is me and Bartholomew. He is art. He will battle the Shadow Swine, and this time he will win."

Atop an Artanian castle, the Thinker nodded.

Chapter 8

"I can't take it anymore," Bartholomew said to Alex as they shuffled out the classroom door "First school, then hours of tutoring with Mr. White. Next dinner, where Mother frets about every crumb and germ."

"I know dude, met her."

"There she reminds me of how Father drowned in a mud puddle before I was born making me feel even worse. So, to make her happy, I take yet another bath, and then when I'm completely exhausted, I get to do my homework."

"Man, that's messed up." Alex shook his head, sun-bleached hair reminding Bartholomew of all the hours at the beach he never got to be part of.

He'd barely set foot on the pier since moving to Santa Barbara the year before. Too many germs for Mother. His life was one horrible division problem with repeating decimals of misery.

"You know if I fail, it's homeschooling again," Bartholomew pulled the hand sanitizer out of his pocket and started it in. He kept seeing that book with the answer key. If only he could get his hands on it.

"That'd suck!"

"I know. I should just cheat," he mumbled.

"What? Are you crazy? Do you know what would happen if you were caught?"

"About the same thing as if I fail math."

"You know; my dad is a math professor. He could help you."

"No one can. I just don't get numbers. I have to cheat. It's the only way."

Just then Bartholomew noticed two shadows out of the corner of his eye; Ty and Conrad circling them.

"What do you jerks want?" Alex said turning to face them.

"You don't own the school, so shut-up." Ty stood up taller, his purple mohawk towering over them.

"That may be so, but this is a private conversation," Alex replied.

"What if I want to join?" Ty challenged, puffing up his chest.

"Then-" Alex put his hands on his hips. "I'd say no."

"And I'd just have to tell Ms. Buttsfert about your cheating plan, wouldn't I?"

Bartholomew gulped. "I don't know what you're talking about."

"Lies. Heard you." Con said with his usual monosyllables.

"We were just talking," he winced. *That was so loud.*

"But you're right." Ty's rat like eyes narrowed into specks. "We should. And then Donkey farts would back off.

"But we don't have the book," Bartholomew blurted out.

"Bartholomew. Why are you even talking to these guys?" Alex's voice grew louder.

Bartholomew knew he should stop right there and then. Say no. Tell those two to go away. They were trouble. Big trouble.

"I…" Bartholomew glanced at Ty whose constant sneer reminded him of a Shadow Swine he'd met in Artania. Ty couldn't be trusted. Still he might be a good partner for the plan. He swallowed hard.

"We'd need to find a way in…" Bartholomew began.

Alex gaped at him unbelieving. "No friggin way,"

"I have to. Don't you see?" He looked away.

"No, you don't. My dad can help you. Come on Bartholomew, let's go."

"Oh, I think he wants to stay," Ty said, his voice like fake silk. "You can leave. Wuss."

Opening and closing his mouth, Alex raised his palms.

Bartholomew would always regret what he did next. How he failed to defend his friend. How instead of telling Ty to shut up, that Alex was the farthest from a Wuss you could be, he'd turned away and immediately began to plan how to steal the answer book. How after long moments, Alex stomped down the hall, angry feet echoing in Bartholomew's ears.

Chapter 9

A light breeze blew back Alex's hair as he and Gwen skated way through the streets of Santa Barbara. But it did little to cool his fears. Mom still sick. Bartholomew ready to make a huge mistake. And what about Artania? That endangered world could call upon him any time.

Then he noticed Gwen popping her board up along a curb for a grind and almost smiled. Until he saw the long cracks breaking the curb into earthquaky bits. Jagged edges that could snag her wheels tripping her into a scraped and bleeding heap.

"Watch out!" he called.

Skidding to a halt, Gwen flipped her board into her hands. "What?"

He pointed at the crack.

She gave him a long look. "Dude, chill. I got it."

"But-"

"Been grinding for a year. Anyhow, don't we have enough to do without you getting all Dad on me?"

"I know. It's just–just–everything."

"Worries. I get it. Hey, how about you show me your kick flip?"

Shrugging, Alex kicked off toward a smooth place in the sidewalk that was perfect for the move. He tried one. Board flew. Tried again. Went down.

Gwen held out a hand to help him up. "See, falling's part of it. Now, put your foot closer to the bolts."

He fell two more times.

Gwen shook her head. "Further up."

Yes!" he cried when he finally got enough air to spin the skateboard and land square on the deck. Bringing a fist down in a victory pump, he curled a goofy lip at Gwen before heading down the street. "Come on. It's around the corner."

A few minutes later they were skidding sideways to halt in front of a wrought iron gate. Immediately Alex's smile faded, replaced by a determined scowl.

The week before, he'd been pretty ticked about Bartholomew taking Ty's side. Wanted to hit that stupid B-3 up side the head. But after he'd had a chance to cool off and started to imagine what might happen, he realized that Bartholomew could get suspended, fail math, or end up full on home-schooled again. Then they'd never get to hang out. So, Alex tried to talk him out of it. Whenever he approached Bartholomew in the halls, he'd start to argue. No dice. The Richie insisted that nothing was going on.

Alex knew better. Zach had overheard B-3 plotting with those two criminals the week before. According to him, the three were planning to steal Ms. Buttsfert's book on Wednesday. Alex needed stop his friend before then.

Glancing at the huge mansion, Gwen whistled long and low. "My dad does alright with his gyms but Dude this place is huge."

"I guess B-3's family is pretty rich," Alex said approaching one of the stone pillars at the bottom of the long flagstone driveway. "Some huge cleaning empire or something." He stepped up to the intercom box and pushed the button.

A voice crackled from the speaker. "Yes? Whom may I say is calling?"

"It's Alex and Gwen from school."

"One moment please."

While he waited for what felt like forever, Alex rolled his board back and forth with one toe. Sighing, Gwen paced back and forth, did a few toe touches, and shuffled her feet on the stones.

Finally, the droning voice returned. "You may enter. But there will be no running, jumping, shouting, or horseplay on the premises."

"You mean no fun," Gwen said under her breath to a nodding Alex.

"Got it," Alex said into the speaker.

When the large gates swept open like great brooms polishing the drive, Alex gave Gwen some quick advice. "Be careful. Mrs. Borax is a clean freak. Make sure your shoes are clean before you go inside."

Inspecting the soles of her high tops, Gwen saluted before tucking her skateboard next to his just inside the gate.

Alex walked a few feet up the long driveway and pointed. "Check it out. The plants are all plastic."

"No way," Gwen argued.

"Way," Alex replied. "Feel one."

Bending down, Gwen rubbed a leaf between two fingers. Then, as if non-believing she felt two more. She shook her head and gaped at the acres of plastic.

"I told you the mom was neat freak," Alex said.

"But we need plants. They clean the air."

Alex couldn't argue that one. Shrugging, he trudged up the long drive toward the mansion at the top of the hill. When they reached the high arched doorways at the entrance he scrutinized their shoes before looking for the doorbell.

"This is new," he said staring at the brass rod hanging from a ball-shaped apparatus. Alex gave the pull a quick yank and a funeral dirge gong toned. At the same time liquid coated his hand. "Yuck!" He jerked his hand away, flicking off the clear gel.

"Hand sanitizer? You weren't kidding when you said neat freak," Gwen said wiping her feet on the mat again. Not that she really needed to. There were seven doormats outside and they'd wiped their feet on every one.

The giant door opened to reveal a butler dressed in a black suit and Alex found himself shrinking back from the white-gloved hands. Behind the servant glared the thin Mrs. Borax, her platinum blonde hair pulled in such a tight bun that the blue veins bulged on her forehead.

"Welcome children," she said in an ice-cold voice.

"Thank you, Ma'am," Alex said feeling about as welcome as a mosquito on someone's arm.

"Bartholomew is upstairs studying with his tutor. But I have given permission for him to break for this…" She cleared her throat as if a bug were stuck in it. "…visit." Mrs. Borax turned to the butler. "Cecil, you may lead these, uhh… children, up to the playroom." She exited without another word.

Alex couldn't help but take a moment to marvel at this palace. Although he had a job to do, the wide staircase lit by a sparkling chandelier looked like something out of a fairytale. Hallways of pale marble tiles led to untold rooms he'd never set foot in. The glass tables arranged at even intervals down the halls were bare except for silver bells in the center of shining trays.

Alex knew from prior experience what those silver bells were for. If anyone tracked dirt inside, they'd ring, and an army of maids would descend on them with mops, sponges, and disinfectant wipes.

Alex gripped the wooden banister for a brief second before he and Gwen followed the butler up the stairs to greet a red-faced Bartholomew and his tutor, the strict Mr. White.

The man in the vanilla-colored suit was a real jerk who seemed to totally enjoy embarrassing B-3. For the past year and a half, he'd been poor Bartholomew's shadow waiting on the sidelines towel draped over one arm every time they had P.E.

Then he'd lead Bartholomew to the stretch limousine parked in the lot. And why a limo? It was so his buddy could take a bath in the tub they'd installed in the back.

Talk about public humiliation.

"Hi guys," Bartholomew said waving weakly as if a strong gesture would get him slapped.

They both mumbled hello and there was a long awkward pause. Surprisingly it was Mr. White's clipped British accent that broke it.

"Bartholomew," he said looking at his watch. "It is now 1:42. You have exactly one hour of rest before we are back at it. I shall expect you in your seat by then."

"Yes sir. Thank you, Mr. White."

The tutor headed for the stairs but then stopped after three steps. Alex held his breath afraid he'd turn and tell them to leave. But Mr. White didn't say a thing. Instead he pulled a fingernail file out and began shaping his nails. After a few moments, he compared hands, and seeming satisfied, marched downstairs.

Now, Bartholomew beckoned Alex and Gwen toward the playroom. Alex wondered why the Boraxes even called it that. There wasn't a single toy in sight. Only a few clear plexiglass desks, a couch next to a big bookcase, and a poster that said, "Cleanliness is Next to Godliness."

Bartholomew closed the door, and Alex heaved a sigh of relief before settling onto the opposite end of the pale leather couch from Gwen.

"Dude, your family is a real trip," she said shaking her head so hard her pigtails hit her cheeks.

"I do apologize for any inconvenience. I was not aware–"

"It's all right B-3," Alex said before quickly adding, "Anyhow, how're ya doing?"

"I am well, thank you." Bartholomew opened his mouth as if to say something more but then clamped it shut again. Alex wondered if he was about to apologize.

"And math?" Alex asked.

Bartholomew shrugged and started to adjust his grey tie. It looked awfully tight and uncomfortable.

Raising his eyebrows Alex exchanged a glance with Gwen before trying a new tack. "Are we still buds?"

"Of course," Bartholomew replied too quickly.

"Then I think you know why we're here."

"Yeah, Dude. We heard what you're up to and it's not cool," Gwen added.

"I do not know what you're talking about," Bartholomew said.

"Bull." Alex crossed his arms. "Zach heard you plotting with those felons. It's all over school."

"Your stealing plan is totally in the gossip mill," Gwen added. "Everyone knows."

"Gossip is often untrue."

"Come on Bartholomew. We know," Alex tried again, louder this time. "And you will get caught. Then what?"

"I was just pretending, trying to keep Ty from bullying me," Bartholomew argued. "You are aware of his behavior. If you don't act like you are going along with him, he makes your life miserable." Bartholomew walked over to one of the clear plastic desks and squirted a dollop of hand sanitizer from the bottle on top into the palm of his hand. Keeping his back turned, he rubbed it in.

Alex narrowed his eyes wondering if B-3 might really be telling the truth. That'd be a relief. Then they could return to their normal routine of Alex painting every morning while Bartholomew sculpted in that secret studio underground. The two of them would protect people's dreams and strengthen Artania.

But Alex had only to glance at his fellow Deliverer to know the truth. Bartholomew's sanitizer rubbing hands told all.

"I don't believe you," Alex said.

"But…it's true."

"And my Dad is a skinny wimp," Gwen said with a sneer. "Not."

Marching across the room, Alex yanked his friend around and pointed at his nervous hands.

"No...I...uh..." A stuttering Bartholomew began.

"Liar," Alex accused.

"No, you're the liar. You and Gwen are making this up," he stammered still rubbing hand sanitizer in.

"Unbelievable. After everything we've been through?"

Gwen leapt between them and held up her hands as if ready to break up a fight.

Shaking his head, Alex took a step back and stared into Bartholomew's blinking eyes. Long moments passed waiting for the Richie to admit the truth. Bartholomew took several quivering breaths but said nothing.

Alex sighed. "Don't you care about *them* at least?" he asked trying to refer to the Artanians without rousing Gwen's suspicions.

Bartholomew kept his obstinate mouth shut.

"Let's go. This is a waste of time," Gwen said.

Alex gave Bartholomew one more imploring look before marching toward the door. Yanking on the handle, he stopped mid-swing to let Gwen go ahead. "Fine!" he called over his shoulder. "But from now on, you're on your own."

Without bothering to turn around, he slammed the door.

Chapter 10

Sharp blades glistened in the sun reflecting triangular lights onto the river. But there was no sign of the Smiling One.

She had completely disappeared.

The Thinker shivered as he made his way down the stone steps. Knowing the peril both she and this painted land faced. Artania's leader looked into his bronze palm waiting for images to shine some light.

But only questions remained.

Later, in the dungeon, a bearded man in hose and soft leather shoes joined the sculpted Thinker. Both stood just outside the iron bars of the dank cell watching Nicolo interrogate the beggar. The Thinker hated seeing one of his people, however wrong he might have acted, being subjected to hours of questioning inside that chamber of horrors.

"For the twentieth time, where is she?" Nicolo demanded from inside the cell.

"On a simple pilgrimage," the beggar replied, a half-smile on his grimy face.

"That is no answer," Nicolo said stepping closer. "Tell me, where is she and who sent you?"

"Do you think I'm a fool?" the man spat. "As a beggar, I learned long ago when to keep quiet. You slave masters will know nothing until it's too late." He glared at Nicolo and wrapped his tattered rags tighter around his head.

"Was it Shadow Swine?" Nicolo asked.

The beggar said nothing. But his eyes betrayed him. He glanced down at the dirt floor as if looking for help from the enemy underground.

"Look and see what happens to people who refuse to answer." Nicolo waved a hand up at one of the room's torture devices.

"But I was only seeking renewal in her smile. Is it my fault she fell in the river?"

"Perhaps the rope will twist the truth from you," the bearded man next to The Thinker warned.

"Leonardo!" The Thinker scolded. "We are Artanians. This is not our way."

"But Leader, she is my daughter. She could become..." his voice trailed off.

The Thinker whispered into his friend's ear. "I understand, Leonardo. But we cannot become Shadow because we fight it." To Nicolo he said, "Continue as an *Artanian* should and report to me later."

Deciding to get Leonardo away from the prisoner before there was trouble, the bronze statue hastened down the hall, waving for him to follow.

The chalk-sketched man padded down the dark corridor glancing back at the cell as he walked.

"He is just like the others," The Thinker said when they were out of the beggar's earshot.

"I don't understand. Why would an Artanian betray us? Without my daughter, our land will turn to white. All will be destroyed."

"Our enemy grows stronger each day. They find ways to turn our kind away. Trickery and lies."

"But the humans. Are they not creating?" Leonardo asked.

"I have not checked for some weeks. Perhaps something is keeping them from paint or clay."

"You know what will happen if we don't rescue her…" Leonardo clutched his long gray beard with an intense stare that moved The Thinker. This man loved his daughter so much.

"Yes," The Thinker said, not adding that she would become a mindless slave. "But remember, hope lies in the hands of twins."

"Yes, yes. Still something is wrong. Don't you feel it?"

The Thinker tapped his forehead with his bronze fist. "Events will unfold when they are meant to," he said raising his head. "Our denial or refusal will not change what is written on the Soothsayer Stone."

"I pray that you are right," Leonardo said, "*and* that young Alex and Bartholomew can reverse the evils that surround us."

Chapter 11

Bartholomew stared at the room number and gulped. *Alex was right. This is crazy.*

"The coast is clear. Come on," Ty whispered.

"I don't think this is a good idea after all." Bartholomew shook his head and rubbed some hand sanitizer in.

"Move. Now."

"Why not just photograph the answers while we're here?"

"Because butt-breath, we don't have time. We need to get in, grab, and get out."

"I can't."

"Oh yes you can. No wussing out now."

"I know but…"

"Either come right now or I knock you flat on your butt and then tell the cops that you were trying to break into a classroom."

Bartholomew took one look at the weasely face and knew he meant it. What a miserable week. Mother was on one of her cleaning rampages. Alex still wasn't speaking to him, and Gwen gave him dirty looks every time he walked by.

And he hadn't been able to sculpt even once.

Swallowing hard, Bartholomew checked the hallway one last time and then darted behind Ty into the classroom. Crouching down as he crept over to the bookshelf.

Bartholomew ran one finger over the titles. *Saving Time for Teachers. Math Fun. California Standards.*

"I don't see it."

"It better be here," Ty said. "Or–"

A knock at the door made them both freeze. Ty yanked Bartholomew under the teacher's desk and clamped a hand over his mouth.

"Yoo-hoo! Doris? Are you in there?" Mrs. Fuller, the English teacher, called as she stuck her head the doorway.

Neither boy spoke. Not that Bartholomew had any choice. The bigger boy's hand was pressed so tight over his mouth that he couldn't breathe much less speak.

"Want to get Chinese, Doris?" To Bartholomew the teacher's voice sounded like a megaphone announcing that the cops had the place surrounded so come out with their hands up.

Ty squeezed tighter. Struggling to breathe, Bartholomew pulled on his arm.

The seconds ticked by. Ty ventured a peek around the desk and released Bartholomew who collapsed onto his knees. Gasping, he rubbed his cheeks where Ty's fingers had left deep imprints.

Bartholomew wheezed. "That was too close. Can we go?"

"Hell no." Ty lifted a fist to Bartholomew's face. "We came for a book. We're getting it."

"O-kay," Bartholomew squeaked. Between a bloodied face and getting caught, one at least left his nose intact. He began a frantic search.

But it wasn't on the shelf.

"Find it, Wuss. Now."

When had Ms. Buttsfert had that book? Tapping his forehead, Bartholomew tried to recall seeing it. The clock ticked overhead. Ty glared. Bartholomew's mind was a blank. Ty's fingers aimed at his throat. Ready to clinch down in a chokehold.

Suddenly Bartholomew remembered the teacher reading off answers at the podium. Jerking away from that outstretched hand, he dashed up there.

"Got it," he said grabbing the book. He peered out the window to make sure the coast was clear before heading for the door. But as soon as he put a hand on doorknob, clicking footsteps approached.

"Hell," Ty said.

Eyes wide in fear, Bartholomew dropped down to his belly. As if lying flat would hide him. Still there was small comfort in imagining his white suit blending in with the floor tiles.

The footsteps grew louder. Bartholomew was sure it wasn't just a teacher outside. It was the SWAT team in full riot gear.

"What now?" he whispered.

Instead of replying, Ty shrugged nonchalantly. Bartholomew guessed for someone like Ty who'd been suspended more times than all the other kids in junior high combined, getting caught in a teacher's class was no big deal. Then it occurred to him that if breaking and entering was no big deal to the purple-mopped bully, he might be capable of all kinds of scary things. The possibilities made him shudder.

Click, clip. CLICK, CLIP.

Bartholomew buried his face in his hands and waited for the inevitable. Suspension. No expulsion. Then prison.

Yep. He was going to prison. Or what did they call it? Juvenile Hall? This was it. No more sculpting. No more time with Alex. His fate was a three-by-five cell with a roommate named Punchy who would beat him up regularly. Probably break his fingers too.

"Just so you know, this was all your idea," Ty warned. "I just followed you here. I didn't even know you were planning to steal the book. Got it?"

With a miserable nod, Bartholomew stood. Hands trembling, he fumbled with the handle until Ty finally shoved him out of the way and yanked the door open. Bartholomew stepped out into the hall and came face to face with... No one?

The corridor was empty. Bartholomew didn't waste time wondering why but tucked the book under his dress shirt and fell in behind Ty who was already sprinting across campus toward the field where Con was waiting with their backpacks.

"You get it?" Con asked.

Bartholomew lifted his shirt and showed him.

"LOL," Conrad said.

Bartholomew tilted his head to one side not getting the joke but Ty, who seemed to think it was hilarious, guffawed loudly.

"Now all we have to do is photograph the answers and return the book at lunch." Bartholomew flipped through the pages until he'd opened the book to the unit they were studying.

"Con?" Ty said, waving both hands to get his husky partner to stop snorting. "Phone."

With a nod of his oversized head, Conrad pulled out his cell phone. "No problem," he said, aiming the lens at Quiz Seven. He pressed the button with a sausage fat finger. "Hey, wuz wrong?"

Ty grabbed the phone away from him. "Your battery is dead, idiot. Why didn't you charge it last night?"

"Dunno." Con shrugged stupidly.

Ty looked to Bartholomew.

"I don't have one. Mother thinks they're dangerous."

"My step-dad took mine away when he caught me downloading dirty pictures," Ty said. Elbowing Con he raised his caterpillar brows. "But those ladies were hot, huh?"

They both started guffawing again as an incredulous Bartholomew gaped. "But now what are we going to do?" he asked, his voice shriller with every word.

"Memorize the answers for tomorrow's test, dumb face."

Knowing there was no point in arguing with these hulks, a panicked Bartholomew spent the rest of lunch helping Ty and Con memorize each answer. All the while, they assured him that the book'd be back in class before Ms. Buttsfert even knew it was missing.

Bartholomew believed this about as much as he believed his mother had run off to join a team of mud wrestlers.

Chapter 12

Alex walked around the easel waiting for that inspiration seed to sprout into a magical vine. It had been days but still no tingling hands made him race over to the shelves where tubes of watercolors and assorted brushes waited to be dumped onto the little table next to the easel.

When he felt a slight vibration under his feet, his heart leapt. He glanced down to realize that it was only Rembrandt dropping a tennis ball, silvery blue eyes begging to play.

Alex sighed. There wasn't going to be any art again.

"Okay, boy," Alex said picking up the ball. He tossed it up and took Rembrandt out back to play catch.

Usually he would have cracked up as soon as that fluffy goof started dashing back and forth, paws skidding across the patio. But this afternoon there were too many things on his mind. Not being able to paint. Mom seeming weak again. And that stupid Richie who continued to hide out plotting with Ty and Con.

These last few days Alex had waited for Bartholomew to walk up and, if not apologize, at least say hi. No dice. Every time they passed in the halls Bartholomew would suddenly tighten his tie or stick his nose in one of those fantasy books he liked.

What's his problem? Alex had wondered watching B-3 sit at the loser table with those creeps at lunch. He almost went over but then shook his head, deciding he was better off.

"Go get it, Rembrandt," Alex called half-heartedly, pulling his arm back for another toss. Rembrandt's grey and white ears perked up as he chased the ball into the bushes and sent leaves flying around the yard.

When Alex heard his Mom call him for dinner, he groaned. The last thing he felt like was eating.

He ignored her and picked up the slobber-covered ball. It reminded him of those slimy Shadow Swine. Last year in Artania one of them had threatened to invade Mom's dreams. If he and Bartholomew weren't creating, how soon before those monsters came after her? Maybe causing another heart attack.

"Stupid Bartholomew," Alex muttered.

"Alex." Mom poked her head into the yard. "Dinner's ready. Tonight, we're doing traditional Chumash" she repeated with a smile before disappearing back through the sliding glass door.

"I'll be there in a minute!" he called tossing the ball one last time.

At the table Alex made hills and valleys in the acorn gruel with prickly pear sauce on his plate. If he'd been a better mood, he would have noticed how interesting the designs were. But he couldn't stop thinking about what would happen if Bartholomew got caught stealing the book.

"And then it hit me, just reverse the sign to positive and suddenly the equation was solved." Dad grinned, proud of how he'd triumphed over the latest theorem.

"Wonderful, honey," Mom said. "Don't you think so Alex?"

"Hmm? What?"

"Aren't you happy for your dad?"

"Sure...congrats Dad."

Mr. Devinci started to smile until his wife lifted her chin toward Alex's full plate.

"Are you okay, kiddo?" Dad asked searching his son's face.

"Fine."

"All you've done is pick at your food for the last twenty minutes. Are you getting a fever?" Mom reached over to feel Alex's forehead.

"No," Alex replied swatting her hand away gently. "Just not hungry."

"Be that as it may, Dr. Bock says that a boy your age needs at least 2,500 calories a day; athletic ones like you even more," Dad said.

"I get plenty."

"Try a few bites. You're looking thin." Mom sounded concerned.

"I don't feel like it," Alex said.

"Try. It's a Native American dish," Dad said.

"Leave me alone,"

"Not our job young man. And your mother worked hard on this meal. Grinding and leaching acorns. Pounding them into flour. The least you can do is eat it."

"And you don't think I work hard? You don't think I have things on my mind?" Alex raised his arms. "Big things?"

"But it's Chumash," Mom said.

"Who cares? It's weird. Why can't you make something normal, like good moms!"

Mom jerked back as if she'd been slapped. She didn't say a word, didn't have to. Alex could see her lower lip trembling as she stared down at her plate.

Alex shoved away from the table knocking his chair over in the process. He dashed out to the garage and stood there glaring at the empty canvas. Why didn't he think before speaking? He wanted to rush after her, say he didn't mean it, that he loved her exotic recipes, really, let her wrap him up in those soft arms.

But he didn't.

It was all the Richie's fault. Alex picked up a plastic bottle of paint, hefting its weight.

"Stupid Bartholomew!" he cried heaving the bottle across the room.

Chapter 13

"Dad?"

Mitch Obranovich looked up from the papers he was working on at his desk. "Yeah Tinker Bell?"

Gwen thought he looked tired. His handsome face looked more like a dad in a flu commercial than his usual athlete on a cereal box.

"I was wondering. Could I keep your cell phone by my bed tonight?"

"What is it Gwenny?" Dad set down his papers. "Missing Mom?"

"No. It's just that I've been having bad dreams."

"That mother of yours. She should be here." He clenched his teeth making the muscles in his strong jaw bulge. Dad lowered his voice and muttered, "Damn her."

Gwen stared down at the carpet.

"I'm sorry." Mr. Obranovich got up from his chair and walked over to her. He wrapped her up in his strong arms and said, "I shouldn't talk about her like that."

"It's okay Dad."

"No, it isn't." He gave her a squeeze. "I tell you what. I need my cell in case of emergency, but I could knock off early to read a chapter from *The Odyssey,* alright?"

Gwen was flabbergasted. Mr. Time-management, take off early? Not knowing what to say, she just nodded.

"...*and Odysseus drove the hot spike deep in the crater eye of Cyclops.* Quite the trick, huh Gwenny?"

"Yeah," Gwen replied sleepily.

Her father bent down and kissed her forehead. "Goodnight Tinker Bell," he said before tiptoeing out of the room.

At first Gwen slept soundly. No nightmares this night. Hours passed with her breath as even as lapping waves on Santa Barbara's shore. Then the Mom Dream began.

It started like it always did with the two of them walking hand in hand. But as soon as they entered the cave, everything changed. Colors faded. Shadows lengthened.

"Let's paint," Mom giggled.

Amidst tinkling laughter, Dream-Gwen dipped a reed brush in the stone pot on the ground and started painting suns and clouds next to Mom's goofy rainbows.

A great shadow fell over the cave entrance and they both froze.

"Who dares enter my home?"

Gwen dropped her pot, but Mom kept painting. Then a creature's giant hands lifted Mom up to his misshapen face. "Stop."

Instead of stopping, Dream- Mom painted a pair of glasses around the Cyclops's single eye. The monster roared and pulled her closer to his great mouth.

Suddenly a leather waterskin appeared at Gwen's feet as a faceless voice commanded her to destroy art. With a desperate kick Gwen knocked over the container, picked up a piece of charred wood from the cold fire pit, and stirred the soil into a dark paste. Then she smeared a long splotch over the joyful paintings they'd just created.

But the Cyclops did not loosen his grasp.

"More. Destroy."

Scooping up a large glob of mud, Gwen threw a handful at the wall. As the disembodied voice urged her on, she splattered more and more. Finally, Cyclops let Mom go and the quivering Rochelle crumpled into a heap on the ground.

Gwen bolted upright in bed and blinked. Although the window was closed, the curtains were fluttering wildly. Stranger yet, her room had filled with gray mist as curls of dark smoke twisted from every corner of her bed.

Gwen shivered.

One wisp snaked over her naked arm like a muddy string over skin. Gwen hunched over, too terrified to even cover her eyes.

Wrapping her arms around her knees, Gwen started rocking back and forth, struggling to shake the nightmare.

But those images haunted her throughout the night.

Chapter 14

Bartholomew's eyes widened. An A. Yes! He wanted to hug the test and feel all those correct answers warm against his chest.

Now it wouldn't matter that he had to bathe in a limo right after P.E. or that his clothes were different from everyone else's. He was passing math. He wouldn't have to be homeschooled again.

Holding it tightly, he glanced over at Alex and smiled. But Alex kept he eyes focused front, and it quickly faded. They hadn't spoken since that one day, giving Bartholomew an ever-bigger pit in the bottom of his stomach.

Then Ms. Buttsfert started riffling through her books, counting each one, and Bartholomew's blood froze. *The Answer Book* was still in his backpack waiting to be returned. Not that he hadn't tried, but Ms. Buttsfert had gone from absentmindedly leaving the door ajar to locking it every time she left.

Leaning over, Bartholomew quietly unzipped his bag. How many times had he done this the last few days? Forty? Four hundred?

Every time he peeked he was sure it'd be gone, whisked away by some police officer that now had it sealed in an evidence room. Or, as an alarm sounded, he'd find himself in the center of a spotlight while handcuffs descended from the ceiling.

Expecting to see a satisfied smile on Ms. Buttsfert's face, he glanced up. Instead she had the same look Mother got when she saw specks of dust.

But there was no reason for her to appear so grouchy. The class was quiet. Even Con and Ty were sitting politely. For once.

Ms. Buttsfert paced the room, eyes crawling over every child. She paused at Ty's desk, and shook her head. Lifted an eyebrow at Con. But then her gaze crept up to Bartholomew and she nodded.

She knew! The color drained from his face. Should he run?

Bartholomew reached down and clutched his backpack. With one leg poised to dash away, he started to inch off the chair. She stomped closer ready to tap him on the shoulder and tell him he was caught.

Get up Bartholomew. Run!

Sweat beaded on his upper lip but Ms. Buttsfert was so close, he didn't dare wipe it away. Gardenia perfume hung in the air. He choked on the sick odor.

Keep going. Don't stop. Please, please pass me. He thought.

Ms. Buttsfert halted right next to him.

He felt a hand on the back of his char. His heart raced, pounding so loud he was sure she could hear it.

"I..." Bartholomew began,

"An A? Hmm."

He didn't dare look up.

Bartholomew opened and closed his mouth to apologize, but nothing came out.

"But you did not show your work. Redo it at break," she commanded, her blonde moustache stretching into sneer.

Bartholomew felt sick. This was a trap. She wanted to get him alone, so she could search his backpack. He had to get rid of that book. NOW.

"Yes, ma'am," he croaked out. As class droned on, his mind raced. *As soon as the bell rings go to the field. Run like the wind.*

When you get to the corner, throw that thing as far as you can. Then come back pretending a bathroom emergency.

When the bell finally rang, Bartholomew dashed out the door. Passing right by a confused Ms. Buttsfert.

He heard her voice but didn't turn. "Bartholomew!" she bellowed. "Come back."

He ran faster. Through laughing students. Past grinning faces. Over the sidewalk. When he bumped into Gwen he mumbled a hurried apology before willing his feet to go ever faster towards the field.

His shoes squished into the recently watered grass. *Mud, yuck.* He leapt to one side but the ground there was just as soggy.

Gazing straight ahead, he focused on that one corner of the fence. Salvation. A place to toss that horrid book. There rays of light shone on the drainage pipe like heavenly beams.

"Bartholomew!" Ms. Buttsfert called.

He glanced over his shoulder and gaped. The shrieking Ms. Buttsfert was getting closer by the second.

He sped up. Then suddenly, one foot stopped. For a split-second time froze. Down he went, splat, right into a mud puddle. Arms and legs all akimbo, his backpack skid across the grass.

Ms. Buttsfert grey slacks flapped like vulture's wings as she descended upon him. "I told you to stay after class," she hissed.

Bartholomew didn't reply. He was in a mud puddle just like the one father had drowned in twelve years before.

"Why aren't you getting up? Are you hurt?"

Bartholomew hadn't thought of this. An injury, huh? He liked it. But where? Head? Torso? Limbs, yes. That would divert attention. He pointed at his right leg.

"Can you walk?"

Bartholomew shook his head. "I can't," he groaned. That *was* the truth. If he got up everything would be ruined.

"You don't look like you're in too much pain to me."

He tried to sound very sad when he said, "My ankle, I think it's broken."

"Pshaw," Ms. Buttsfert blew as the nurse and Dr. Stricklin arrived with a wheelchair for the moaning Bartholomew.

He tried keeping up the act until, to his horror, he saw Ms. Buttsfert pick up his unzipped backpack and follow alongside. His eyes never left the bag as they bumped over the field toward the office.

As if staring could magically keep everything inside.

But as soon as they parked him inside the nurse's office, the answer book tumbled onto the floor with a thud. Several of the adults chatting nearby stopped mid-sentence. The school secretary, Mrs. Boltnice, tilted her head to one side and pointed. Dr. Stricklin shook his balding head.

Bartholomew tried moaning again.

Ms. Buttsfert didn't miss a beat; snatched up the answer book and shoved it in front of his face. "You lying little cheater. So that's how you got the A."

Bartholomew stared at his mud-splattered slacks as cold prickles of shame pierced his every nerve.

This was the end.

Chapter 15

The Lord of the Shadow Swine stared out from the throne room on the top floor of his castle. Carved from Subterranea's largest stalagmite, it was twenty stories high, giving him a perfect view of Caustic Cavern. He had named his tower Sickhert's Stalagmite, so no one would ever forget who ruled in this underground land.

He glanced at the obsidian clock. Its crystal hands told him it was nearly time. Many humans would soon be drifting off to sleep and with so few Knights of Painted Light it would be easy to invade their dreams.

Turning toward the miniature volcano in the center of the throne room, Lord Sickhert reached out. He admired the way his albino hands contrasted with the black surface as his long claw-tipped fingers scratched and caressed the smooth sides.

While steam rose from the waist high basin of lava in front of him, he recited the ancient chant. "Lava Pool Gramarye. Help me search for happy dreams. To twist and turn and drain away. While tormenting humans with thoughts of gray."

The lava began to bubble. Twisting tendrils of white mist filled the room, and hung suspended, like hundreds of ensnaring spider webs. Then as if the spiders had all woken at once and shot silk from their spinnerets, each took shape, filling every corner with ghostly human figures.

Lord Sickhert pointed a bone white finger at one of the misty shapes. The image of a young girl with short pigtails floated toward him. She had her eyes closed and was smiling as if having a happy dream; a dream that would soon be bent and warped by his minions.

"Fly, fly through the air. Straight into my Shadow Swine's lair," he hissed running a tongue over double rows of jagged teeth. "And art will become your worst nightmare."

Sickhert drove his fist into the girl's spectral face. Immediately the apparition recoiled and flew out the misshapen window. Grinning savagely, Lord Sickhert watched the dream child drift toward his Shadow Swine's army barracks.

He loved this high perch. From here he could see all of Caustic Cavern. To the west was the Great Window of Red where lava dribbled down a high wall. On the opposite side, stepped dams, called Gour Pools, caught the mucous-filled slime trickling from the ceiling. Next to them, a labyrinth of tunnels cut into the cavern wall led to the army barracks.

A hunchbacked soldier emerged from one of the caves in the wall and snatched the wraithlike figure of the floating girl from the air. With a salute, he disappeared back into his hole.

"He will find his work easy this night," Lord Sickhert said.

In the southern valley, other Shadow Swine were gathered on the banks of the River of Lies breathing in the sulfuric fumes of lava and water: the vaporous mixture that fueled their dream draining. The soldiers swayed back and forth as blue-grey steam filled the air, their piggish nostrils flaring with each breath.

"Go, my minions," Lord Sickhert said. "Power. Gain it now."

The creatures below panted and blew as more dark mist filled the air making the slime covering on each of their faces thicker and more viscous. Their yellow eyes glowed through the steamy haze while they swayed in a trance-like dance of breathing, hissing, and moaning.

"Yes," Sickhert rasped, rubbing his long hands together. "More." He turned back to the Lava Pool Gramarye and repeated his spell. Soon the outlines of mothers, uncles, and sons appeared, each representing a human dreamer on Earth. Lord Sickhert sent them all to his waiting army.

"Creation thoughts will be drained white this day."

One by one the Shadow Swine below trapped a human dreamer beneath a dark cape. With hunched backs heaving, they opened their cavernous mouths and blew. Scores of dark smoke escaped from blood red lips.

Then, like rising floodwaters on a horse-filled plain, the twisting smoke shot beneath the folds of all those dark cloaks. The fabric rose and fell in jerky waves as if a hundred stallions were drowning underneath.

His albino eyes grew wide reflecting the scene below. *Glorious.* Sickhert thought. *Almost as beautiful as the day that father drowned in mud. Ridding us of another artist.*

The cries of nightmares filled the air and his jagged grin widened. With a satisfied sigh, Sickhert lowered himself onto his black throne. But his work was not yet done. He pulled on a stalactite lever that hung next to the royal seat and a sob yowled throughout the castle. Adjusting the folds of his white robe, he waited.

The sound of clawed feet scratched up the staircase. A moment later, Sludge and Scum entered the throne room and dropped to their knees.

"What is your will, my lord?" Sludge gurgled, his mouth full of foam. Crawling closer, he dribbled spittle onto his master's feet.

"Many dreams are being turned this night," Sickhert said accepting Sludge's honorific spittle by rubbing his maggot white toes together. "The Deliverers' friends turn from art. But a few are resistant. You must find their every weakness and use them to your advantage"

Sludge glanced at the stairs leading to the torture room and touched one of the blisters on his face.

"You had best remember my Correction Chamber," Sickhert warned, his voice like a den of slithering snakes. "Or those burns will feel like a Gour Pool bath compared to what you will next receive."

"We have invaded their dreams, sire," Sludge assured him.

Scum nodded his bulbous head. "Ya, ya. We got em good."

"I expect nothing less. Now go!"

Crawling backwards the two Shadow Swine made their way to the door of the throne room, spitting reverently all the while. When they exited, Lord Sickhert rose from his glassy black chair and returned to the Lava Pool Gramarye. Stroking either side of the mini-volcano, he watched the twisted dreams unfold.

With every nightmare, his serrated smile grew wider. Then he started to laugh, louder and louder. Soon his dissonant howls filled every inch of Subterranea.

And beyond.

Chapter 16

The school nurse shook Mr. White's hand. "I have examined his ankle and can't find any swelling or signs of a break. I think the fall frightened him more than anything."

"That remains to be seen Miss. The family doctor will let us know."

The blood drained from Bartholomew's face. Doctor? She'd probably put one of those blood pressure cuffs on him and pump it until he spilled the truth all over the examining table.

"I have brought clean clothes for Bartholomew. His mother gave me explicit instructions that he was to change before leaving.

Bartholomew glanced around for Mother.

Mr. White read his mind. "Your mother awaits you in the car, young man. She could not bear to see you in the clothes your principal described over the telephone." He handed Bartholomew a plastic bag. "If you would be so kind as to slip into these, we'll be on our way."

The nurse's jaw dropped. She stared at Mr. White as if he'd just suggested they toss a baby out a window. Bartholomew knew why. Not that many families would ask a child to change before rushing their kid to the doctor. But of course, Bartholomew's family was not like other families. Although she seemed shocked, she closed the blinds and stepped outside to let Bartholomew change.

He looked in the bag. Pajamas! He had to wear pajamas at school? And these were the jacquard silk ones. They didn't even look anything like the cartoony sweat pants other kids wore on pajama day.

He started stripping down, tossing his mud-caked clothes into the bag. He knew where they were going. The garbage.

When he stepped out into the hall a minute later, the nurse and Mr. White both turned to him simultaneously.

"As you can see," the nurse said. "His ankle is fine. Just scared him."

Oh no! He forgot to limp. Well never too late. He started hobbling over to Mr. White and held out a hand for support.

"Fine indeed." Mr. White glared at the nurse. "Come along Master Borax." He held out an arm for Bartholomew to lean on and lead him toward the door.

Luckily there were only a few kids in the office. And most were at the other end of the hallway. There was a preschooler sitting next to his mom in the waiting area, but Bartholomew didn't care what little kids thought. He even managed a smile for the mousy-haired boy.

"Hey! The urchin called. Why you got your PJs on?"

"I'm hurt."

"Oh," the boy said before going back to playing with the zipper on his sweatshirt.

Keeping a pained look on his face, Bartholomew limped to the parking lot.

Inside the stretch limousine Mother waited facing front as if she didn't dare look in Bartholomew's direction. Although steam had filled the inside of the car it added no color to her cheeks. If anything, her face was paler than usual.

Bartholomew hung his head and waited. For some word. Anything. Mr. White squeezed his shoulder. It seemed that he too was dreading Hygenette Borax's wrath.

She pivoted her head slowly toward them. As soon as she saw Bartholomew she put one hand to her forehead and swooned. "FILTH! MY BABY IS FILTH!"

Her words echoed so loudly Bartholomew thought he saw the office walls shaking. God, he wished he could disappear.

Leaping from the limo Mrs. Borax started hopping around frantically like a grasshopper between two pecking birds. "My baby. My beautiful clean baby. What have they done to you?"

"I am quite alright Mother."

"Probably infected. A horrible illness."

"The nurse said his ankle looked fine," Mr. White broke in.

"I can see that! He's walking, isn't he? But he needs disinfecting. The germs. The bacteria. The disease!" She gathered up the stack of towels on the car seat and threw them at him. "Bathe, at once!"

Bartholomew caught them, crawled miserably into in the limo, and sat next to the full bathtub. Waiting for them to close the door, he cleared his throat loudly.

Still open.

He did it again, louder this time.

Still ignored him.

"The boy will be right as rain in no time Mrs. Borax."

"Oh, the dirt. The filth. Just like when Bartholomew Junior ...," she muttered between long hiccups.

Did she have to mention Father? He felt bad enough. Now he was her making her relive that horrible drowning. The guilt knife twisted deeper.

Well upset mother or no upset mother, he was not going to strip with the door open and the privacy glass down. He was twelve, after all.

"Bartholomew." She poked her head into the limo. "Get in the bath.

"But–"

"No buts. Go!"

Now Bartholomew had put up with a lot in his twelve years. But getting naked in front of the whole school? That was where he drew the line. He stuck out his lower lip and crossed his arms.

"NO!" he said.

Mrs. Borax froze. Their mouths agape, Mr. White and the chauffeur stared at him incredulously.

Bartholomew sighed. Were they that oblivious?

"The door is open!" he cried. "And the glass is down."

The door slammed in his face and Bartholomew heard another scream.

It was somehow soothing.

Chapter 17

Alex looked down at his hands. No paint under the fingernails or on his sweatshirt sleeve. No smell of turpentine from his rags. Even the calluses on his left hand were shrinking. He had stopped painting and it was driving him crazy.

Why had B-3 been so stupid? If he had just accepted help they wouldn't be in this mess. Bartholomew'd be in the now empty seat, they'd still be friends, and their art would be protecting both Earth and Artania.

And now with that note to all the parents about cheating Mom and Dad were looking at him as if he were some kind of criminal or something. Even though he had nothing to do with it!

Alex heard Gwen's shoes squeaking on the steel legs of her desk a few rows away. That girl never sat still. Then he glanced at the vacant seat next to hers.

The desk had been empty for a week now; ever since Bartholomew had gone into the principal's office. Had he been suspended? Expelled? They didn't send kids to juvenile hall for stealing books, did they? Alex had no a clue since they still weren't speaking. Even though he was still full on mad, he didn't want Bartholomew to be trapped in that mansion, again.

"-and remember that each line of a sonnet has ten syllables, so–." Mrs. Fuller stopped mid-sentence.

All eyes turned toward the door. Alex's jaw dropped open. There stood Bartholomew beside that British tutor of his. With his blonde hair slicked back, sand-colored suit with a tie, and white shoes to match, he looked like a mini Mr. White. Alex couldn't help but felt so sorry for him. Dorkville all the way.

"A-hem. Mrs. Fuller," Mr. White began. "I do apologize for interrupting, but it seems that Bartholomew here needs a day or so here while I gather the appropriate materials for his home-schooling transition."

Staring at Mr. White as if he were a magician struggling with a magic trick, Mrs. Fuller's mouth made weird shapes. She raised her thin eyebrows and blinked. "Well of course Bartholomew is welcome. You say he's going to be home schooled?"

"Starting Monday. But there are a few necessities that I must attend to first."

Alex knew just what Mrs. Fuller was thinking. It was written all over her face. Alex waited for her to protest and fight for his friend.

Tell him, Mrs. Fuller. Tell him how Bartholomew needs to be around other kids. How crazy he feels being cooped up in that mansion all the time. Come on.

But instead of arguing, she smiled that fake teacher smile and told Bartholomew to take a seat. Then she just continued with her poetry lesson letting Mr. White exit without a word.

Rustling her binder paper loudly, Gwen gave Alex a meaningful look that he returned with a sad nod. Man. Only a few days. Then his fellow Deliverer would be locked away. This sucked big time.

When the bell rang Bartholomew didn't even look his way as he slouched to the doorway and shuffled down the hall.

"Crazy, huh?" Gwen said watching B-3 go.

"I know," Alex sighed as the two of them followed the line of kids heading to lunch.

A few feet down the hall Ty and Con had just exited another class when they spied Bartholomew and began trailing him.

"We better see what they're up to." Keeping to the shadows Alex began following the lumbering pair through the hallways toward the gym.

"Why is B-3 taking the long way?" Gwen asked.

Alex's reply was cut short when Con glanced back, and he had to yank Gwen into a doorway. He put a finger to his lips and she nodded. They both craned their necks to listen for approaching feet before continuing to trail the bullies.

As soon as B-3 was behind the gym with no adults were in sight, Alex saw Ty halt. "Hey Rat," Ty called.

Bartholomew turned, his face as pale as death. Glanced around. He tried to dash toward the doors, but Ty stepped in front of him while a cross-armed Con blocked him from behind.

Bartholomew twisted right. Left. But there was no escape.

Still yards away, Alex quickened his pace.

"You told," Ty accused taking a step closer.

"No. I swear…"

Ty closed in, his mohawk's spikes denting Bartholomew's cheek. "I think you did."

B-3 shrunk back.

"Yeah." The hulking Con grabbed Bartholomew's wrists and crossed them behind his back.

"Here is a reminder of what will happen if you do." Ty lifted a fist.

A trembling Bartholomew closed his eyes.

Blood boiling, Alex rushed toward his friend. But he was too late. B-3 was already doubled over gasping for air.

When rat-face wound up for another Alex head butt him in the chest. The bully staggered back.

Meanwhile Gwen snap-kicked Con from behind. Legs buckling, he stumbled, releasing Bartholomew, who crumpled to the ground.

Ty leaned back on one foot, fists raised. "You want a piece of this?" Ty cried brandishing his knuckles at Alex.

"I'd love it, jerkface," Alex growled. "But I'm not an idiot. I'm not going to take the fall for you like Bartholomew did."

Ty feigned a punch, but Alex didn't flinch.

"Gwen, you were right about him," Alex said.

Gwen sighed. "Stupid as a toad."

"Yep," Alex blew out a nonchalant breath. "He'll hit me, campus police will come, and I'll be forced to tell them all I know about the stolen book. He'll be busted for bullying *and* stealing."

"I guess his I.Q. does match his shoe size," Gwen said.

A few kids had now gathered with scattered chuckles. Ty narrowed his eyes while Con scratched his head. Heather Gomez, the biggest tattletale in all of Santa Barbara, already had her cell phone out.

"I'll let you get away this time, Wuss. But you just wait." Ty shook his fist one more time before grabbing Con and strutting off.

When most of the chuckling kids had wandered away to look for more excitement a red-faced Bartholomew rose to his feet.

"Are you alright?" Alex asked patting his shoulder.

Nodding, Bartholomew pulled out the hand sanitizer from his pocket and rubbed it in. Shuffling his feet, he said, "I made a mess of things. I'm sorry Alex, I–"

"Forget it," Alex held up a hand to cut him off. "I'm just glad you're okay."

Bartholomew hunched over and drew a circle on the concrete with his shoe. An uncomfortable silence ensued. When the last chattering kids drifted away, Alex was surprised that Gwen stayed. She usually was all over the quad.

"Maybe if you talked to your mom, she'd let you hang with us," Gwen suggested.

"You have met my mother. Do you really think that would do any good?"

"Well, there has to be something. When I get in trouble I usually try to do something good, so Dad thinks I learned my lesson."

Bartholomew's eyes met hers. "Like what?"

"Oh, chores around the house. Volunteering at the daycare in Dad's gym. Stuff like that."

"Mother does speak about upholding the Borax name a lot."

"I know! The Student Store always needs help. We could go there."

When Bartholomew gave an I-don't-care-shrug Alex decided that it was time for action. Anything was worth a try. He started jogging back toward the Campus Store.

"Come on slowpokes!" he called over his shoulder.

Along the way, Gwen started teasing B-3 and Alex about how ridiculous they'd looked facing those two bullies while Alex shot back with his own insults. Pretty soon all three were clutching their guts in laughter.

When they arrived at the Student Store, a chortling Gwen went first saying she knew the faculty advisor. "He's my P.E. teacher and pretty cool," she said opening the door.

Alex peered inside. The room was empty. All the Las Brisas Bears pennants, pencils, and folders were locked away. Someone had drawn a school bus with the words, *Field Trip!* on the white board and the chairs were stacked neatly in one corner. On the wall, a half-finished fall dance poster with a rainbow-colored disco ball in the center hung from blue tape.

"Bummer," Gwen said, turning to go.

The heavy steel door blew closed silencing all three. Now the only sound in the air-conditioned room was the robotic ticking of a large wall clock.

Alex shivered. Was he mistaken or had the temperature just dropped twenty degrees?

Gwen rubbed her bare arms. "Well there's always... hey what's that?" Gwen pointed behind Alex and Bartholomew.

Alex spun on his heels. Something he knew all too well was floating above the closed door.

The color drained from his face. It was the same blue jewel that had led them to Artania the year before.

"What is *that* doing here?" Alex gasped.

"I don't know but it's cool." Moving underneath the flashing jewel, Gwen swiped at it with one hand. It hovered over her then bobbed through the air towards the other end of the room. A giggling Gwen skipped after it.

"I think you should leave that alone, Gwen. It could be dangerous," Bartholomew warned, giving Alex a meaningful look.

"Yeah." Alex nodded, before adding quickly. "Anyhow, we should go. We don't want to get caught in here without a teacher."

"No way. It's awesome." Gwen leapt into the air and swiped at it again.

Like a balloon in a dust devil, the jewel circled her head. Gwen spun around, arms outstretched. Then it grew brighter.

And Alex's stomach turned.

The ever-lighter gem bounced through the air toward the fall dance poster. There it began a slow spin. Gwen took another step closer and reached up. "Amazing."

"Don't touch it," Alex warned.

Pulsating, it spun faster shooting rays of red, green, and purple in all directions. Then the painted disco ball began to hum and grow. The mirrored lights swelled as colored bands flashed on the walls.

You'd think Gwen would have stepped back. Instead she said something about being a dancing queen while pointing at the air in a silly disco pose.

"Gwen, stop!" Bartholomew said.

Later Alex would wonder why he hadn't acted. Even though every muscle was set to spring, he just stood there.

Twirling, Gwen danced with the flashing colors that were coating the floor. Then she threw her head back and bent her knees. "It's like a living rainbow," she said.

Alex's friend and was halfway through a leap when her smile suddenly disappeared. Feet stuck, she jerked right and left. But the bands of rising color held her fast. In two seconds, she was submerged up to her knees. In four, her hips. Then the rainbow gave a lurch and began to pull her forward.

Right into the poster.

Black and orange braces opened and closed like a Halloween fish. Green eyes wide, Gwen implored Alex to do something.

By the time he acted, it was too late.

There was a brilliant flash and the entire room filled with blinding light. Alex squeezed his eyes shut and when he opened them again Gwen had disappeared.

Sighing, he turned to Bartholomew. "You know what that means."

Bartholomew nodded. "Here we go again."

Chapter 18

Years of skateboarding had taught Gwen something about how to fall. So, when the crazy roller coaster disappeared, and the ground rose to meet her, she tucked into a roll. After a few bumping somersaults, she sprang to her feet.

The student store, jewel, and dance poster were gone.

"What the...?"

There was no sign of Mr. Clean or Alex.

"Hey, where are you guys?" Gwen called.

There was no answer, just echoes over the barren earth. Or was it even Earth? It looked more like a spooky cartoon than any place she'd ever been. Reaching out a tentative hand, she touched the ground. It felt like dirt, kind of. But as Gwen crumbled the earth between her fingers it fell away in tiny balls of brown play dough.

The raucous caw of a vulture pierced the silence. Gwen glanced up and realized that it wasn't really a bird. At least not like any she'd seen. This thing flapping through the sky had paper wings and an aluminum foil beak. It was a sculpture!

This isn't real. I'm dreaming, Gwen thought as she crossed her arms defensively across her chest. *Get a grip, girl.* She turned toward the black hills on the horizon for calm.

"Okay hills are normal." Gwen let out a breath. Then she squinted. Opened and closed her eyes. The mountains weren't real either. Cardboard, like some back-lot Hollywood set.

"Impossible."

She spun around searching for something that wasn't freak show crazy. Trees made of construction paper? Rocks sculpted in bronze? A wood-carved bunny hopping around?

Her breath caught in her throat. She felt light-headed and unsteady on her feet.

"No...way," she choked out. *It's just like those horrible dreams.* Gwen thought, teetering back and forth.

Loud cries filled the air. Gwen gaped at the falling objects but didn't move. Until she realized that they were directly over her.

Gwen screamed and fell to her knees, clasping her hands behind her head.

Thud! Crash! The ground shuddered. Keeping her eyes squeezed shut she waited for the fireball to pass.

"Hey Gwen." She felt a hand on her shoulder. "You okay?"

She lifted her head. Alex was standing over her, his face a knot of concern.

"Alex?"

Nodding, he pulled her to her feet. Beside him a worried looking Bartholomew, his white slacks streaked with dirt, was rubbing a dollop of hand sanitizer into his palms.

"Where are we?" she asked, her eyes darting from one to the other.

Alex and Bartholomew exchanged a glance. Bartholomew shrugged as if to say we might as well tell her now.

"Artania," Alex said.

"Art what?" *Like those nightmares with strange creatures?* Gwen's breath quickened making her dizzy again. Hyperventilating, she bent over, hands on her knees.

"Hey Gwen, take it easy. Just breathe," Alex assured her. "We'll try to get you home real quick."

"But people are gonna worry."

"No, they won't because time is frozen on Earth while we're here," Bartholomew said.

"Frozen? Go back? Artania?" Gwen straightened her back and curled her hands into fists. "What's going on? "I want some answers!"

"We're in another dimension," Alex explained. "It comes from people's art."

"Whenever people paint or sculpt, those beings are born." Bartholomew pointed at the paper vulture flying overhead.

"No way."

"Way," Alex replied. "It is another realm, but it's connected to Earth. Humans' creative energy keeps this place alive."

Gwen didn't believe it. No siree. She was dreaming. She never went to school that day. Nope. She was still back at home sleeping in her cozy bed with the skateboard sheets. When she woke up she was gonna laugh at all this. *Wake up.* She told herself. *Come on. It's just a dream. Open your eyes.* She pinched her arm. *Ouch!*

"Gwen? Hello." Bartholomew asked her before turning to Alex. "Has she gone into shock?"

Alex took off his sweatshirt and slipped it over her shoulders. Shrugging him off, Gwen rolled her eyes. Even in a dream he could take the hero business too far.

"I'm fine. And as soon as I wake up I'll be even better."

"But you're not dreaming. This is real."

Defiant, Gwen shook her head.

The sound of clattering hoof beats made her turn, but she didn't see any animals trotting over the hills. She heard a loud cry and then the sky brightened. She looked up.

A team of white stallions with flaming manes whinnied as they flew overhead. Pulling what? A gold cart with a dude dressed in a white chiton that reminded Gwen of the Greeks they'd studied in sixth grade.

She blinked. *I really need to wake up now.*

"Greetings young ones," the driver called as he reined the horses downward.

Gwen stood back as they landed. The pale steeds snorted and pawed at the ground while their burning manes dimmed to a sunset glow.

"Apollo!" Alex and Bartholomew cried rushing up to greet him, hugging him each in turn.

Gwen crossed her arms and shook her head. *Okay this dream is getting too weird. The hero and Mr. Clean know a sun god? Right. Where do I come up with these things?*

Apollo turned to her and bowed. "Greetings Gwendolyn Obranovich, friend of the Deliverers, skateboarding enthusiast, and child of strength."

Gwen ignored him. She was not about to get into a conversation with a dream.

"Earth to Gwen. Hello." Alex waved a hand in front of her face.

"Leave me alone so I can wake up."

"We told you. This isn't a dream. It's real."

She shook her head. It couldn't be. Gwen was not the wish on a star type kid. She was logical. You work out, you get stronger. You practice goofy foot grinds you learn them. You take your vitamins you stay healthy.

She'd learned a long time ago that wishing for magical things didn't work. It didn't keep her parents from getting divorced. It didn't bring her mother home from Paris.

"Young one, your belief or disbelief does not change the way of things. We are in need and must make haste. Come." Apollo gestured toward the chariot.

Gwen stared unbelieving at this guy, if you could call him that. He didn't have skin. Instead he was stone like those sculptures at Bartholomew's mansion. His head was covered in a tight cap of soft curls and his body had nice muscle tone.

Must work out, she thought. *If marble men do that.* His nose was straight, and his jaw was strong with white perfectly aligned teeth. Gwen ran a tongue over a mouth full of braces for a moment reminded of how crooked hers were. Oh, this dream was freaky weird.

Shrugging, she took her place next to Bartholomew. If she was gonna be in crazy land, she might as well have fun.

Bartholomew gave her a knowing smile like a kindergarten teacher getting a five-year-old to play nicely. "Hold on. It might be a little bumpy."

What did he know? He couldn't even skateboard.

She had no idea.

Chapter 19

Bartholomew noticed his crème-colored jacket was torn and had large splotches of dirt on it. He shrugged knowing it wouldn't matter. Stains and tears didn't stay on when you left Artania. He'd return home just as clean as he'd been that morning. He was more concerned about Gwen. Why was she here?

She wasn't an artist.

He glanced down at the quilt-like landscape, marveling once again at the magic of this strange place. The living paintings and sculptures constantly changed like weather patterns rearranging the sky. One moment the heavens were dark and thick oil paintings while next they became light and airy colored chalk. But the sky didn't look like different pieces of paper pasted next to each other. Not at all. Each change edged in soft clouds was so gradual that it all fit together perfectly.

He remembered how Alex had tried to get him to relax when they'd journeyed into Artania the year before. It didn't work. Bartholomew had shied away, wanting nothing to do with this inexplicable place.

In those a few short days, he became a different kid. Strong, heroic, confident. But when he returned to Earth that kid disappeared. Replaced by the sneaking, cheating, lying kid he was now.

Bartholomew shook his head. If it hadn't been for Father's drowning, things would be so different.

Apollo jerked the reins to the side. The glowing stallions reared their heads and began their descent toward an ancient building floating in a cradle of clouds.

"Mount Olympus." Apollo lifted a strong chin at the Greek structure. "Home."

The rectangular building below was made of white stone with tall marble columns supporting a triangular roof. There an assortment of Greek gods milled about and waved at them. As they drew close, there was a flash of light and all the gods on the fascia disappeared.

Gwen jumped back and crossed her arms over her chest making her skinny muscles bulge.

"Don't worry." Alex gave her a gentle punch in the arm. "Stuff like that happens all the time around here. You'll get used to it."

Bartholomew nodded. He wished he could come up with reassuring words like his friend. Alex, always the hero, always able to come up with a plan.

Descending through the clouds, the stallions reared their heads once more and glided to a landing in front of the Parthenon. Apollo hopped down from the chariot and went around to the lead horse.

Snickering softly, he unhitched the steed and rubbed his nose against its velvety muzzle. Next, he ran a hand over its fiery mane snuffing out the flames with his caresses. He patted it on the rump before repeating the process with all six stallions. When the last white horse had trotted off toward a distant stable, he turned to Gwen.

"Come. It is time to meet my family," he said leading them into the Greek temple.

The space between the Doric columns supporting the building made Bartholomew think of doorways that could lead to anywhere. He only had to choose which way to go.

Here he could sculpt animals that came alive or paint a magic spell to free trapped pharaohs. It helped him to forget his own prison of obsessive cleanliness.

"Dudes," Gwen said, her green eyes darting nervously. "You said you'd try to get me out of here."

"We'll ask, okay? Don't worry," Alex said.

"It's perfectly safe." Bartholomew cleared his throat and added in a lower voice. "Here, at least."

Gwen opened her mouth as if she were about to ask something but, seeming to decide against it, clamped it shut again. Wrinkling her freckled nose rabbit-like, she trudged after Apollo, tennis shoes slapping against the marble floor.

Inside, a bearded god sat on a wooden throne carved with female sphinxes fanning him with their wings. Flanking him were the gods and goddesses that had just disappeared from the building. Each wore a different colored chiton draped over their shoulders and nodded reverently as Apollo and the trailing kids entered the room.

"Greetings Deliverers," the bearded god said.

Bartholomew wanted to rush up and hug him. The summer before, when he'd had his birthday party at the Yacht Club, this man had surfed the waves and shook Bartholomew's hand. That vision had inspired Bartholomew to his greatest sculpture yet. Then, on his first trip into Artania he'd nearly fainted when he discovered that the kind surfer was in fact Zeus, king of the gods.

Apollo pointed to a row of stools facing the stony assemblage. "Sit, young ones. Be comfortable."

As Bartholomew lowered himself onto a seat he glanced over to see if Gwen was all right. He couldn't tell since she was staring straight ahead ignoring Alex who kept trying to wink reassuringly at her.

Apollo took his place next to his father and Zeus raised his scepter waiting for the room to quiet.

"We thank the Deliverers, for venturing once again into our land." His deep and noble voice warmed Bartholomew to the core. "As you know the first battle may have been won but the war is not yet over."

"The Thinker said we'd have more missions," Bartholomew said.

The beautiful crowned woman next to Zeus paused from petting the peacock in her lap and spoke. "The Second Task awaits your skills."

"Ahh but I am remiss in my duties," Zeus said. "Let me introduce my wife. This is Hera, queen of the gods, mother to Mars, god of war."

An armor-clad god two chairs down stood and bowed.

She is also mother of Vulcan, the smith-god."

At the other end of the row, a man with a hammer in one hand pounded the anvil at his feet. A loud clang filled the air.

Bartholomew loved reading the Greek myths. He could relate to the gods and had often thought how he was most like Vulcan. Bartholomew worked in his studio below the ground of Santa Barbara like Vulcan worked at his burning forge inside of Mount Etna.

"And you've met my son Hermes before. Remember the messenger god, who gave you the key for your first entry?" Zeus asked.

When the god in winged sandals stood up and bowed, Hera's face immediately clouded over, and she glared at Zeus. Bartholomew knew that Hera had a reputation for being jealous. But it was deserved. Zeus was known as a womanizer who had all kinds of children with other ladies. Hermes was just one of them.

"Yes, well there are many Olympians here." Hera cleared her throat. "And time is of the essence."

Bartholomew counted at least fifteen gods and goddesses around her and agreed it would take too long to introduce them all. His eyes fell upon the sculpted Athena, goddess of wisdom. She touched her breastplate and tipped her helmet at them. Next to her stood Poseidon, his crown of pearls catching the light. He smiled and raised his triton in salute. But it sure would have been fascinating to hear their stories.

"So, what's up?" Alex asked.

"And if you don't mind my saying, I believe there has been a mistake. Our friend..." Bartholomew's voice trailed off and he turned to Alex.

"Gwen isn't an artist," Alex said, picking up Bartholomew's train of thought. "Somebody messed up. She's not supposed to be here."

Exchanging a glance with Zeus, Hera set her peacock down and stood. Her sky-blue gown rustled softly as she glided over to face Gwen. The goddess bent down and took Gwen's face in her hands.

"Don't touch me," Gwen snapped, brushing her hands away.

Undaunted, Hera folded her painted hands in front of her gown and spoke in an even voice. "Child, believe it or not, you have a destiny. Just as your friends do. You may not be a Deliverer, but you have strengths that will be needed." She gave one of Gwen's red pigtails a gentle tug and returned to her throne.

Gwen's face was so pale that even her freckles blanched. But she didn't look scared. Her face was white-hot with anger.

"I don't care. Send me home. Now!"

Bartholomew looked at Gwen's raised fist and groaned. *Here we go again.*

Chapter 20

Yep. She told them. Now she'd wake up from this weird dream and find Dad sleeping right up the hall. Gwen tapped her foot and waited. One second went by. Two. Four. Those gods kept staring at her. *Jeesh. Take a picture why don't you.*

Okay talking didn't wake her up. Why not try some action? Gwen got up from her chair and faced Zeus.

"Hello. Didn't you hear me? I said, send me home."

Zeus smiled and pointed his long scepter with an eagle on top at her. "I cannot."

"Can't or won't?"

"I did not open the doorway. Our leader did."

"Then tell *him* I want to go home."

"It does not work that way." Hera stroked the peacock in her lap. "The doorway cannot open again until the task is complete."

Gwen dashed to the empty stool next to Alex and lifted it over her head. "If you don't send me home, you'll be sorry."

Why weren't they acting scared? They just kept sitting there like they were watching a movie.

"Fine. Have it your way." She threw the chair on the ground and it broke into a dozen pieces.

Gwen blinked repeatedly. But no matter how many times she opened her eyes, she was still in that weird room on Mount Olympus.

She picked up one of the broken sticks and raised it. Ready to strike Zeus, she pulled her arm back. But suddenly she couldn't move. Gwen spun around.

"Alex! Let go!"

"Mellow out. Just chill."

Gwen tried to jerk away but Alex held fast. She was tempted to kick him. This wasn't Alex anyhow. It was just another nightmare. But then she looked into those soft brown eyes and couldn't. Even a dream Alex was her friend. Gwen released her grip and the stick clattered on the floor.

"Why can't I wake up?" she whispered in his ear.

"We've tried to tell you. This isn't a dream. It's a real world."

"And it's in trouble." Bartholomew came up next to Alex. "Terrible trouble, needing our help."

"You?" Gwen raised her eyebrows. "You can't even skateboard."

"But he's an artist. And that's what they need."

Bartholomew nodded.

Could it be true? Gwen's glanced from one face to the other. Could she really be awake right now? But if she was surrounded by art wouldn't she be attacked soon like in those nightmares? She cocked her head, waiting for everything to turn into a horror movie. A place where every nice face morphed into monstrous sharks or a Cyclops.

"Fear not, human." Hera laid a hand on her arm. "You are among friends."

Gwen didn't know what to believe. But it seemed she had no choice.

"O-kay," she said slowly. "What's the plan?"

"The Renaissance Nation is in peril," Zeus said. "You must go there."

"Rena- what?" Gwen asked.

"The Renaissance. You know that European time when art, writing, and technology grew so much?" Bartholomew asked.

"No." Gwen looked to Alex.

He shrugged. "Bartholomew's the bookworm. Not me."

"It started in the 1400's and lasted a couple hundred years. Western Civilization's most famous art comes out of that time. The David. The Mona Lisa. Things like that."

"Interesting you should mention her," said Hera. "For it is the Smiling One who needs your help."

"What!" Alex cried. "The Mona Lisa is here!"

"But, of course."

Alex's mouth was open, and he was shaking his head back and forth. It seemed even Mr. Hero could be rattled.

"We think she's still alive." Zeus draped an arm over his wife's shoulder. "But we do not know for sure. She disappeared three days ago."

"She was in The Fortress." Hera nodded. "We thought she was safe. There were so many guarding her. But on the eve of the Equinox she vanished."

"Why were you guarding her in the first place?" Bartholomew asked.

"There had been attempts to kidnap her," Hera replied.

"Shadow Swine," Alex spat.

"Possibly, or it could be those who align themselves with Sickhert's Army," Zeus said.

Gwen felt like she was watching a ping-pong match where the ball kept turning invisible. One minute she thought she was following the conversation but the next she had no idea what the heck they were talking about. Shadow Swine? Sickhert's Army? Renaissance Nation? This place was full on jumbling.

Bartholomew gave her a look that said he understood. Had Mr. Clean felt this way when he'd come here before? Or was he just happy to escape that neat-freak mother of his?

"How can that be?" Bartholomew asked turning to Hera. "I thought there were just two sides. Sickhert's and yours."

"Some Creations have trouble living in our world," The goddess explained. "They desire more, and thus become spies for Lord Sickhert hoping to someday transform into Mudlarks."

"Crazy," Alex said, shaking his curly head.

"Crazed with power," Apollo said. "As it has always been, in both our worlds. Those with such desires have long done irrational things to gain them."

Gwen thought about her mom. Off in Europe to get her own kind of power, a super model who was so famous she was known by her first name.

"I want to be a star again," Mom had said before abandoning her family two years before. "Everyone will know the name Rochelle."

And Gwen supposed it was happening. From the runways of Paris to the catwalks of Milan, Mom modeled the latest designs. In ads for everything from perfume to make-up Rochelle posed with that ever more famous pout.

Gwen kept a hidden scrapbook under her bed of magazine clippings featuring Mom in all kinds of poses. She didn't know why she cut them out. She hated those kinds of magazines anyhow. Make-up? Hair dos? Fancy clothes? Yuck! But somehow, she felt closer to Mom when she pasted those photos into her book. Even closer than when Mom had been home.

"The Deliverers will need the strength of the gods to rescue Mona Lisa," Zeus said. "You will need the trickery of Hermes, the light of Apollo, and the love of Venus."

"With the forging powers of Vulcan and the war attributes of Mars you will have powerful allies," Hera added.

Zeus nodded. "My wife and I will watch over you from our respective thrones. But be ever diligent."

"For if you fail, the Renaissance Nation will be pulled below," Hera said. "The land of art's rebirth will become nothing but white shadow."

"You can count on us," Alex assured them. "You know that."

Gwen had no idea what they were talking about. But she did get that the stakes were high. If they messed up, this land called Renaissance Nation could crumble away.

Maybe she was still dreaming. But a battle? It might be cool.

Chapter 21

From Apollo's chariot, a confused Alex went over the last hour in his mind. Why was Gwen there and how the heck was he going to keep her safe? Just protecting B-3 was enough to give him the shakes.

Staring off into the clouds, Alex ran his fingers over the scalloped detailing of the gold railing. The cool surface reminded him of a snake.

He shivered.

Alex clenched his jaw. *No fear. Focus.*

"Florence," Apollo said jerking the chariot's reins to the right. "The cradle of our rebirth."

Below them brick colored tile roofs cast shadows over the cobblestone streets. And Alex could see people. Well not exactly people. Artania was filled with tapestries, sketches, and paintings.

But to Alex they were as human and anyone he'd ever met. Some even more so.

A long river snaked its way through the medieval town. In the center, a stony bridge topped with what looked like toy apartments spanned the water. Alex wondered how these buildings kept from falling into the river. They didn't look like they were attached very well.

As soon as they landed on the cobblestone walkway in the center of bridge, all the strolling people froze. Then, as if in response to a distant bell, in unison they turned away, and marched off the bridge.

"Some greeting," Gwen muttered under her breath.

Although sparkling jewels and gold shone from windows in every jewelry shop, shopkeepers were nowhere to be found. Alex gave Apollo a questioning look.

In response, the marble statue began to shimmer. Then, as if a match had just been lit at his feet, Apollo developed color. It started with his strappy sandals and drifted up his chiseled form until his whole body shone. Now he was an oil painting, his head haloed in soft blonde curls and eyes that sparkled a light blue.

Gasping, Gwen took a step back.

"Hey, he's all right. He does that because lots of people painted him, but only one can exist in this dimension. He can morph whenever he wants, kind of like changing clothes."

"That's not how I change, Dude."

"You're human," Bartholomew said. "Different rules apply."

Gwen shook her head like Rembrandt after a bath.

Suddenly Apollo rushed up to greet a man with a flowing gray beard and hair that tumbled past his shoulders. "Leonardo, my condolences. The Smiling One is beloved both near and far."

"Let's not be too hasty Apollo. My daughter is not a Mudlark yet."

"You know such a thing?"

The man who looked like a reddish-orange painting placed a hand on his chest. "I still feel her presence."

"Of course." Apollo nodded, then turned to Alex and his friends. "Forgive my manners. Let me present those tasked to rescue our Mona Lisa."

Bowing, Leonardo told them that his creator was also a Deliverer in his time. Then he pointed a gnarled hand at Gwen.

"Another? But the Soothsayer Stones says, 'Hope will lie in the hands of twins,' It says nothing of triplets."

"Her talents will become evident in time. The Thinker sees much in his bronze palm," Apollo said.

"That he does." The old man smiled. "*Ciao bella bambina. Ciao bello bambini.*"

"Chow?" Alex asked.

Apollo smiled. "It is Italian for hello, and goodbye. Surely the Deliverers have knowledge of the language where art was reborn?"

"Is this Italy?" Bartholomew stepped up.

"This is Florence, yet not. It is Italy, yet not." Leonardo replied clasping his hands in front of his long cloak. "We have the greatness of the Florentine painters, architects, and sculptors here. But our geography is not exactly like Earth's. You should know that by now."

Alex thought back to his first visit into Artania when he'd gone to Ancient Egypt. But it hadn't been like the Egypt on any map he'd ever seen. It was made from the art of the time and it didn't have any modern technology.

He glanced around. Florence was the same. No cars, power lines, or planes overhead. It was just as if he had stepped back in time five hundred years to a place made completely from art.

"Florence, cradle of the Renaissance." Mr. Encyclopedia grinned and began to recite some factoids. "Home to the greatest masterpieces of all time. Artists such as Michelangelo, Raphael, and Leonardo da Vinci." He puffed up his chest obviously proud to have remembered the names. Then he stared at the bearded man in front of them. "Hey, are you THE Leonardo da Vinci?"

"He who birthed my creation was. I have his knowledge and talents."

Bartholomew's pale blue eyes widened.

Alex was speechless too. This place continued to blow him away. On his last trip here he'd spoke with gods and pharaohs, and now he was in the presence of that genius, Leonardo da Vinci? Even a twelve-year-old couldn't escape hearing that name. Anyhow, Dad said they were related, Sort of. Some distant cousin or something.

"Did you know that Leonardo da Vinci was called the true Renaissance man because of all the things he could do?" Bartholomew started listing more facts. "He was a painter, inventor, architect, and scientist. He even studied the human body by dissecting cadavers."

"Gross," Gwen said making a face.

Alex agreed but guessed doctors did the same thing.

"His drawings were way ahead of his time with things like flying machines, a robot, and a submarine."

That Alex could relate to. He'd always drawn things from his imagination too.

"But they did not prevent my daughter's disappearance," Leonardo said his wrinkled face crumpling into a frown. "Come let us go to the Fortress. Perhaps the Delivers can find clues that escaped these old eyes." He turned to Apollo. "Thank you, god of light."

Apollo nodded and stepped back into the carriage. "I pray for the Smiling One's return." He snapped the reins and soon melded into the whiteness of the sun.

Chapter 22

A quieter Bartholomew glanced around as Leonardo led them off the bridge. From Apollo's chariot he'd seen scores of Artanians strolling along, but now the streets were empty.

Every shutter and door were closed tightly. Bartholomew cocked an ear but couldn't detect even the scarcest of whispers. It was eerie. Their feet shuffling over the flagstones announced their approach like a herald. But no dog's low growl rumbled nearby.

Mr. da Vinci seemed wary. His ancient eyes narrowed making those lines around them look even deeper. Then he lifted his strong Roman nose, sniffed the air, and turned full circle.

Bartholomew raised his eyebrows at Alex.

"Sir, where *is* everyone?" his friend asked.

Leonardo put a crooked finger to his bearded lips. "Ears are everywhere, bambini. Wait."

"Shadow Swine here?" Bartholomew gasped drawing up closer to Alex and Gwen.

"Shh!" Leonardo warned.

Bartholomew clamped his mouth shut and focused on his feet. *It's okay.* He thought. *You have powers here.*

Leonardo entered an arched opening where a narrow stairway twisted up the center of a Fortress wall. Stroking one thick eyebrow, he smiled reassuringly at the children before starting up the well-worn stone steps.

"I'm cruising in a castle. Cool," Gwen said.

They emerged in an open area on a high wall. From the parapet surrounding the Fortress, Bartholomew could see the river below lapping against a wooden dock. Long thin rowboats which Bartholomew immediately recognized as gondolas were moored to the pilings. Next to them, armed men with swords perched on their shoulders marched in groups of two and three.

"Now it is safe to talk," Leonardo said. "Please forgive the creations of Florence. They are afraid that your presence brings danger."

"Us?" Alex looked confused.

"Sickhert has spies everywhere." Leonardo glanced backwards as if expecting one of these spies to come running up the stairway. "Come." Leonardo gestured as he made his way over the parapet walk. More soldiers marched here but they ignored the three children trailing the ancient man. Their eyes were focused beyond the battlement walls, ever watchful.

Inside one of the square towers they entered a large room with a flagstone floor. Here, wooden models of strange flying machines hung from the ceiling and scattered drawings littered a long table, while shelves held beakers, pulleys, and a few yellowed bones. The whole place looked like a magician's workshop.

"My laboratory," Leonardo said with a slight bow, "where I continue the work of my creator. Delving into the sciences he so loved to explore."

"Neat toys," Gwen said, nodding appreciatively.

"They aren't toys bambina, they are inventions. But please be seated. We have much to discuss." He pointed at a grouping of wooden benches and three-legged stools in the corner.

"So, what's the plan?" Alex asked when they had all made themselves comfortable.

"Ahh, directness. And singularity of mind. Good attributes of a Deliverer."

Alex tapped one foot on the floor. "Well?"

Bartholomew couldn't help but nod. This all might be cool, but he was eager to get on with it.

"Did you notice any differences here?" Leonardo pointed from one side of the room to the other.

Bartholomew scrutinized every corner of the room. It looked exactly as he'd imagined Leonardo's studio might. He glanced at Alex who shrugged.

"This looks newer," Alex said, lifting a chin at the ceiling.

"Oh yes," Bartholomew agreed, noticing the light color of the wood.

"That is because this Fortress was just built." Leonardo stroked his long silky beard.

"Why?" Alex asked.

"There had been threats against my Mona Lisa. Letters left at her doorstep. Ruffians following her. Then one night she was nearly snatched from the piazza by a band of pirates."

"You thought she'd be safe here?" Bartholomew asked.

"That was our hope. But then three days ago she disappeared in the river. Soldiers to the east and west, but she vanished without a trace."

"Shadow Swine," Alex said lifting on eyebrow knowingly.

"Or those in their league. Yes."

"Shadow Swine?" Gwen leapt up and started waving her arms around in circles. "Deliverers? What the heck are you all talking about?"

"Have your friends told you nothing?"

"Cha!" Gwen gave him an exasperated look.

Leonardo sighed and smiled. He tried to lay a hand on Gwen's shoulder, but she jerked away and glared at him, green eyes blazing.

"Well?"

"Your friends are Deliverers." The old man pointed at Alex and Bartholomew. "Chosen at birth. They use art to keep both humans and Artanians safe."

"And Shadow Swine?" Gwen asked.

"The evil destroyers of artistic inspiration. We have battled them as long as Artania has existed."

Bartholomew didn't want Leonardo to tell Gwen too much. She may be tough but if she knew how horrible the Shadow Swine really were, even she might get scared. "But we defeated them last time," he said quickly, nudging Alex. "Didn't we?"

"Yeah. We kicked their butts," Alex added.

Leonardo cocked his head quizzically. "Yes, well. That was but a single battle. The War is yet to be won."

"We know, we know." Bartholomew held up a hand. "Their task will be long with seven evils to undo."

"But our world will be saved if their art is true," Alex said reciting the final line of the Prophecy.

"Okay, so you dudes beat these bad guys. And now these same ones have this chick, Mona Lisa. Right?"

"It seems so," Bartholomew replied.

"And in order to get her back, you first have to find her."

"Of course."

"Well, whenever I'm working on a new skateboarding stunt I always go back to what I know. Like when I learned to ride goofy-foot I just thought back to what is was like when I rode regular. Then I reversed it in my mind." Gwen pivoted on her feet as if reversing her stance on a skateboard.

"I do the same thing," Alex said.

"So, we go back to what we know. And get clues there."

Bartholomew looked from Alex to Gwen and back again.

"But of course." Leonardo nodded in understanding. "Come. I will lead you."

Although he had no idea where they were going, Bartholomew didn't ask. He didn't want to look stupid. Anyhow they were inside a fortress. What could happen?

Chapter 23

When Alex reached the dock, several soldiers in striped bloomers, and metal helmets marched up to them and bowed.

"*Buongiorno*, Deliverers," the tallest one said, his straight form reflected in the river water below.

To Alex *buongiorno* sounded like bone-jern-o. He guessed it meant hello. After nodding at the soldiers, he turned to Leonardo. "Is this where you saw her last?"

"Nicolo was guarding her at the time." Leonardo said tilting his head at the soldier who had greeted them.

"It was quiet." Nicolo nodded. "Not a gondola rowing in sight. I thought all was well. Then the beggar appeared and grabbed her. Kicked her into the water and she immediately disappeared. We captured him and have tried interrogation, but he refuses to answer." He shook his head. "I blame myself."

Mr. da Vinci laid an ancient hand on Nicolo's puffed sleeve. "You were ever watchful. We know that."

Alex pondered for a moment. "Where exactly was she?"

Nicolo pointed to a short pier about twenty feet from them. Trying to think like a detective, Alex bent down to look at the wooden planks that made up the floor. Between the cracks he could see the posts sinking into the water below.

Then, something that looked like a thick spider web caught his eye. Alex scrambled down the stairs beside the pier to get a closer look.

"What is it?" Bartholomew asked following him.

"It looks like a scarf." Alex stretched an arm, but it was just beyond his grasp. He inched out a little farther. Still out of reach. "Hey Bartholomew, hold my legs so I can get it."

"Give me a second," Bartholomew said bracing his back against a post. He grabbed Alex's ankles. "Okay. I think I have you."

Alex extended an arm and swiped. No luck. "Closer," he called.

"My hands are cramping, but I'll try," B-3 said, lowering Alex until he was barely perched on the dock.

Wiggling his fingers Alex grasped the cloth. "Got it! Pull me up."

He felt a shudder. Bartholomew's fingers spasmed open and closed. Alex slipped an inch. Two.

Then he was in the water.

Alex lifted his head gasping for breath. Tried to swim.

Only one leg moved.

The other one was trapped. He tried to kick free, but something was holding it down. He jerked right and left but still couldn't break away.

"I'm stuck!" he cried, barely able to stay above water.

Bartholomew dove in, popping up beside Alex a second later. "Which one?"

"My left. I think it's wedged under something."

Bartholomew disappeared beneath the river's ripples. The water swirled and churned.

Alex sputtered. He felt a tug and was suddenly flying. Blue sky filled his vision. Then, he landed flat on his back with a painful thud. Groaning, Alex rolled over and glanced around.

Where was Bartholomew?

Chapter 24

Gwen scanned the churning water one hand shielding her eyes.

"Where is he?" Alex cried, dashing down the path.

"I don't know. He never came back up," Gwen replied.

Gwen stood to jump in, when a green back rose out of the swirling currents.

"A river monster!" Nicolo cried.

About twelve feet long with a long snout like a wolf, it had shiny scales, a fluted tail, and fins like sharp razors. But Gwen couldn't tell if it had teeth or not. She prayed it didn't.

That was no monster. It was a giant fish. And it had Bartholomew in its mouth!

The wolf-fish raised its head with what seemed like a sneer before pulling Bartholomew back under the swirling eddies.

Gwen's blood froze. She considered leaping into the Arno, but there was no way to wrestle Mr. Clean from its jaws.

With a flick of its tail the creature swam downstream.

Fighting the sick feeling in her gut, Gwen grabbed Alex's hand. "Come on!"

The fish twisted round and round like a sea snake.

"Mr. Clean's face. So pale," Gwen said while jogging along shore.

"Hang in there, B-3. We're coming," Alex called.

Keeping her eyes pinned to their friend, Gwen ran ever faster until suddenly her shoulder hit something hard. She staggered back, stars spilling in front of her eyes.

She blinked. They were facing a huge gate.

And it was closed.

Gwen tried to lift the heavy wooden bar, but it wouldn't budge. *No way!* She looked around, called over her shoulder. "Help me!"

Alex joined her moments before Nicolo raced up with two other soldiers who helped hoist the long wooden bar and toss it aside. When it clattered on the flagstone path, they all leaned against the huge door.

As soon as there was a crack in the opening, Alex wriggled through, followed by Gwen. The duo sprinted to catch up with the fish, soldiers' boots padding behind.

When the creature some came into view, Gwen willed his feet faster. *Hold on Mr. Clean.* She thought as hot sweat ran in her eyes. But the next scene turned her blood to ice.

This fish wrenched Bartholomew to one side. But it wasn't necessary. Her bud wasn't fighting. Or moving. Slack jawed, his body was limp, eyes closed; Gwen couldn't even tell if he was breathing.

She skidded to a halt. "Is he..." Her voice trailed off.

"Don't say it."

"We have to get him away. Now. We need a net, or harpoon or ..." Gwen glanced back at one of the soldiers behind them and waved. "Hey, you with the crossbow, come here."

Alex nodded in understanding. "We'll have to get ahead of him. To the bridge. Come on." Zooming up to to Ponte Vecchio, he dashed inside one of the attached jewelry shops, and threw open the shutters. "In here!"

Gwen took her place at the window. "Give me the crossbow."

The soldier handed it the weapon to her. It had a stirrup on one end with two cranks at the other to pull the bowstring back.

Gwen set the stirrup on the floor and put one foot through it.

Alex pointed. The scaled back of the great fish crested on the water as it began its roll. "Here he comes."

"Help me crank this." Gwen leaned back and placed both of her hands on one of the windlass handles.

Alex positioned his hands on the opposite one and began to pedal it with her, straining to curl the rope around the roller. When they had finally wound it tight, Gwen unlatched the winch and tossed it aside.

"Now the bolt."

The soldier pulled one from his quiver and handed it to her, its triangular blade looking more like a dagger than any arrow she'd ever seen. She fletched it atop the bowstring.

"Gwen, if you miss-" Alex's words stuck there.

"Don't worry," Gwen assured him. "I've been doing this since I was four. I can hit a bull's eye from a hundred yards."

Alex stared at the razor-sharp end.

"Chill. I got this." Gwen rested the crossbow on the windowsill and got down on one knee. Placing her cheek up against the back of it as if it were a rifle, she closed one eye. Then she placed a finger on the trigger.

Alex gripped her t-shirt. "It's rolling back," he said.

"One...two..." she said.

Bartholomew's lifeless face bobbed above the surface.

"Three," Alex whispered.

The arrow catapulted through the air. Closer and closer to their friend.

Chapter 25

Atop his stalagmite tower Lord Sickhert's long clawed fingers scratched the obsidian surface of the mini volcano. He smiled while the lava in the small basin in front of him flashed images of the Great Fish pulling the Deliverer below.

Everything was going according to plan. The traitors had been successful. Mona Lisa was in chains, rough metal scraping those delicate wrists. Her captors were heading toward the meeting place and soon would reach the doorway.

Then the Renaissance Nation would fall. And the Blank Canvas would take the place of all this sickening color.

He passed an albino hand over the top of the Lava Pool Gramarye and the scene before him changed, descending through dark clouds until Sickhert could see the Arno River west of Florence. To Sickhert, the snaking waters looked like a viper seeking prey, its fanged head ready to strike.

The view altered as the Gramarye showed him Italian cypress and olive trees near a tower tilting comically over a stony village. He had heard the Artanians say The Leaning Tower of Pisa was a symbol of their constant fight. A beautiful tower to climb. But to Lord Sickhert it was a joke.

"The Deliverers have long thought themselves brilliant," he sniggered. "But they can't even build straight!"

Sickhert's scoping view took wing until it focused on the sleek galley ship cruising west. Reveling in its cargo, Lord Sickhert rubbed his bone white fingers together.

"Soon the Betrayers and their prisoner will be at the Portal."

Sighing like a wolf after a kill, he ran a tongue over his jagged teeth. Sickhert bent over the Lava Pool Gramarye. Steam condensed on his maggot-white face, pooling on the bridge where his nose should have been. The droplets passed over the two nostril slits and dripped back into the pool.

"Obstruction? No." Lord Sickhert hissed. He pulled on the stalactite hanging from the ceiling and a mournful howl sounded. Immediately, the sound of jackboots drummed up the twisting stair.

The spike-headed Captain Sludge entered the room and dropped to his knees. He opened his mouth to release the honorific spittle.

"Not now!" Sickhert waved a hand. "Fool! Did you not look at the river before sending her on?"

"I-what?" Those usually ruthless eyes stared back at him with surprise while reddish slime beaded on his forehead.

"The river is silted up. Now Mona Lisa cannot reach the sea." He raised an ashy hand to slap that ambitious soldier across the face but hesitated when Sludge had the presence of mind to respond quickly.

"I will call upon the Saracen Slaves. They will dredge it, Lord." Sludge said backing up.

"You had best, or feel the Correction Chamber's lash," Lord Sickhert warned. "And be sure to avoid the Thinker's watchful eye. Make all work appear innocent."

"It is done." Sludge bowed and exited the Throne Room.

Lord Sickhert smiled. Once again, he had thwarted disaster. Soon the ship would be at sea, where few Artanians could follow. He returned to the Lava Pool Gramarye, inhaled the bitter mist of sulfuric fumes, and dreamt of the day when all Artanians would breathe this acrid gas.

And he would be Lord of them all.

Chapter 26

Thump! Bartholomew heard the muffled sound of metal against metal. He felt a jolt of pain ripping through his arm as the Fish loosened its grip. Knowing he had precious seconds, Bartholomew shot to the surface.

"Swim Bartholomew!" He heard Alex cry from somewhere.

Gulping a mouthful of air, Bartholomew aimed for shore. Heavy arms dragged as he recalled what his swim coach had told him years before.

"Angle your hands as they enter the water. Then pull in the shape of an S until your arm is past your body."

Before the monster had a chance to clamp down on him again, Bartholomew sped up. Then he felt a nudge behind him. The Fish!

He remembered Coach's words. *"Flutter kick, Bartholomew. Straight legs. You are a sleek ship gliding through the water. Not an anchor pulling it down."*

Bartholomew kicked furiously. As he turned his head for a breath he ventured a glance. Dust bunnies! He was in the middle of the river. Going the wrong way.

Vowing to aim for shore, Bartholomew twisted into a turn. *S-pull. Flutter.*

The current pushed against him making every stroke feel like five. He slowed his pace and let his legs drag behind him.

"Come on Bartholomew. Faster!" Gwen urged.

Her words were like fuel powering his legs. His feet splashed as he closed in on shore. *Fifteen yards. Ten.*

His lungs burned, but he didn't dare waste time breathing. He pulled harder. Soon he felt pebbles under his feet. Only now did Bartholomew turn to suck in a quick breath.

"Watch out!" Alex shouted.

But it was too late. Wolfish jaws pulled him under. Water filled his mouth and nostrils.

He blew little bubbles to keep from choking then grabbed hold of one of the flaring fins. Bartholomew yanked back. Then he jerked it to the left with all his might.

Nothing.

That fish had to have a soft spot somewhere. He kneed the beast's underbelly. It was like hitting steel. Bartholomew drew his free arm back and punched its wolf face.

The jaws slackened.

He started to pull his arm free, but the wolf-fish clamped down before he could escape.

Desperately he kicked, but in his struggle, he forgot where he was and swallowed a huge mouthful of river water. He sputtered as bubbles whorled around his face. Fire filled his chest.

Gurgling, the foam confused his mind and vision. Brown fizz simmered.

Bartholomew's body convulsed in an oxygen-deprived spasm. Desperate to breathe, he sucked in another lungful of the river as a faint ringing filled his ears.

Bartholomew felt the strength fade from his body. The last thing he remembered were teeth piercing flesh before everything went dark.

Chapter 27

Gwen heard the bow strings hum as the arrow sailed through the air.

When the bolt met its mark, the monster released Bartholomew. Letting the crossbow clatter to the floor, Gwen raced to catch up with Alex who was already in waist deep water. He had his arms wrapped around Bartholomew's waist and was trying to drag his limp body to shore.

"Help me!" Alex cried.

Splashing into the river, Gwen gripped one of Bartholomew's arms. Using all her eighty-two pounds, she leaned back to help lift the listless Bartholomew to the riverbank.

Alex knelt in the mud. "Breathe, Bartholomew, breathe."

Gwen stared. Bartholomew's face was so pale. But she thought he had magical powers here. Now she was beginning to wonder. Could people die in this world?

"Just one breath B-3," Alex's voice was choked with emotion.

"Maybe we should–"

Her words were cut short when Bartholomew spasmed. He gave a lurch and shuddered. Then he coughed once and started sputtering.

Alex placed a hand under his head and rolled Bartholomew on his side. A long stream of brown foam erupted from B-3's lips. Alex patted him on the back and waited for the spasms to subside before helping him to sit up.

"All right?" Alex asked the still pale Bartholomew.

Spitting out another mouthful, B-3 nodded.

Gwen felt as if she were seeing Bartholomew for the first time. This wasn't the super wimp from school. No whining or running away. He'd been the one to jump in and save Alex. She realized how she'd misjudged him.

"You had us going there for a minute." Alex gave Bartholomew a friendly punch in the arm.

Bartholomew smiled weakly. "I thought I'd try to replace Zach as Mr. Entertainment. What do you think?"

"I give it a three."

"No," Gwen continued with a playful smirk. "2.8. Your hurl wasn't colorful enough."

Bartholomew chuckled until a fit of coughing made him spit up more brown gunk.

"Now you're just showing off," Gwen said.

Bartholomew shook his head and river water splattered Alex and Gwen. They all started cracking up.

When the laughter had died down, Leonardo beckoned them closer. "I am glad you are safe, young Deliverer," Leonardo laid a hand on Bartholomew's shoulder. "But now we must seek understanding. Tell me about the beast."

"Well, it had a strange way of swimming. It kept rolling on its side like it needed to take a breath."

"I noticed that too." Alex said.

"Do you think it was trying to breathe or was it helping you?" The bearded man asked.

"Don't know. But why would it want to keep me alive?"

"Now you are thinking like a scientist." Leonardo nodded.

"Hey, it wasn't going to eat Mr. Clean," Gwen blurted out. "It was taking him somewhere."

"I have to agree. Now we must ask where and why?"

Gwen rubbed her chin chewing over Da Vinci's words. She glanced at B-3, his white dress shirt all streaked with mud. Then she noticed his sleeve. Had that creature torn it? She bent down for a closer look.

"I know that I must be quite the spectacle," Bartholomew blushed smoothing his matted hair, "but you don't have to–"

"What is that on your arm?" Gwen pointed.

Bartholomew glanced down. A piece of thin fabric was wrapped around his wrist. He untwisted it and held it up.

"That looks just like what I saw under the pier," Alex said.

"I believe I know what this is." Leonardo removed the fabric and rubbed it between his fingers. "Alexander, please show me the other one back at the Fortress."

When they were back at the dock, Alex pointed out what he'd been reaching for before he fell in the water. This time Nicolo used his lance to retrieve the fabric and handed it to Leonardo. The old man held it up next to the one that had been wrapped around Bartholomew's sleeve.

They were a perfect match.

"What is it?" Gwen asked.

"Ahh." Leonardo fingered the fine fabric. "That, young ones, is a veil, my dear Mona Lisa's. I gave it to her on her birthday." His voice cracked on the last words.

Feeling awkward, Gwen stared at her feet. She never knew what to say at times like these. Dad didn't deal with sad topics at her house. After Mom left, he never mentioned that empty place at the table. He stuck to subjects like work-outs or sports.

"But why was it on the fish?" she asked, suddenly breaking the silence.

"If I knew that, perhaps I would also know my daughter's location."

"Okay," Alex began, thinking out loud. "So, we know that Mona Lisa disappeared here and that this fish grabbing people."

"Right." Gwen nodded her head.

"Then," Alex said slowly. "I think it captured her." Alex turned to Leonardo. "But why?"

"Sickhert uses trickery to turn Artanians to spies. That beast must have been one of them."

Gwen shook her head. "A fish as a spy? Come on."

"I told you. Artania is different from Earth," Alex said.

"Yeah, but a fish?"

"I think," Bartholomew interrupted. "We should stop arguing and try to figure out where that thing was going."

Agreeing, Leonardo suggested going to a library for research. As they headed out, Gwen started to smile but then Mr. da Vinci turned toward her.

"But beware." Leonardo stopped her advance with one hand. "If there is one spy, there could be others."

Chapter 28

Alex glanced around. The streets were filling with chattering people. Women in long flowing gowns and veiled heads emerged from doorways. Squires in two tone tights and belted tunics whispered in each other's ears. Men in black and red caps jabbered away excitedly. People pointed and stared.

"Did you hear?"

"Yes. The Deliverer was almost carried away."

"The water beast was two men long."

"I heard three."

"But still he defeated it."

While poor Bartholomew's face turned as red as the apples in the fruit-sellers basket, Alex covered his mouth, hiding a smile.

A couple of minutes later they turned toward a large domed church. Leonardo bowed, and then lead them through multiple arches. "The Vestibule," he said with a sweeping motion of his hand.

Alex thought the staircase in Bartholomew's house was cool, but this one stopped him mid-step. "Why are there frames but no windows?" Alex asked staring at the wide steps that lead to a dark landing. "It's so gloomy in here."

"It is because we enter the Library. We step from the darkness of ignorance to the light of knowledge."

"Grinning, Bartholomew held up one finger. "Symbols! Artists during the Renaissance used to have one thing stand for another. For example, laziness was painted as an armless man who cannot work."

"Gross," Gwen said, wrinkling up her nose.

"Maybe," Bartholomew agreed. "But it inspired people to do the right thing. Especially when they saw justice as something like a lovely woman floating on a cloud."

"Okay Mr. Encyclopedia, Thanks for the lesson," Alex said, holding up a hand. "Now, we are all enlightened."

Just then a shadow fell across his face. Alex couldn't make out what it was at first but when his eyes adjusted, he saw a furrowed brow and deep-set eyes.

This painted man stopped his pacing and growled as if disgusted by the interruption.

"Need my help?" he asked Leonardo with a cool glance. Before the older man could reply he raised one eyebrow and turned into the room. "Of course, you do."

Leonardo entered first followed by Gwen and Bartholomew and then Alex. He felt a little dizzy stepping onto the tiled floor with its intricate pattern of flowers, curlicues, and diamonds.

"So many books!" Bartholomew gasped.

Alex knew that a place like this was heaven for his friend. Here hundreds of ancient books lay atop rows of slanted wooden desks. Alex wandered over to one of the rose-colored stands where one book was open to a beautifully illustrated page framed with curling branches and leaves. In the center, a man dressed in red and purple robes wore a stocking cap. He held a small golden organ on his lap and had a serious look on his face. Alex reached out to feel the paper.

"Scusi!" The painted organist on the page slapped Alex's hand away. "I work here."

"Do not touch the manuscripts!" the thin man growled. This guy was cranky.

"Sorry," Alex said, rolling his eyes so only Bartholomew could see.

Now, young ones let us to the task at hand. My…" Leonardo cleared his throat as if a piece of old meat were in it. "…associate may have information that will help us in our quest. Michelangelo?"

So, this man was the famous Michelangelo! Alex hit Bartholomew's shoulder with the back of his hand and they both smiled.

"It is bad enough you interrupted my work." Michelangelo growled again. "Now you bring me children who cannot even pay attention?"

"They are Deliverers just as our creators were."

"My creator would have had better manners."

"Your creator was a–" Leonardo paused.

"A what?"

"Never you mind."

"It is because you are unwilling to speak the truth." Michelangelo said. "That my creator was the greatest sculptor, architect, and fresco painter of all time!"

Alex knew that Michelangelo might have done all these things but to brag like that to Leonardo. Jeesh. What an ego.

Leonardo's face clouded over with anger. "No, he was an arrogant, brusque, loner who delighted in making fun of mine!"

"Are you still going on about that incident on the bridge? It was folly, a joke."

"I did not think so. Your first made fun of the fact that I could not quote Dante, then called me a quitter! And the ideas my creator had. You never understood them!"

"So! How many paintings did he make in his lifetime? Nowhere near what mine did."

"He only wrote thousands of pages of scientific philosophy!"

"Guys." Gwen jumped between the two men and held up her skinny arms to push them apart. "Come on. You are worse than my parents before the divorce. I thought we were here to save this Mona Lisa chick."

Leonardo's face softened. "But of course. The daughter of my heart." He turned to Michelangelo. "You have heard?"

"Few enter my Laurentian Library. Is she not safe?"

"Gone." Leonardo shook his head.

"What? But we built the Fortress to protect her!"

Michelangelo listened while they quickly explained about the beggar, the fish, and the discovery of the veil. When they finished, he stopped rubbing his forehead and suddenly slammed a fist on a desk.

"We cannot let her become a Mudlark!"

There was an awkward moment of silence.

"What's a Mudlark?" Gwen asked, breaking it.

"Surely you know?" Leonardo looked at her quizzically. "Have the Deliverers explained nothing?"

Gwen shook her head.

"A Mudlark is a twisted creature," Alex began.

"But it wasn't always," Leonardo continued. "Once it was one of us. A citizen of Artania. A son or daughter."

"Before being transformed into a zombie-like slave for Lord Sickhert," Alex said, remembering a vacant-eyed creature he'd battled on his last trip.

"Can't they be changed back?"

"No, never," Leonardo said. "That is why we must find my daughter, soon."

Michelangelo held up a finger and went over to the book Alex had looked at earlier. Gently, he picked up the manuscript.

"Ahh a codex," Leonardo said. "Squarcialupi?"

"Of course," Michelangelo replied with a smug smile. "What else would it be?"

Alex sighed. More big words and riddles. But still he had to know.

"Okay, I'll bite. What's that?"

"Here lies the greatest music of Italy from my time," Michelangelo said. "My friend Landini will demonstrate." He opened the book and held it up the page for all to see.

The man in purple and red robes on the page took a bow. Then he sat on a wooden chair and began to play the golden organ in his lap. The room filled with an eerie melody like something from a dream. Or the dream of a dream.

Alex began to sway to the music as a warm mist filled the air. His eyelids grew heavy. Then the room faded from view.

Chapter 29

Bartholomew blinked and glanced around sleepily. Just a second before he'd been in Michelangelo's library, now he was back in Leonardo's lab. What happened? Alex and Gwen were a few feet away looking just as dazed as he felt.

"What the heck?" Alex muttered.

"You see," Michelangelo said, lifting one eyebrow. "It has powers to hypnotize."

"What powers? How did we get here?" Gwen demanded, her green eyes flashing.

"The last thing I remember was haunting music," Bartholomew said.

"Landini's organ hypnotized you. Then you walked here," Michelangelo explained matter-of-factly.

"I did not!" Gwen sniffed and stuck out a petulant chin.

"Worry not bambina. It was but a test. To see what powers the other arts could have on the creators." Leonardo flicked his long white beard at her. "And it was successful."

"But it did not work on us." Michelangelo held up the illuminated page from the book where Landini sat looking very pleased with himself. With a smug smile, he pulled his purple robes tighter around his waist.

Bartholomew felt like the butt of a giant joke. Was he some sort of clown for their entertainment? He crossed his arms and eyed the Artanians warily.

"Nor will it have powers, unless the Deliverers recreate it," Leonardo said, pointing at a huge easel in the corner.

"Oh," Bartholomew said. "I see where you are going with all of this. We need to get that fish to lead us to Mona Lisa without arousing suspicion."

"And the only ways are to scare it, convince it, or hypnotize it," Gwen said.

"For sure. Come on B-3 Let's get to work." Alex picked up a ladle-shaped stone and started to walk over to the table where a grinding bowl and various colored rocks, minerals, and jars of powders sat. He picked up a reddish pebble and was about to start grinding it when Leonardo interrupted.

"The design must be proportioned. You cannot begin without a plan," Leonardo instructed.

"I thought I'd just copy that other page," Alex said.

Leonardo shook his head. "You must sketch lines first and make a design."

"If the perspective is not just right, the music will not hypnotize," Michelangelo agreed. "Come let me show you." Walking over to the table, he picked up a quill pen and dipped it in ink before drawing two connected squares on a piece of parchment paper. Next to these he made a larger square with sides equaling the rectangle's length. Then he repeated the process again and again until he had filled the paper with connecting squares, looking kind of like plans for a house.

"He is making a grid so that the perspective is correct," Leonardo said. "You must make sure that if something is further away it appears smaller. There is a direct mathematical relationship between how far away something seems to be and its size."

"Oh no!" Bartholomew groaned. "I hate math."

"But you are a Deliverer." Leonardo smiled. "You use mathematics daily, whether you realize it or not."

"Yes." Michelangelo nodded. "All artists do." He pointed to the center squares. "This place will become your vanishing point. The music must come from there for the hypnosis to work."

Bartholomew felt a pit in his stomach. If the numbers weren't just right they couldn't hypnotize the fish? He'd had trouble with math all year. He shook his head and stared off into space.

"I can't," he whispered.

"Don't tell me that." Alex glared at him.

"You know that math is what got me in trouble in the first place."

"So, suck it up. Try."

"You go ahead. I'd just mess it up."

Alex reached for a quill, but Michelangelo blocked his hand.

"Our world was born from the magic of two. Not one."

"Both must create equally for the magic to work," Leonardo added.

Bartholomew's face grew hot and he felt the red rise in his cheeks. He wanted to help but he wasn't good at math like Alex.

"Come on, I'll help you." Alex gave him a friendly nudge.

"All right. But I'm not making any promises."

"That's okay." Gwen grinned. We wouldn't have believed you if you did."

"Very funny." He curled his lip at her then turned to Leonardo. "Now, where do we begin?

Chapter 30

"Okay, be extra careful now. Don't drop it," Bartholomew advised.

Gwen stared at him incredulously. Mr. Mess-Up-Seventy-Six-Times while everyone had to wait was telling her to be careful? She started to retort, but something about Bartholomew's face made her stop. She nodded her readiness to Alex and lifted her corner of the painting.

As Alex backed up toward the doorway, the painted organist on the canvas started to warm up his voice. To Gwen his counting to three in Italian sounded like, "Oono, dooay, tray." It was catchy, and she found herself singing along. "Uno, due, tre, uno, due, tre," she trilled.

Alex grinned at her. "I didn't know you could sing."

Gwen blushed. She could. The one thing Rochelle had done that was motherly was sing lullabies. When Gwen was by herself she often sang; it made her feel less lonely. But she usually didn't do it in front of people.

"Gwen, you have a beautiful voice," Bartholomew said.

"Whatever. I'm just trying to keep this Landini dude happy, so he can hypnotize the fish."

"Scusi!" Landini said with an indignant snuffle. "I no-a-need-a child to make-a my music. It-a sublime on its own."

"I think you might have offended our composer here," Leonardo said with a hearty laugh.

Gwen grinned, glad to have the focus back on the job. Not on some of her girly singing.

Twisting the painting through doorways and around corners, she and Alex followed Leonardo down the steps of the Fortress through the cobblestone streets of Florence.

"Watch out, people," Bartholomew cautioned from behind.

"We got it," Gwen said.

"There's a dog. Oh no. Don't let it get too close. It might urinate on Landini. Shoo pup, shoo." The blathering Bartholomew mopped his brow with a stained handkerchief.

"Alex?" Gwen muttered through clenched braces. Bartholomew's constant fussing, fretting, and flinching at every fluttering leaf was driving her crazy. She was tempted to drop her side and bop him on the head.

"I know. I know. Just deal."

When they reached the Ponte Vecchio Bridge, the Fish was nowhere in sight. But several people they asked said that they'd seen it swimming up and down the Arno River earlier.

"Now what?" Gwen asked.

"We wait," Alex replied as the two of them propped the painting up against a shop wall. He stepped inside a jewelers' shop and peeked out their window. Gwen followed scanning the water below.

Nothing. Not even a splash.

After about twenty minutes, they regrouped near the center pier of the bridge.

"Well, it was seen earlier." Leonardo smoothed his thick eyebrows with a finger. "It may return."

In the silence that followed, Gwen's stomach growled. Alex stared at her and sniggered.

"What?" she snapped. "I'm hungry."

"Actually, so am I," Bartholomew agreed.

Leonardo glanced at the water again then smiled at the children. "Come. I know of a tavern close by." Ducking his head inside a jeweler's shop he told the shopkeeper they'd be at Signor Pastori's before leading the children down a narrow street to the restaurant.

With the painting safely tucked in a corner they settled themselves on long wooden benches. Gwen breathed in through her nose. The pungent smell of spices made her mouth water.

"I can just taste the pizza. I'm thinking pepperoni."

"Me too." Alex nodded.

"Pizza?" Leonardo gave them a blank stare. "What is that?"

"You know, pizza," Gwen replied. "That bready pie with thick tomato sauce, bubbling cheese, and mmm, mmm spicy pepperoni."

"I do not know it."

"But this is Italy. You have to have pizza."

Bartholomew sighed as if Gwen were a spaz who had just fallen on her butt. "Pizza was not invented until the nineteenth century," he said.

"Okay Mr. Encyclopedia. Then what do we eat? I'm starving," Gwen said.

"Pasta or rice dishes were popular during the Renaissance."

"And how do you know this?"

"When you're home schooled there's lots of time to research obscure facts. The Italian Renaissance has always fascinated me."

"Didn't you ever, like watch cartoons or play video games?"

"I am a Borax. Mother says we rise above such things."

Gwen stuck a finger beside her nose as if she were picking it. "Boring."

"Their macaroni with saffron and chicken is very good," Leonardo snapped his fingers at the bald man in a sea green tunic and leggings. "*Signore. Vorrei pasta i pollo.*"

"*Cierto.*" Senor Pastori bowed and passed through a door next to a large stone fireplace.

"I love macaroni and cheese." Alex smacked his lips.

Gwen totally agreed. "But not the stuff in the school cafeteria. Yuck."

"Too sticky. Like it's got glue in it."

"Kroft is the best," Gwen said.

When the heaping platter arrived, it looked nothing like either Kroft or the school mac and cheese Gwen was expecting. First it wasn't macaroni, but spaghetti. Second, it was a pasty gray instead of yellow. And third, it smelled so spicy she didn't know if she could eat it. She sniffed at it doubtfully.

"You can't always skate at the park," Alex said. "Sometimes you gotta hit the streets."

Gwen sighed. "I'm so hungry I could eat anything."

Gwen scooped up a single strand and stuck out her tongue to test it. It wasn't half bad; a little hot but she liked it.

"Gwood," she mumbled shoving in another forkful. Soon she was munching away greedily with the rest of them.

Gwen was in the middle of t a long draught from a tankard of water when she saw him in the doorway. Water started to dribble down the side of her mouth. She sputtered and covered her mouth.

Then she covered her eyes.

"What?" Alex asked from across the table.

Keeping her eyes covered, Gwen pointed behind him. She heard Alex cough and Bartholomew squeaked.

Right behind them was a giant. And he was absolutely naked!

Chapter 31

"Faster! Dig!" Sludge hissed from his hill perch. He wished he had a whip; then he'd show these peasants a thing or two. But Lord Sickhert had been clear about how to keep these traitors on their side.

"Encourage but do not incite fear," his overlord had said.

Sludge sneered. In their tattered tunics and muddied leggings, these peons dug, picked, and hauled away buckets of soil with no idea that they were betraying their own kind. They actually believed that they would become lords of the manor when the Change came. As stupid as the humans who created them.

"*Mama, mia.*" One peasant mopped his brow with a dirty rag. "I am-a tired."

"*Si*," his partner said setting down the bucket of mud in his hands." Me too. Here, take some of my water." He removed a goatskin bag from his shoulder and handed it to his friend.

The painted man drank greedily, letting water spill down his chin and onto his brown tunic. "*Grazie*," he said.

Sludge fought the urge to gag; these Artanians were disgusting. At least he wouldn't have to deal with their sickly sweetness for long. When Lord Sickhert gained control, the air would fill with sulfuric mist.

At least these peasants were steady workers. After dredging the silted-up river all day, the Arno nearly connected to the Mediterranean Sea.

But time was running out. The Deliverer had escaped the Fish and was drawing closer to Mona Lisa. Her ship must reach the Portal before the humans found it.

If only he could transport her over land. But she glowed with the light of Creation and would shine like a beacon to anyone searching for her.

Sludge growled. How could he encourage speed without pain?

Of course. He cupped his slime-covered hands over bulbous lips. "Remember peasants," Sludge called down into the ditch. "You were painted as slaves. For centuries, you have repeated the same tedious tasks again and again."

"I have served the Medici family long and well," the man with the goatskin bag grumbled. "Yet still I am not free."

With as voice as smooth as a pupa's skin, Sludge said, "But Lord Sickhert will remove those bonds. Making you new."

Just as Sludge expected, a few angry faces filled with hope. Those idiots in the aqueduct below believed his every word. It was so easy to deceive these Artanians. They thought that they were suffering when in fact they were happier than any Shadow Swine he knew.

"Faster," Sludge crooned. "For your just reward."

The picks and shovels rose and fell until soon the first trickles of water broke through.

"More!" Sludge said.

When the river flowed freely to the sea, the Shadow Swine captain sighed. Now the pirates could sail. Then Mona Lisa would enter the Portal and the Renaissance Nation would fall.

Sludge's yellow eyes glowed in anticipation.

Chapter 32

Bartholomew was glad he wasn't eating like Alex and Gwen when he turned around. While they sputtered and choked, all he had to do was avert his eyes.

But Leonardo acted like a naked giant stopping by during lunch was the most normal thing in the world. And come to think of it maybe it was. Bartholomew had seen tons of Renaissance art with nude or semi-clothed people in them.

"*Ciao* David!" Leonardo called.

"*Buongiorno*," the giant said bending at the waist, so he could peer through the doorway.

"Are you hungry? Perhaps some macaroni?"

"Thank you, no. I am here with news."

Bartholomew couldn't help it. His curiosity made him turn around. Oops. Too much information. He turned back, his cheeks beet red.

"What is it David?" Leonardo asked.

"The Fish has been seen just west of Florence."

"Let's go. Come on." Alex pushed away from the table and motioned for Gwen to help him with the painting.

As the naked giant lead them along, Bartholomew tried to look away. Of course, if you don't watch where you are going, you trip. Especially over cobblestones.

Gwen seemed just as embarrassed. But since she and Alex were carrying the painting it sort of blocked their view. Bartholomew wished he had something like that.

Then he realized he did.

If he were just four steps behind, the painting hid the most embarrassing part of the David's anatomy. Then he could pretend that David was just a man in swim trunks and he could focus on walking.

"Where is the Fish anyhow?" Bartholomew called out after several minutes. "We're way past Ponte Vecchio."

"Yeah," Alex agreed. "Almost past the city."

David pointed a marble finger at the river below. There a single fin sliced through the water.

Bartholomew thought the sight of the creature that had nearly drowned him would make him tremble, but that wolfish face just infuriated him. *Try to hurt my friend, will you?* He fumed, remembering how it'd trapped Alex.

"The painting, quickly," Leonardo ordered.

Gwen and Alex propped the canvas up against a boulder facing the river. Then they all waited for Landini to sing.

And waited.

But the musician did not begin his hypnotizing song.

"Hurry, it's getting away," Alex urged.

"I must-a warm up," Landini said humming a few bars.

Gwen raised her arms in exasperation. "Come on!"

"Greatness, takes-a time."

The fish's tail flicked as it moved further downstream. Soon it wouldn't be able to hear any singing much less be hypnotized by it. Bartholomew glanced at Alex who had clapped a hand to his head.

He tried to keep his voice calm. "Mr. Landini, Please!"

With an exaggerated yawn, the man stretched his arms over his head and cracked his knuckles. Landini repositioned the portative organ in his lap, opened the bellows, and placed his fingers on the keyboard.

Could he go any slower? This wasn't a concert for all of Italy.

Five more me-me's and seven knuckle cracks later. Landini finally began. Hauntingly beautiful music filled the air and floated down the river.

With a relieved smile, Bartholomew turned to his friend. Instead of smiling back, Alex shook his head and pointed down river.

The fish was nowhere to be seen.

Chapter 33

Now Landini sings. Alex wanted to scream. And he would have if he thought it'd do any good. "Come on before it gets away!" he called. Grabbing one end of the painting, he started dragging it behind him as Gwen fumbled to pick up her corner.

Once she had it on her shoulders, he quickened the pace, tramping along the bank while a light breeze ruffled the rainbow-colored folds of Landini's robe. Although the singer trilled in a clear voice, it did little to cool Alex's anger.

I put up with Bartholomew's whining, cranky Michelangelo, and almost drowning. Still this diva waits to sing? Alex thought clenching the painting tighter.

"There straight ahead." Gwen pointed with her chin.

Cruel eyes rose out of the water and scanned the shore. Alex ducked down.

"Strange," Bartholomew said after a few moments. "It's not reacting at all. Maybe it's immune."

"Louder Landini, it's not working!" Alex urged.

The tiny maestro glared at Alex, who glared right back. Harrumphing, Landini trebled in ever higher notes. The timbre of his voice rose into the air.

Still the Fish swam on.

"No!" Alex kicked at the dirt.

"Let's get closer," Gwen suggested.

The fish slapped its sharp tail against the surface in seeming rebellion before diving beneath the rippling foam.

Landini's organ moaned but the beast didn't slow.

Alex was perplexed. They had used Divine Proportion. This creature should be snoring away by now, if fish did that.

Just when he thought things couldn't get any worse, he heard a loud groan from Gwen.

"What?" he asked, turning in her direction.

Gwen jerked her head up hill.

"Seriously?" Alex said staring at the thicket of thorny brambles.

"It must be six feet tall." Bartholomew said.

Gwen sighed. "There's no way we're getting through that."

Alex wanted to throw the painting on the ground and stomp on that slowpoke Landini. He glanced around looking for something to entice or at least to scare the creature in their direction.

Nothing.

He was about to make a mad dash up hill, when David ambled up, the afternoon breeze rippling the fabric of the sling draped over his back. For some reason Alex thought about the David and Goliath story that inspired this marble sculpture. In it, a boy defeated a giant with a single stone.

"That's it!" Alex hit Bartholomew with the back of his hand before calling to the eighteen-foot statue. "David, find a rock, a big one."

"*Nessun problema*," David said, scanning the hillside. He soon found a cannonball-sized one and loped up, his long marble legs covering the distance in three strides. Hefting it in his huge hands, he placed it in his sling.

"Perfect," Alex said.

Ordering everyone to stand back, David began to twirl the sling. Faster he twirled, neck and arm muscles bulging. Then, leaning back, he closed one eye, and threw.

The speeding rock jet higher, lighting up the sky like a shooting star.

"Whoa," Alex said, watching its meteoric rise and fall.

When it hit the water, the fish reared up, long whiskers twitching.

"Please," Alex said trying to keep his voice controlled. "Can you sing now?"

Thankfully this time the maestro didn't do any warm-ups but burst into loud song. As soon as the beautiful melody filled the air, the Fish slowed. Swimming in time to the music, its v-shaped tail swayed back and forth. After a few moments, its eyes rolled back in its head and it glided to shore.

Leonardo, who had just arrived, hobbled over to the riverbank. He began to speak to the hypnotized fish in low tones as the creature slowly lifted its fins on one side and the other. When it started to swim in slow circles, the bearded man turned to Alex and his friends.

"It is done. The entranced creature will follow your command."

Bartholomew's eyes widened. "But you are coming too, aren't you?"

"That which was etched in the beginning of time, cannot be undone. The Soothsayer Stone requires you go on alone. Besides, I am old and would be little help," Leonardo said.

Alex couldn't argue. Leonardo would be someone else to worry about. He shook the old man's gnarled hand, handed David the Landini painting, and thanked them both for their help.

He trudged up the mountain feeling heavier with each step. Bartholomew. Gwen. Mona Lisa. The entire Renaissance Nation. A lot of responsibility for a twelve-year-old.

Halfway up the hill, he turned. Leonardo and David had disappeared, but the Fish was still swimming in circles, waiting for them to emerge on the other side of the brambles.

The ripples below made a maze of circles on the Arno River, reminding Alex of a watery labyrinth. One he hoped he wouldn't get lost in.

Or fall into.

Chapter 34

Gwen wished Mr. Clean would go faster. Even though she and Alex were making their way back down hill to the river Bartholomew was still at the top.

"Come on Dude!"

Bartholomew waved but kept tiptoeing. It was annoying how he stopped every few seconds to reach in his pocket for that empty bottle of hand sanitizer. She had no idea why he didn't just throw it away.

It didn't seem to bug Alex though. With a quick wave, he sprinted down to the Arno to order the Fish forward before leading them along shore.

She followed that river for what seemed like hours. And the fact that the guys barely spoke as they passed olive orchards, stone houses, and fields of waist high sunflowers, made it seem even longer. Alex looked like he was deep into tactical plans while Bartholomew went from smiling at the clouds to tripping over rocks.

Yawn.

But as soon as they entered the shadowy forest of ash, beech, and oak trees, Gwen's annoyance turned to a feeling of foreboding. Every twisting branch reminded her of her bedroom furniture seeming to swell and shrink in the darkness before the nightmares came.

She had just halted when she noticed the Fish start to swim around in figure eights.

"What is it doing?" she asked.

Then she saw the triple masts swaying back and forth.

"Hide!" Alex rasped.

The three of them ducked down behind an outcropping of rocks at the edge of the woods. Gwen gaped at the long and lean sailboat with *Red Raven* painted in crimson letters on the stern. As its pointed bow bobbed on the river turbaned men milled about on deck.

Alex jerked his head toward the ship. "I bet Mona Lisa is in there. Probably in the hold."

"Maybe," Bartholomew said, chewing on his lower lip. "But how do we check? In case you two didn't notice, those are pirates. And they have weapons."

Gwen swallowed. Those curved swords looked scary. And the sneers on the pirates' faces told her they wouldn't hesitate to use them. Even though this place seemed like a cartoon, she'd learned that you could get hurt here just as easily as on Earth.

"We need a diversion," Alex whispered.

Bartholomew nodded.

"The fish?" Gwen suggested.

"Nah." Alex shook his head. "We need to get them as far from the ship as possible."

"We need something like a bullhorn," Bartholomew said.

All Gwen saw were rocks and trees.

"You got it B-3." Alex smirked.

"I did?"

"Sure. Maybe not a bullhorn, but something *like* it." He started to scoop some mud up from the riverbank.

Bartholomew stared at him blankly at first. Then his blue eyes lit up and he smiled. He ran a hand over the ground touching different stones on the ground as if searching for a good skipping rock. When he found one about the size of Gwen's foot, he set it next to where Alex was working.

"Perfect," Alex said before molding the mud into a long thin shape. Bartholomew knelt at his side and started rolling the opposite end of what Alex was working on.

What happened next made Gwen's jaw drop.

Alex and Bartholomew's hands sped up and soon their arms were just a blur. It only took a few seconds but when Gwen blinked to clear her vision, Alex was leaning back smiling at the axe in front of them.

Sculpting an axe in twenty seconds was weird enough. The crazy thing was that it was no longer made of mud and stone but had transformed into a steel blade with a real wooden handle.

"Nice job B-3," Alex said and then turned to Gwen. "Bartholomew might be good at sculpting, but I think you should handle this."

Looking at him blankly, Gwen shrugged her shoulders. Alex didn't explain but just kept smiling as if waiting for something.

She shrugged. "What?"

"The diversion, of course." Alex pointed at a tall cypress behind her.

Then she got it. They'd made the axe to fell a tree. Okay, no problem. Alex was right; she did know how to handle one; Dad had taught her to chop wood up at their cabin in Big Sur. She'd even helped him cut down a Christmas tree at that farm up Highway 101.

"No problemo." But when she went to pick up the axe, it was heavier than it looked. Gwen lifted weights but, man. "On second thought, couldn't you dudes work your magic on this thing and make it lighter?"

"No, it doesn't work that way," Alex said shaking his head. "But I'll help you if you want." Hefting one end of it, he helped her carry it over to the tall beech tree.

Gwen set her end down and circled the tree three times. "Hmm," she mused before explaining how to make wedged cuts to get the tree to fall where you want.

"Okay," Alex said. "As soon as the toppling tree makes the pirates come, I'll run downhill to board the ship."

"No, I'll go," Bartholomew said.

"I don't think so," Alex said doubtfully.

"I'm the better swimmer."

Alex clenched and unclenched his fists. Gwen could tell that he wanted to say no. He searched Bartholomew's face. "Are you sure?"

"Positive," Bartholomew replied.

A hesitant Alex agreed. Clenching his jaw, he watched Bartholomew give them a thumbs up and trot through the trees down to the embankment.

"Let's do it." With Alex's help, Gwen hoisted the axe onto her shoulder and widened her stance. Leaning back, she swung. A bit of bark chipped away.

"Now knock that sucker over," Alex said.

Gwen went around to the other side and tried a few short chops but barely broke bark.

"Put more power into it."

She flexed her wiry muscles and struck. Still only splinters. She shrugged.

"I know," Alex said. "I'll come around behind you and we'll make our arms work as one."

"Sounds like a plan."

But when Alex positioned his arms over hers, Gwen wished she hadn't agreed. Her face turned red and her heart started pounding.

"Ready?" Alex asked.

All Gwen could do was nod weakly. Her throat was too dry to answer.

"Swing!" he cried pulling her arms back.

Gwen tried to focus but those curls brushing against her cheek were making her light-headed. She'd never noticed how adorable Alex's sun-streaked curls were before. And his arms felt so strong.

Staring off into space, she imagined the two of them in the middle of the gym at the school dance.

"Gwen, you okay?" Alex nudged her with his shoulder.

Blinking, she shook her head and grumbled that she was fine before raising her arms for a third strike.

"Now, swing."

With this strike, the swaying tree toppled over and crashed right next to the ship. The surprised pirates shouted an alarm.

Even when they set down the axe Gwen could still feel his warm arms on hers. Pretending to brush the dust off her pants, she turned away. No way was she going to let him see her blush.

"Okay, here they come. Get ready."

Gwen nodded. Right then she would have flown to the moon if Alex had asked her.

Chapter 35

From his crevice between two granite boulders Bartholomew peered at the ship. He tried to imagine the men on deck as clowns in balloon pants, but it didn't work. He had read enough about pirates to know what they'd do if they caught him. They'd poke at his toes with long pikes, slice his shirt with t curved scimitars, and then cut his hair, or more, with sharp daggers.

Bartholomew gulped.

When the last of the roaring men surged down the gangplank chasing Alex and Gwen, five pirates were still left on deck. Bartholomew had no idea how to get past them.

He couldn't approach from the bow, they'd see him if running along the shore, and he sure as Saniclean couldn't use the gangplank. He only had one choice. Oh well, maybe it'd wash some of the stains out of his clothes.

Scrambling atop the largest boulder, Bartholomew sprang into a long racing dive. When he hit the icy river, he glided under water toward the ship.

He finally surfaced downstream near the Fish some twenty yards behind the galley. There he ordered it to keep swimming in circles until he emerged later. Bartholomew wasn't sure if the blinking creature understood but he didn't have time to worry about that now.

Keeping an eye on the posted sentries, he sculled closer. Unable to find a way aboard at the stern, he swam toward the front of the sleek ship. When he reached the bow, he found the anchor chain leading up to the deck.

He slipped his shaking fingers through the links and ascended a few inches, his muscles straining from his heavy wet clothes.

The sound of approaching boots made Bartholomew freeze mid swing.

"What taking 'em so long?" a gravelly voice asked.

"You think I know? Captain tell nothing."

"What's that?" The first man leaned over the bow right above where the terrified Bartholomew hung.

"Aw just that fish," said the first pirate.

"But it be acting strange," replied the second.

"That's because it's on our side, tuna breath."

"For the twenty-third time, I don't have tuna breath."

"Oh yes you do. Even Aruj Barbarossa says so."

"I'll not stand here and be insulted by a Spanish slave!" he said before the sound of stomping feet told Bartholomew he'd headed for the stern.

The second man chuckled heartily when his comrade marched off. *Twenty-three, twenty-four, twenty-five,* Bartholomew counted waiting for that second pair of boots to shuffle away. Instead the pirate started whistling off-key.

The discordant sound compounded with stretching arms made Bartholomew feel like he was on a torture rack. His clothes grew heavier by the second. On finger slipped.

Bartholomew fought to hold on but if he didn't move soon he'd be in the river. With a huge splash. Another finger slipped.

Bartholomew began to pray.

Just when he was sure he'd be splattering water like a beacon, the second man ambled off.

Kicking his legs, Bartholomew swung up on deck and landed with a soft thud. Immediately he inched behind one of the cannons mounted on the platform to get a good view of the guards milling around on deck.

So far, so good.

The weather worn deck had a couple of lifeboats, some rigging, and barrels but no lady anywhere. There was a hatch mid-deck leading to another space. Maybe Mona Lisa was below.

Bartholomew crawled over. Holding his breath, he raised the hatch an inch. Waited. He lifted it a bit more. No pirates.

Lowering his legs into the square opening, Bartholomew dropped silently onto the wooden floor. Expecting an attack, he ducked down.

None came.

After a few moments, his eyes adjusted to the dim light. Here in the hull, a few hammocks and oil lanterns hung from the ceiling. On the floor, rows of benches were topped with the wooden oars that powered this ship.

Then he saw a head bowed as if in prayer. Bartholomew half stood as a painted woman turned toward him.

The first thing he noticed was how the filtered light gave her cheeks a soft glow. Her peach colored lips were turned down but her hazel eyes were rimmed in tears that reminded him of amber droplets.

Bartholomew was mesmerized.

When she opened her mouth to speak, Bartholomew put a finger to his lips. She nodded in understanding.

"*Buongiorno.*"

"Shhh," Bartholomew whispered as he tiptoed over to her. "I'm here to rescue you."

"A bambino?" She raised her nearly invisible eyebrows.

Okay he was being called a baby again. But it didn't make him angry; a curse would sound like an aria coming out of this lady's mouth. Her mustard-colored sleeves draped gently over her arms. With long auburn hair curled around in a gentle frame, her face was somewhere between oval and heart shaped.

Perfect. He couldn't help but stare.

Mona Lisa finally cleared her throat.

He blinked. "Sorry." *Be careful, and methodical, like Alex.* He thought glancing down at her wrists shackled to the bench.

"A key?"

Mona Lisa pointed to the ring hanging on the wall and Bartholomew padded over to retrieve it.

The handcuffs fell to the floor and she rubbed her red and bruised wrists. "Now we must fly."

"I don't know if the coast is clear yet. Let's wait."

"No bambino. Redbeard might return at any moment," Mona Lisa began to tug on Bartholomew's sleeve.

"My friends are distracting him. Let me check first." He set a knee on a bench and peered out the crack between the oar and the ship's hull. The fish was still swimming, and the footprint covered bank was empty. Still there might be a pirate just out of sight.

"Regardless–"

"Quiet, please. Let me look." Bartholomew shuffled over to the starboard side and peered through a different porthole. The empty river flowed peacefully and the only thing on opposite bank was a deer nibbling on leaves. But he knew that could be an illusion. He refused to take Mona Lisa out until it was perfectly safe.

Mona Lisa came up behind him and tugged on his sleeve again. Cocking an ear, he tried to ignore her. Several seconds passed in silence.

"Now?" Mona Lisa looked at him with wide eyes raised her hands in exasperation.

Bartholomew paced aft and stern, listened one more time. He would be a strategist, just like Alex.

"It is time, young one." Mona Lisa grabbed the ladder and put a foot on one of the rungs.

"No," he rasped, pulling her back as gently as he could. "I'll go first." He stepped up to the second rung of the ladder and poked his head out. Clear. Then he reached down to give her a hand and they crept over the deck before ducking behind the cannon at the bow.

The Fish was still making that dizzying figure eight. In a low voice Bartholomew explained how they'd use the fish as camouflage while swimming to shore.

They lowered themselves into the water, barely making a sound.

Crack! The roar of gunfire filled the air.

Bartholomew dove under pulling Mona Lisa with him. After a few strokes, it looked like they were going to escape unnoticed but then something about the calm water made Bartholomew turn.

The Fish had stopped its dazed swimming. Now it was blocking their way.

And it looked mad.

Bartholomew punched the beast in the nose.

"Quick, my lady, swim!" he cried.

Mona Lisa started to kick wildly while the Fish splashed. It was so loud he was sure they could hear it on the ship. He tried swimming around it.

Then Bartholomew heard a new sound.

It was laughter. And not the tinkling giggles of a beautiful lady escaping her captors.

This was a pirate's sniggering.

"What have we here?" the red-bearded man in the rowboat asked.

Grabbing Mona Lisa's hand, Bartholomew turned. But before he could swim a single stroke, the net covered them both.

Chapter 36

Pressing his body against the ash tree, Alex waited for the shouting pirates to appear. He glanced at the pile of rocks at his feet and then at Gwen, who seemed excited by the prospect of a fight. As soon as the pirates crested the hill, they would pelt them, then move up the mountain to draw them further away.

He swallowed hard, remembering the monsters with swords, axes, and daggers he'd faced last time he was in Artania. They knocked him flat, bloodying his nose and breaking Bartholomew's arm, but because they were Deliverers, they'd healed at will.

Alex realized that Gwen couldn't fix wounds by imagining it. She was just a regular girl. A skinny twelve-year-old who had no idea what she was getting into. One that could be seriously injured or worse. He started to reach for her hand and pull her away from all this.

Then he heard a grumbling roar barely yards away.

"Ready?" a grinning Gwen whispered as she picked up a rock.

Alex gave her weak thumbs-up, wishing he could see more but from this vantage point. With no idea how things were going, he could only hope that between the hypnotized Fish and Bartholomew's skillful swimming, everything would go according to plan. Bartholomew could be a wimp on Earth but last time they were in Artania he'd really proven himself.

Alex tested his rock's weight and huddled further into the hollow of the tree. A turban emerged on the rise. He held a finger up. Another red-capped head rose.

He extended a second finger. Took a deep breath. "Now!" he cried flinging his stone.

It missed by a mile, but Gwen's hit one right in the head. The man in the stocking cap swayed and fell.

"Yes!" Alex cheered, gathering another handful of rocks in his t-shirt.

The turbaned man with a long scar on one cheek drew closer and Alex hurled a stone, sure it would meet its mark. But it brushed right past his head.

Alex groaned.

Gwen had better luck tossing beechnuts three at a time. Two of them hit Turbanhead, leaving a matching scratch on his other cheek. The pirate clutched his face and charged up the hill, cursing so bad Alex's Mom would have told him to wash his mouth out with soap if she'd heard.

Alex heaved another stone. Not even close. Baseball was not his sport.

Then that brute made a beeline for his friend.

"Gwen!" Alex didn't think but released his t-shirt as rocks tumbled to the ground and rolled away. The he pivoted on one foot and charged down the hill.

He thought he'd be a battering ram knocking that jerk over but instead he hit a brick wall chest. Scarface didn't budge; instead he grabbed Alex under the arms and lifted him overhead.

"Let me go." Alex slapped at the pirate's shoulders.

"Certainly."

Alex blinked. "Really?"

"As soon as you've done a lifetime of service as a slave." He threw his head back and sniggered.

Narrowing his eyes, Alex kicked. His foot connected but it might as well have been a feather for all the good it did. The brute didn't even flinch.

Alex refused to call for help. Gwen was here by mistake and had to get to safety.

But it looked like that red-head friend had other ideas. She was already tiptoeing up, dragging the axe behind her. She winked at Alex, who nodded.

"Ow! Ow! Ow!" Alex squealed. "You're hurting me."

"Quit your squawking kid."

"Ouch! My arms!" Louder this time.

Inching closer, Gwen stole behind the pirate. Then she swung the wooden handle at his ankles. Scarface fell over taking Alex with him.

Now it was the pirate's turn to squawk.

Alex grabbed Gwen's hand and plunged deeper into the forest.

Chapter 37

Bartholomew sat in the hold, chained to a wooden bench. *Stupid, stupid.* He cursed inwardly. *Should have gone faster.*

Head bowed, Mona Lisa was directly opposite him on the same seat she'd occupied before. This beautiful woman did not deserve being soaked to the skin, auburn hair matted.

"I am so sorry."

She gave him a smile that just made him feel worse. "There is nothing to forgive, bambino." Her eyes were so kind, even now.

"I should have–."

"Stop." She cut him off. "It was a valorous attempt."

"I am not the brave one. That's Alex's department." Bartholomew stared at his shackled hands.

"Alex?" She gave him a puzzled look.

"My friend. He's out there right now waiting for us." Bartholomew shook his head. "*He* wouldn't have let himself get captured."

"Some events are unavoidable."

"Tell that to Alex, or jeez, Gwen for that matter."

"You appear different from the rest of us," Mona Lisa changed the subject. "Are you from the Photography District?"

"What?"

"You are neither painted nor sculpted. You look like one from the land of photos."

"I don't know what that is."

"How could you not?" Mona Lisa asked. "We are all created with the knowledge of the lands."

He shrugged.

"But every Artanian from the Photography District to the Renaissance Nation knows his or her place."

"But I am not from here. I am human."

Mona Lisa gasped. "One of the Deliverers?"

Bartholomew nodded. Then he explained how this was his second journey into Artania. How the year before he and Alex had stood side by side to rescue pharaohs. The words came easily, tumbling out of his mouth like pebbles down a stream.

He then shared how his father had drowned in a mud puddle, turning Mother into a germophobe who had only recently allowed him to go to school to finally get friends like Alex and Gwen.

"And when we met Leonardo, he just knew you were still alive. He said he could feel your presence in his heart."

"He must have heard my prayers," she said. "Poor Papa."

"Ha." The harsh voice made Bartholomew jump. "He won't just worry. He'll be destroyed when he hears of your Mudlark transformation."

At the foot of the ladder was the same red-bearded pirate who had captured them. Even though he had a ridiculously loose turban and a shiny gold earring in one ear, his beady eyes gave him such a sinister appearance that Bartholomew had to look away.

"So, this is your rescuer?" the pirate guffawed. "A Photography District coward who cannot even meet my gaze?"

Mona Lisa started to protest until Bartholomew shot her a glance and shook his head. He didn't want the pirate to know who he was.

"At least I have not betrayed my own kind," Bartholomew said, not daring to look at the man.

"What know you, Photo?"

"The Prophecy."

"A bedtime story for children," the corsair said with a sneer. "I will be stronger than any Artanian when Lord Sickhert makes me a Mudlark."

Bartholomew shivered. He had seen firsthand just what happens during a Mudlark transformation. First, an enormous mouth in the ground smacks its bulbous lips, waiting to close in. Then it swallows him or her, and the morphing process begins. And when Mudlark Maker finally spits the Artanian back out, it's no longer a beautiful creation but a zombie slave.

"Child, meet Aruj Barbarossa, better know as Redbeard."

"You forgot to mention my other names." The turbaned man placed his gnarled hands on his hips. "Greatest pirate of the Mediterranean. Scourge of the Barbary Coast, Sultan of Algiers, and brother to Hizir."

"Of course. How could I forget?" Mona Lisa replied with a sarcastic smile that Redbeard completely missed.

"Wow!" Bartholomew gushed trying to widen his blue eyes. "I didn't know you were famous."

Redbeard puffed up his paisley tunic and stroked his velvet cloak. "Not meaning to boast but I am feared both near and far. Everyone trembles at the sight of the *Red Raven*, the swiftest galley of the Mediterranean."

"Have you been in lots of battles?"

"One or two," he chuckled. "Actually, it's in the hundreds but who's counting?"

Bartholomew realized that if they were ever going to escape, he needed more information. But he had to proceed carefully.

"Will there be one I can watch when you take us to, to–," Bartholomew paused to segue slowly into the question. "By the way, where are we going?"

"Venice." Redbeard stared off into the distance. "No, sadly this journey is just a delivery. Although it would be fun to attack a few merchant vessels on the way, eh?" He poked Bartholomew in the ribs.

"You bet!"

"I might just be able to accommodate you." The captain turned to go, but then as if thinking the better of it, spun back. Glaring at Mona Lisa, he bent close to her ear. "See how much more fun we can have if you cooperate?"

Mona Lisa glared at him. "Never. *You* are a traitor, Aruj."

"And you, my dear, are a fool." He stood up and waved in Bartholomew's direction. "At least he understands my greatness." He raised a sword and shouted, "Hizir, prepare to set sail." With a dramatic flick of his cloak Aruj Barbarossa exited.

Mona Lisa smiled at Bartholomew.

"I wish I had thought of that, bambino."

Bartholomew blushed. Maybe he wasn't a complete failure after all.

Chapter 38

Gwen shuddered as she slowed to catch her breath. The trees here had that surreal look that made her feel so uneasy. Even with Alex at her side she couldn't shake the feeling that something was wrong with this place.

Coming to a sudden halt, Alex put his fingers to his lips.

The air was still. A few sparrows twittered here and there but there were no drumming feet or loud curses. They should have heard more angry pirates chasing them.

Gwen sidled up closer and whispered in Alex's ear. "Maybe they're trying to sneak up on us."

He didn't respond but stared into the grove of trees they'd just come though. Alex rubbed his forehead. "Something's wrong. I'm going to check it out."

Gwen started to protest. But before she could get a word in, Alex had disappeared in the underbrush. Leaving her alone in this dark place.

"Okay girl, everything's fine," Gwen muttered. "Alex'll be back in a minute with this Mona Lisa chick in tow. Then we can all go home."

Gwen took a deep wishing she could believe her own words. It didn't work.

"So, nightmarish art is everywhere. You're okay, aren't you?"

As if in answer to her question, the ground in front of her started to split in two. At the same time, the trees shriveled and turned brown. Dead leaves crumbled and showered down into her hair.

She turned to run but an even larger pit opened behind her. Teetering, she held out her arms to avoid tumbling in.

Something like a rising river of dark magma, erupted from the fissures. Then two muddy heads atop hunch-backed monsters surfaced. Fighting the urge to scream, Gwen spun round and round.

But there was nowhere to run.

"Hello human," one slime-coated creature rasped. Not much taller than her, its spiked hair was like black thorns. The thick gnarled fingers ended in werewolf claws and it smelled like a nasty science experiment gone wrong.

Brushing the debris out of her hair, Gwen crossed her arms and tried to glare at the fiend. Her toughness was just an act, but it made it easier to face those eerie yellow eyes.

"What? Art got your tongue?" the pig-nosed thing grinned at its partner, brown lips curled back to reveal shark teeth.

The second creature started to hoot and snort like a drunken hog.

Gwen tightened her arms around her chest. This voice sounded familiar, like something out of a dream. No, out of a nightmare. The worst kind of nightmare. The kind that wakes you up in a cold sweat feeling a muddy string snake over your naked arm.

The spike-haired thing leered at Gwen. "How is your mother, human?"

"Mother gone, boss," his comrade giggled. "She chased by art."

No sound escaped as Gwen opened and closed her desert-dry mouth.

"We don't need her to speak, do we Stench?"

"No sir, Captain Sludge."

"We just need her to remember what we can do."

"Yeah, yeah." Stench stepped closer and bobbed his slimy head up and down. His matted braids dripped brown ooze on her arm. "Sharks. Cyclops. Mama run away."

These things knew about her nightmares? Shivering, Gwen brushed some slime off her arm. "What do you want?" she demanded.

"Ahh, she can speak." Captain Sludge bent closer to whisper in her ear. His hot breath on her neck was as rank as poison gas. "There will come a time when your friends will ask you to act. But you won't."

"Yeah right."

"You will stand frozen, as if in fear." He flicked his cape and backed away. "Exactly like you are now."

Gwen glanced down. Her arms were crossed so tightly her veins bulged.

Stench's hand cupped a bat-like ear. "Captain, someone coming!"

Sludge waved his hand and the fissure widened. He and Stench started to sink below the soil. "Tell no one. Or else," he warned just before his head disappeared into the closing ground.

Gwen shuddered. A dream-invading monster? She clenched and unclenched her fists.

Her heart was still racing when she heard birdsong. She looked up. Fluttering sparrows and wrens had started circling the trees warbling Landini's haunting melody.

As they sang, a rainbow of flowers and ferns burst from the cracked ground the monsters had left behind. Next, the barren trees morphed into an orange orchard heavy with painted fruit.

When tinkling giggles came from the blossoming trees, Gwen blinked at an approaching trio of women in long gossamer gowns. Hand in hand they skipped and twirled as they sang with the painted birds overhead.

One of the goddesses from Mt. Olympus strolled behind them. No, she didn't stroll, she glided, her sandaled feet barely touching the ground as flowers bowed before her. When they drew closer, the skipping women spun around three times and sat down cross-legged in a circle.

Gwen shook her head. This place just kept getting weirder.

Floating nearer, Venus smiled down at Gwen. "Hello child."

The goddess reminded Gwen of Mom; a perfect oval face with flawless skin, not a freckle anywhere. But where Rochelle's gaze seemed aloof, Venus's was warm. Her smile made Gwen feel like she was curled up next to Dad in front of a cozy fire.

"What's going on?" Gwen asked.

"I have been sent to help you find the Smiling One," Venus said.

"We don't need any help. My bud is rescuing her right now."

Venus shook her head sadly. "If only it were so."

What did this painted lady know that Gwen didn't?

There was a rustling in the trees. Gwen glanced over, expecting to see Alex with Bartholomew and Mona Lisa.

But only one face emerged from the underbrush. And it was as white as that monster's sharp teeth.

Alex didn't need to say a word. His eyes said everything.

"The ship is gone. And so is Bartholomew."

Chapter 39

Bartholomew was chained next to Mona Lisa on deck. Two days earlier Redbeard had said that they needed fresh air and sunshine. He figured that it had more to do with showing off his prized prisoners to the crew than their health but kept his suspicions to himself.

Alex is never going to find us. He thought, shaking his head. *We've been at this for days.* They'd already passed the Leaning Tower of Pisa, skirted around the Elba and Corsica, and now were anchored off Sardinia Island to load supplies.

As the pirate crew rowed back and forth in the bay filling empty kegs and barrels with water, hardtack, and dried fish, Bartholomew mused about how strange it was that Artanian people needed food. Since they were living art, you'd think that they wouldn't need to eat. But in many ways, they were as fragile as the humans that made them.

Mona Lisa's hands resting peacefully in her lap with long delicate fingers as pale and smooth as Hygenette's. But while Mother's hands were nervous and fidgety, Mona Lisa's were as calm as beach glass.

"Worry not, bambino. Rescue will come."

"If only I had your faith."

"It has been foretold," Mona Lisa said. "*Our world will be saved if their art is true.*"

Bartholomew didn't remind her of the line that preceded it: *And many will perish before they are through.*

A ship's boy shuffled up to him, a wooden tray of grapes, bread, and dried meat in his small hands. Bartholomew ignored him until he realized that the boy's hands were trembling.

"Hello," Bartholomew said with a reassuring smile.

Instead of comforting the boy, his hands increased shaking until Bartholomew was sure the cups on the tray would topple over.

Bartholomew reached for the clattering platter. "Here. Let me hold that for you."

The boy jumped as if Bartholomew were a snake ready to strike. Eying Bartholomew nervously, he backed away.

"Don't go," Bartholomew coaxed.

"W-why?"

"I thought perhaps we could talk."

"No!" His mop of hair bouncing as he spoke. "C-Captain said I no t-t-talk. That you be d-dangerous."

Bartholomew set the tray down and held his palms up. "Look. No weapons."

"And what could I do to you?" Mona Lisa's mouth turned up in that famous smile. "Whip you with my veil?"

"I no know." The little guy started to draw a circle with one barefoot toe. He glanced up at Bartholomew shyly. "Is it t-true?"

"What?"

"That you come from f-faraway lands?"

"What does he mean?" Bartholomew whispered to Mona Lisa.

"He looks so strange," Mona Lisa explained, "because he is from the Photography District."

"But it b-be forbidden. No one passes his own b-border."

Now Bartholomew understood. Each of the Artania lands was separate and they stayed that way. The Renaissance Nation never mixed with the Photography District and visa versa. He smiled. Maybe this taboo would work to their advantage.

"I was given permission." Bartholomew paused and leaned forward; hoping his next words would hit the mark. "By the Thinker."

The boy nearly dropped his tray.

"What's your name? Bartholomew asked quickly.

"Name?" The boy stopped and stared before taking another step away.

"Yes. What are you called?"

"They call me Ship's Boy."

"But don't you have another name? From your parents?"

He shook his head. "No p-parents. Some call me S-Stupido. Or they c-cry Piccolo when I be working slow."

Bartholomew looked to Mona Lisa for a translation.

"*Piccolo* means small," she said.

It was true; this ship's boy was little. He only came up to about Bartholomew's chest. But he didn't look weak, more wiry and strong, kind of like Alex.

"I think we'll call you. Mmm. Pico. What do you think?"

A smile crept up at the corners of the child's mouth as he tried out the sound of the name. "It b-be pleasing."

"Then Pico it is." Bartholomew reached out and shook his hand. Before he let it go he asked, "Pico. Do you know who you work for?"

"C-Captain Barbarossa."

"Do you know who *he* works for?" He released his grip and looked directly into Pico's brown eyes.

"No one. He b-be captain."

Mona Lisa shook her head.

"No?" Pico looked confused.

"He works for the enemy," she said.

The child raised one eyebrow then the other like a perplexed puppy. "The Spanish?"

"If only it were someone as gentle." Bartholomew sighed.

Pico blinked.

"Who is the worst of all?"

"Not..." He brought a hand up to his mouth.

"Yes," Bartholomew paused so the next words would sink in. "The Shadow Swine."

Pico gasped, and his legs buckled beneath him. Bartholomew held out an arm to steady him, but the poor boy was shaking so much he could barely stand.

"No! It c-can't be!"

Mona Lisa began to utter something soothing, but her words were cut short by a shout from the stern.

"Stupido! Feed them prisoners and get up here!"

Cringing, Pico stumbled toward the sneering pirate. When the little guy rushed past, the turbaned man cuffed the back of his head.

Bartholomew felt his temper flash and started to open his mouth in protest. Then his anger sparked an idea. He exchanged a glance with Mona Lisa and she nodded.

A solution to their problem had just fallen into his lap.

Literally.

Chapter 40

Keeping his head bowed, Sludge rubbed the honorific spittle into Lord Sickhert's taloned feet until they shone like polished bones.

"You may rise," Lord Sickhert murmured contentedly.

Sludge got to his feet but kept his eyes downcast.

"Report."

"They have rounded the island of Sicily without incident."

"And the young Deliverer? Has he been a problem?"

"The Barbarossa Brothers say he just sits there, shaking like a fly in a web." Sludge smiled imagining a horrified Bartholomew in chains.

"Good, good." Sickhert rubbed his ashy hands together. "And the other?"

"We have been unable to locate the second."

"What! You have but one task. Get Mona Lisa to the portal."

"She is on her way," Sludge protested.

Lord Sickhert's white eyes narrowed to slits. "But she is not there yet. And you know all too well what will happen if you fail."

Sludge squirmed beneath his cloak, the welts on his back rubbing against the fabric. Those Correction Chamber's burns would be blistering for weeks. "But I have planted seeds of fear in his companion," he said quickly. "The girl will betray him."

"You don't know this. Humans are unpredictable."

"I invaded her dreams many times," Captain Sludge argued.

"Insufficient."

"Ahh, but in the forest, I made things, shall I say clear?"

Lord Sickhert leaned closer. "And she shivered in terror?"

"Like a lamb in a tiger's jaws." Sludge took a deep breath enjoying the memory of a quivering Gwen.

But Lord Sickhert didn't seem to share his pleasure. He gave Sludge an even stare. "As gratifying as human suffering may be, do not let it deter you from the mission."

Sludge tried to straighten his hunched back. "Of course, my lord."

"These Deliverers can create weapons here that even I have no power against," Sickhert warned.

Sludge knew this all too well. He may have been defeated once by their *true art,* but not this time. This time he would be victorious. This time the humans would be the ones with welts. Then he would rule at Lord Sickhert's side.

"Now go," Lord Sickhert said. He rubbed his boney feet together and leaned back against his shining black throne.

"Yes, my lord." Sludge bowed before marching down the twisting stair.

Outside of Sickhert's Stalagmite castle he strutted over to the steaming River of Lies. Here other soldiers paused from their dream draining to salute. He nodded to a few of them before stopping briefly in front of some new recruits.

"You call those nightmares? Why they wouldn't scare toddlers, much less teens."

"But Captain, it big dog," a soldier with an unusually small hump explained.

"Oh, a sweet puppy. That's terrifying. No. Make it wolf-like with red eyes and dripping fangs."

The small-humped soldier blew, and a wisp of smoke shaped like giant wolf escaped from his mouth. With snapping jaws, it took shape and lunged at the floating image of a teenaged girl who ran in terrified circles to escape. But Sludge knew there was none.

With a curt nod, Sludge continued down the river until he found a boiling eddy. Here grey steam rose and snaked over the irregular stones. He bent over a flat outcropping of shale and began breathing in the sulfuric fumes that'd fuel his journey. He pictured the long oars, lateen sails, and gun battery of Redbeard's ship.

The vision grew clearer in his mind and Sludge began to fade. He raised a muddy fist in the air. "Terror. Horror. Panic. Fear. Make nightmares of what they hold dear."

The frenzied grunts of the Shadow Swine filled the cavern as the nightmares continued.

Chapter 41

Alex leaned over the railing of the ship. The blue Mediterranean reminded him of Bartholomew's eyes, his friend, now captive with Mona aboard the *Red Raven*.

Like glaucous gull wings beating the sky, the mainsail flapped in the wind above him. Higher still, attached to the top of the mast, Gwen stood lookout in the crow's nest. With cupped hands, she shielded her eyes from the sun as she scanned the horizon.

I'm coming B-3. You just hold on.

Although they'd seen plenty of fishermen in rowboats, merchant vessels, and galleons, there had been no sign of Barbarossa's galley. Their own vessel, *Vento Buono,* or the Good Wind, was a caravel explorer. It had three masts: a mainmast at the center, a foremast at the bow, and a mizzenmast at the stern. The two forward sails were square, but the mizzen was triangular. Alex had just learned that the triangular one was called a lateen sail, designed so ships could travel upwind.

He also was proud of learning that the sides of a ship had special names. Left was port, right starboard while the front was called the bow and the back the stern.

In any other situation Alex would have been thrilled to be sailing across the sea. Since their ship looked just like the Santa Maria, he should have felt like Columbus on his famous voyage across the Atlantic. But he wasn't looking for some shortcut to the East. He was tracking his best friend, and he had no idea if Bartholomew was okay. Had those pirates hurt him or tortured him in some horrible way? Alex grimaced until a rustling sound made him turn.

"Your friend still lives. Fear not young Deliverer," Venus said resting a milky white hand on his shoulder.

Alex wished he shared her optimism, but too much had happened this past year. Bartholomew caught stealing, Mom still weak from that terrifying heart attack, Dad trying to hide his worries about Mom by quoting Dr. Bock even more. *Why does everyone I care about have to suffer?*

"Yeah, well," Alex grumbled, wanting to step away from her kind touch. "What does that homing power of yours tell us now?"

Venus breathed in slowly as her eyes got a faraway look. She exhaled with a soft whistle. "South. The ship sails south. Islands many it has passed, and they approach another. It is…" She paused and laid a second hand on Alex's other shoulder. "Sicily. They are near Sicily."

Chapter 42

Bartholomew munched thoughtfully on a grape and watched the pirates work the galley. It really was fascinating to observe the sailors pull on the ropes attached to the sails. When he learned how each had its own name; *mainsheet, halyard,* or *backstay*, he imagined shouting commands as he captained his own ship. His triangular lateen sails would billow like great clouds while he cried, "Ease the mizzen!" or "Trim the mainsheet."

Bartholomew shook his head. *Stop daydreaming.*

Knowing that he needed an ally, Bartholomew had tried to gain the ship boy's trust. But every time he started a conversation, someone would order Pico back to work. Mona Lisa didn't fare much better, although the small boy did seem less nervous around her.

Bartholomew wasn't surprised. She had a calming effect on everyone. Heck, even the pirates sneered less when they walked by her. And every time he looked at her beautiful face he was filled with a sense of peace.

But nice feelings wouldn't help them escape.

He watched Pico bring the pirates flasks of water. Even though they treated him like rotten squid under their boots, he seemed to sincerely care about his fellow sailors.

When one corsair tripped and scraped his knee, Pico sprinted over and began pouring fresh water on the wound.

"Get away Stupido!" the pirate growled, knocking him back with a swipe of his arm.

Bartholomew could relate to Pico. His whole life he had tried to please Hygenette, but no matter how many times he bathed, it was never enough.

Filth.

Bartholomew looked down at his hands, so black with grime. If Mother saw him now she'd probably faint. Hunching over, he started to rub them on his now grey slacks.

"H-how b-be you, Photograph?" Pico asked.

Bartholomew lifted his gaze to Pico's puppy face. Without thinking he answered, "Not good."

"S-sick?" Pico lifted one eyebrow then the other.

Bartholomew blinked. No, he wasn't sick. But maybe if he pretended to be he could finally win this little guy's confidence. Trying to make his voice sound scratchy, he coughed twice.

"W-where h-hurts it?"

Sell it. Bartholomew thought. He took a slow labored breath and winced. "Everywhere," he choked out.

It wasn't a lie. He'd made such a mess of Mona Lisa's rescue it physically pained him to think of it.

"P-poor Photo." Pico pulled out a rag that was tucked into his belt and dipped it in a bucket of water. Wringing it out, he applied the stained compress to Bartholomew's forehead.

Fighting his revulsion, Bartholomew summoned up a thankful look. Pico's soft brown eyes met his and they both smiled.

It was a beginning.

For the next two days Bartholomew put on his best sick act. It wasn't hard; he'd done it many times before. Mother was so terrified of germs that she believed every story. Heck, he could say, "ingrown toenail" and she'd put him to bed.

And there he finally got to have privacy. No Mr. White droning on about some boring math problem, maids dusting every five minutes, or Mother scolding, "Start acting like a proper Borax."

Now Pico came running with every sniffle. And Bartholomew had no idea why, but this boy seemed to think that grapes were the cure for everything. If Bartholomew's stomach hurt, Pico would tell him to eat a green grape. If he complained of a headache, Pico shoved a purple one in his face. And whenever Bartholomew coughed, black grapes ended up in his lap.

Bartholomew popped the dark fruit into his mouth. Maybe Pico was right. the sweet juice did make him feel better. He closed his eyes, savoring the moment. Then a shadow fell over him and he raised a shackled hand to shield his eyes.

Redbeard stood over him, waving his velvet cloak dramatically. He glanced over his shoulder and, as if on cue, all the pirates stopped what they were doing and leaned against masts, rigging, and cannons.

"Well Photo. Never let it be said that Captain Redbeard Barbarossa isn't a man of his word."

"Of course not, sir," Bartholomew gushed.

"Ha. Ha." Redbeard puffed up his chest.

"Tell 'em, Cap'n!" three pirates cried in unison.

"A battle you wanted. A battle you'll have."

"Really?" Bartholomew made his eyes wide. "Wow!" He searched the pirate's face to see if he was laying it on too thick. But Redbeard was obviously so conceited that Bartholomew could have told him he was the handsomest man in all Artania and he'd believe it.

"A merchant vessel is just beyond the horizon." Captain Barbarossa pointed over the port bow and waited for every eye to fix on the sea. "Full of rich booty. Gems. Spices. Silks."

Bartholomew nodded enthusiastically.

"All is ready," a shorter pirate who looked a lot like Redbeard said as he strode up. "Just give the word."

"Photo, meet my brother, Hizir." Redbeard put his arm around the corsair.

"Honored sir," Bartholomew said with a bow of his head.

But the younger Barbarossa didn't even acknowledge Bartholomew. Obviously, he wasn't as easily flattered as his vain brother. Instead he adjusted his faded brown turban and repeated his report.

"Hizir." Redbeard chuckled and patted him on the back. "All business." He grinned at Bartholomew and gave him a conspiratorial wink. "But in this case, he's right. I didn't win all those battles on my good looks alone."

"So?" Hizir drummed his fingers on the hilt of the curved sword strapped to his waist. "When?"

"We will strike at dusk when the setting sun is in their eyes."

"From the west?"

"Of course. All they'll see is a cool shadow."

Hizir grinned showing his five remaining teeth. "But they'll feel the heat of our blades, eh?"

"Aye brother." The captain turned on his heel and called to the gathered pirates. "Ready the ship! There are riches to be had this day!"

Cheering, the pirates began bustling about with a new-found intensity. As the sails to caught the morning wind, they burst into song. With a half-smile, Bartholomew glanced over at a trembling Pico who clung to the main mast like a drowning child.

Poor little guy. He hates battles, probably imagines that every one is his last.

Just then Bartholomew had a thought, *How do pirates attack?*

Pico's pale face answered his question.

Bartholomew wanted to slap himself. He hadn't thought about the people on the other ship. They could be hurt, or worse.

Not if I have anything to do with it. Bartholomew vowed.
Of course, that only left one question. How?

Chapter 43

Gwen woke with a start, her hammock swaying. Holding out a hand to steady it, she squinted in the dim light. People on wooden bunks snored beneath flickering oil lanterns.

Bump. There it went again, unmistakable this time. Heart pounding, Gwen slipped out of her hammock and tiptoed over to Alex's bunk.

"Alex. Wake up," she whispered.

He groaned and tuned over. "Leeme alone."

"Get up." She shook him.

"What?" Blinking slowly, he covered one eye with the back of his hand.

"I heard something."

"This ship's always noisy. Go back to bed." He pulled the gray blanket over his head.

Gwen tugged it back down and crossed her arms. She'd wait until sunrise if she had to.

"All right. Jeez." Alex threw back the blanket and trudged over to the ladder that lead to the deck. He started to climb but when Gwen stayed next to his bunk, he raised his eyebrows. "Well?"

She shrugged, afraid of what she might find.

"Are you coming?"

She'd didn't want to go up there, but Mitch Obranovich hadn't raised a wimp. So, she swallowed her fear and followed Alex up the ladder.

The previous afternoon they'd dropped anchor to load supplies in the bay and the deck had been full of chattering work. Now, with everyone asleep, it was quiet. The loose folds on the tied-back sails flapped in the warm breeze and water lapped against the wooden hull.

Gwen glanced up at the clear sky. A map of stars, so perfect they must have been measured to the millimeter, twinkled overhead. On the horizon, the crescent moon was setting, its sickle shape reflected on the Mediterranean Sea.

Alex paced back and forth on the wooden deck where nothing so much as moved. Not a single rat scurried along the rigging.

"See, everything is fine. Can I go back to sleep now?"

Gwen would have said yes if that prickling at the nape of her neck wasn't there. "Can you look just a little more?"

Alex groaned but Gwen knew he'd stay. She'd been friends with him long enough to recognize his sounds. This one meant he may not like it, but he'd chill a few minutes more. Anyhow, Alex never said no to someone that needed help. At school, if a kid was hurt he was the first one there asking if they needed the nurse. If Ty and Con were shoving in the lunch line it was Alex that ordered them to cool it. And if there were some creep hanging around the skate park, Alex would insist on accompanying Gwen home, not leaving her side until she was safe at her front door.

Wishing for Dad's big arms, Gwen hugged the mainmast. She couldn't shake the feeling that something horrible was waiting just beneath the calm waves.

Gwen could tell Alex's patience was wearing thin when he came up to her. "I don't see anything. Probably just a dream."

"No, it wasn't." Gwen shook her head. "I heard something."

"There is nothing around," he said in a controlled voice. "I'm going back to bed, but you can stay up here if you want."

Alex started to lift the chain for the access hatch when suddenly the ship lurched. Arms akimbo, he tumbled back, bouncing on his butt as it slammed shut. "What was that?"

"The nothing," Gwen said hugging the mast tighter.

The calm surface had suddenly become a stormy sea. Huge waves splashed onto the deck in trickling snakes. As the foamy serpents made their way toward Gwen, she curled her toes back.

Dashing to the starboard side, Alex peered over the edge. He shouted for her, but Gwen could barely hear his words over the crashing water. "Come here!" he cried again.

She didn't want to let go of that mast. It was her security, her safety from whatever was lurking below. But Alex needed her. Tensing every muscle, she released her grip and took a step.

Bump! The ship lurched again. Gwen fell to her knees. The leaning ship now felt like a steep mountain.

Scooting on her rear over the slippery floorboards, she made her way toward Alex. "What is it?" she asked, grabbing a hold of the railing.

Eyes glued to the sea, Alex shrugged.

The black sea rippled as a swelling mound rolled from the waves.

Gwen swallowed hard. "A whale?"

Alex squinted into the lathering ink.

A large head, dripping saltwater and foam surged from the sea.

Gwen didn't remember beginning to scream. Glowing red eyes filled her vision as her throat strained.

Then the hand clamped over her mouth. Gwen struggled, arms shooting in all directions in the scuffle to escape. The kicking girl connected with a skinny shin before Alex wrestled her to the ground.

"Quiet! You'll draw it towards us."

Clamping her mouth down, Gwen bit her cheek, tasted blood. This thing rose higher and higher its huge head like something between a horned dinosaur and an eel. But the scales were sharper than any creature she'd ever seen.

Or even imagined.

"We need the guns!" Alex rasped, pointing at the hatch.

Half-crawling, half-wriggling, they made their way to the closed trapdoor. Alex tugged on the chain. But just as it started to open, a huge wave splashed overhead. Flipped on his back, Alex swept across the deck toward the railing.

The ship was going under. And Alex with it.

"I'm coming Dude!" Gwen cried. Using her feet like flippers, she slid down the slippery deck. Then, wedging herself between the railing and her floundering friend, she turned.

"I'll give you a boost," she shouted. "Be ready." Drawing her legs in, Gwen curled into a ball. Then in a single thrust she straightened them, sending him back up towards the hatch. She launched right after.

Gwen's hair was plastered to her head as she tugged on the chain. But the hatch wouldn't budge.

"Put some weight into it!" Alex urged.

It lifted, but then the ship lurched.

"Again!" Alex cried.

Gwen tensed her muscles and pulled.

When it lifted a crack, she wriggled through, Alex right behind. They scrambled down the ladder and found their shouting crewmates running around in circles. One sailor pulled up his pants while hopping across the hold. Another was picking up the tankards and dishes that had been tossed onto the floor. A third was dabbing at a bleeding gash on his forehead.

"Move more ballast to the starboard side," Michelangelo bellowed. "We'll ride out this storm!"

"It isn't a storm!" Gwen cried.

"What?" Michelangelo looked at her as if she were crazy.

Alex dashed up to the older man. "It's a monster..." He quickly told Michelangelo about the creature in the sea.

"Sickhert." Michelangelo's brooding eyes darkened. "He knows we seek Mona Lisa and sent the Leviathan." Raising his voice, he shouted, "Load the cannons! Prepare to fight!"

Chapter 44

Grunting, Alex hefted the iron ball to the muzzle of the cannon and shoved. He listened for the *ting* sound it made as it rolled, then poured the bag of gunpowder into the muzzle and stepped aside so the gunner, Marco, could ram the long staff with a brass end down the barrel.

"Fire in the hole!" Marco cried touching the portfire stick to the fuse.

With wide eyes Alex watched it sizzle and spit red sparks. He jumped out of the way and plugged his ears.

Boom! The iron ball shot out the gun port.

Alex peered out the porthole. The ball missed the Leviathan by a good twenty feet. He turned back to tell the crew, but they were already priming the cannon for a second shot.

The ship shuddered. Splinters of wood rained down on them.

"We are going to break up if we don't stop that beast soon!" Michelangelo cried.

Alex grabbed a second bag of gunpowder from the pile of sacks. The gun captain nodded his readiness and Alex repeated hoisting the ball into the muzzle and putting in gunpowder before Marco rammed it in.

They shot. Missed again. Three whole minutes to reload and nothing?

Gwen was at another porthole helping Michelangelo and Leonardo load muskets, but the small lead balls just bounced off the Leviathan's scales.

Okay, cannons and muskets didn't work. They were anchored and couldn't run so they needed a new plan.

"Where is Venus?" Alex called out.

Leonardo pointed to a place in the corner. There Venus stood in the center of the Three Graces, her face so serene that you'd think she was at a picnic.

"We need your help," an out of breath Alex said.

"Our world will be saved if their art is true," Venus replied as the Graces began to hum a soft tune.

"I don't have time for riddles. We need weapons."

She folded her hands in front of her. "Only a Deliverer can create what is needed."

Alex had no idea what she was talking about. He didn't have any brushes or paint. He shrugged and turned back toward the gunners.

"Only you have the power." Venus placed both hands on his shoulders turning him toward the crew.

Alex tried to shrug her away, but she forced him to watch them all failing.

At the bobbing porthole Leonardo strained to lift his musket and take aim. Sweat rolled down Gwen's cheeks as she tamped in gunpowder with the long staff and waited for yet another ball to miss. Even Michelangelo seemed insecure as he paced back and forth shouting out orders that didn't make much sense.

Alex rolled his hands into fists, took a deep breath, and closed his eyes.

Crack! The sea monster smashed against the hull again.

He clenched his jaw. How could they fight a creature that could wreathe, bob, dive? Swords, pikes, or lances would have to be so large that no one could heft them. The cannon had horrible aim. And musket balls were like flecks of sand.

No, the only thing that could beat this sucker would be a dinosaur. Yeah, like he could call one from the sea. *Here dino, come on boy, help us fight the monster.* He shook his head as the three Graces hummed louder.

"Hope will lie in the hands of twins–," the trio sang. "–hands of twins."

"I'm sorry Venus. I–" he began. Then all at once the word *twins* flashed in his mind. Alex raised a finger then scrambled down the forecastle stairs. "Please let it be burning," he muttered as he bent over to touch the cook's firebox. "Hell! Where is that flint?"

Alex glanced around.

The ship lurched again. Alex grunted and began to search. His eyes scanned the floor and upward until he found it on the top shelf.

"First, pick up the iron bar and put it in your right hand. Then take the flint rock and hold it so that the sharp edge faces upward," he said trying to remember what the cook had said the day before about making fire.

Boom! The cannon's backfire almost knocked Alex over. Steadying his stance, he picked up the flint like Cook had shown him.

Hold the char cloth atop the flint, then hit the rock with your strike-a-light bar.

Alex tried to remember what char cloth was. He didn't see any fabric in the box. Were they out? He wished the cook was there to help him, but all hands were on deck battling the monster.

He took a finger full of golden flax in the box, held it atop the flint, and began smacking the strike-a-light against it. Once, twice, three times.

No flame.

Alex repositioned his hands and struck again. A metallic odor wafted into his nostrils. It was working!

When he saw a spark, Alex blew softly. The flame singed his fingers and he almost dropped it. Steeling himself, Alex set it on the grate and blew again. A beautiful blaze lit up the box. It warmed his face.

And promptly went out.

"No!" Alex kicked the iron stove, stubbing his toe. "Ow. Stupid thing!" He picked up the flint box and threw it across the room.

It smashed against the galley wall with a clang and the contents spilled out all over the floor.

Alex stood there fuming, until he realized that this was the cook's box, not his. And if they didn't sink the cook was going to be pretty ticked off to find his stuff strewn everywhere.

Alex flipped the container back over to put the items inside. Flax, the extra flint and strike-a-light bar, some pieces of bark. Then he picked up a couple of blackened squares of cloth that had fallen out.

He held one up and examined it. It reminded him of the charcoal Dad used to barbecue with. Then he hit his head with the back of his hand. Char cloth! Like *char*coal. He felt about as clueless as Bartholomew looked on the first day of school.

Grasping the char cloth atop the flint between his thumb and forefinger, Alex struck. He smashed his knuckles, drawing blood but didn't cry out. Instead he struck again. This time more furiously than the last.

He had to get sparks.

"Come on, hit harder."

In the distance, he could hear the faltering cries. Faster he hit. One spark flew. Another.

"Light char cloth. Come on!"

A pea-sized glow appeared on the black square. Alex blew gently, not wanting to kill this infant flame. Leaning over the stove, he held the tiny ember against the tinder of flax and blew again. Flames wormed their way upward. Then he piled a few small twigs on top. His fire grew taller. Now it was time for the larger sticks and logs.

While the flames lapped up the fuel, Alex dashed back to Venus.

"I need your husband. Can you call him?"

Venus gave him a smile that would have made any man fall in love. And although Alex was still a boy, puberty had been rearing its ugly head lately. He looked away.

"I anticipated your need," Venus said, stepping aside.

There stood Vulcan a hammer in one hand and a heavy anvil at his feet. Explaining how he needed Vulcan's forging skills, Alex picked it up. Then, leaning back to balance the weight, he waddled back toward the galley, while outlining what he wanted to sculpt.

"A fine plan," Vulcan said, telling him which supplies to gather as he stoked the fire. His strong back dripped with sweat as he squeezed the bellow handles making the room so hot Alex was relieved to go and collect materials.

When he returned with his final load, the wall of heat that assaulted him was so intense it stopped him at the door.

Alex tried to remember that he was a creator. Even in this sweltering heat he could generate a pocket of safety. Bringing his hands together, he envisioned cold air. His heart beat once. He imagined a refrigerated suit and the sweat evaporated off his skin. His heart beat again, and his red cheeks cooled. By the third heartbeat, a wintry breeze blew his hair back.

He pulled his hands apart and cracked his knuckles.

"Let's make a monster."

Chapter 45

Bartholomew watched the sun move across the sky. Dreading every changing shadow. Soon the pirates would attack that unsuspecting vessel and poor people would get hurt. Maybe die. He stole a glance at Mona Lisa.

Her usual smile was gone. Replaced by a tight-lined mouth.

Bartholomew wanted to tell her everything was going to be all right. That soon she'd be home laughing with Leonardo.

What a dummy he was! He strained against the shackles and the clanking metal dug into his raw skin.

"I too seethe," Mona Lisa said.

"If only I hadn't opened my big mouth."

"Gaining Redbeard's trust was wise."

"But I should have thought about the consequences."

Mona Lisa shrugged, rubbing her hands over each other as if stroking a sick child.

They sat in silence, a sharp contrast to the surrounding sounds of loading muskets and sharpening swords. The pirates told nasty jokes and slapped each other on the back as they all chattered away.

All, that is, except one small boy.

With shaking hands Pico carried bags of gunpowder, musket balls, and kegs of water to the raised platform called the forecastle.

Those wide eyes reminded Bartholomew of his last trip into Artania. Everyone had expected him to be a hero. But when faced with a Shadow Swine holding a pharaoh captive, he didn't strike. And by the time he moved, it was too late.

He could still see the pharaoh's dying eyes. Burned in his memory.

Some hero he was, encouraging a pirate to attack innocent people so he could escape in the confusion.

Bartholomew felt a lurch as the rowers below silently extended their oars. Twenty-four paddles slipped in and out of the sea like killer whales on the hunt.

Mona Lisa remained silent, but her clasping and unclasping hands screamed Bartholomew's failure. At the same time, the last remnants of the afternoon sun burned dismay into his skin.

The sound of marching boots made Bartholomew turn to see Captain Barbarossa strutting across the deck, velvet cloak billowing behind him. He halted in front of Bartholomew and adjusted the turban on his head.

"Sir," Bartholomew said without meeting his eyes.

"Now you'll see some real action, Photo." Redbeard said with a cocky grin.

Bartholomew cringed.

The captain twisted both sides of his long moustache and puffed up his chest. He tapped his foot. When Bartholomew said nothing, he grunted. "Cat got your tongue boy?"

Bartholomew was so worried about the battle that he'd forgotten to compliment Barbarossa. He straightened his back and tried to put on a better face.

"Action, wow," he said in a dull voice.

"You don't sound very excited." Redbeard's eyes narrowed.

Make it good or he'll put you below. Bartholomew thought, but said, "Oh, I'm just a little tired."

"I'd heard tales of Photo's being weak. You be printed on such thin paper."

"Not strong like you, Captain Barbarossa." Bartholomew managed a wan smile.

The pirate chuckled. "Ahh, you'll be seein' just how strong I be in about–" He paused and looked to the west. "–two minutes."

Bartholomew felt his heart sink and the shackles around his wrists grew suddenly cold. It couldn't be time already. Beside him Mona Lisa shook her head sadly.

"What be your problem, lady?"

"You," she said, pointing an accusing finger at him. "How can you be so cruel to your own kind?"

"Baah!" He waved a hand. "What know you? So weak."

No, I'm the weak one. If I'd been stronger we wouldn't be here. Bartholomew thought.

"Cap'n! The ship!" one of the Moors called.

Redbeard withdrew his sword from its sheath and waved it in circles. "Rowers pull! Gun captains ready your teams. The time to attack is *now*!"

He dashed up to the forecastle, and with a dramatic leap swung around the foremast and pointed his scimitar out to sea.

Bartholomew tried to raise a shackled hand to shield the sun from his eyes, but the chains were too tight.

Bartholomew swallowed hard as the three-masted ship, sails unfurled, approached. It was still too far away to make out any people, but Bartholomew imagined them all smiling away. Happy souls floating unaware.

Oblivious to the coming horrors.

They drew closer. Now Bartholomew could see a boy in the crow's nest of the other ship.

"Does he see us?" Bartholomew asked Mona Lisa in a low voice.

"I don't know."

Both waited for him to aim his spyglass at the *Red Raven*. But he never turned in their direction.

"Do something," Mona Lisa whispered.

Wishing for a miracle, Bartholomew glanced around. Nothing caught his eye. A few more seconds and Redbeard would be attacking. In desperation, he started to scream.

"PIRATE SHIP! LOOK OUT! PIRATES!"

"GO BACK!" Mona Lisa cried, joining him.

"PIRATE ATTACK. STAY AWAY!" Bartholomew called.

"PIRATE SHIP!" the two of them shouted in unison.

"What be this?" Redbeard pivoted away from the cannons toward the shrieking Bartholomew and Mona Lisa. "Bahh! Brother, gag the prisoners!"

"PIRATES! PIRATES! PIR–" Bartholomew screams were cut short when Hizir shoved a bandana into his mouth. Even then, his throat strained with muffled screams.

He tried to see if the other ship had heard but Hizir moved in front of him, blocking his view. He shot the pirate a dirty look and kicked out with his feet.

"I knew you couldn't be trusted." Hizir leaned in and backhanded Bartholomew. His long nails left bleeding marks on the boy's cheek.

Bartholomew felt his face grow hot where the man had struck. Blood dripped onto the gag adding the taste of iron to the bitter cloth.

The rowers quickened their pace, closing the gap between the two ships. Mona Lisa gave him a nod of appreciation, but he still didn't know if they'd been heard.

Boom! A cannon ball burst from the merchant ship. A slight smile tugged at the corners of Bartholomew's mouth.

Their warning had worked.

"Port rowers pull. Starboard rest," Hizir ordered.

The *Red Raven*'s bow pointed like a battering ram.

The merchant ship fired three more cannon shots, but each fell short. As he watched the hopeless splashes Bartholomew realized that it was nearly impossible to hit their galley. It was such a narrow target.

"A fly to swat! Ha!" Redbeard burst out laughing. He shouted orders at the gun crew and three cannons fired simultaneously.

Let them miss. Please.

Crash! The iron balls pierced the ship's hull.

"No!" Bartholomew choked through the cloth.

"Again!" Redbeard cried.

Cracking wood splintered. Through the gaping holes Bartholomew could see the sailors scrambling to get out of the way. Men shouted frantic orders as they clutched at wounds in their sides.

Bartholomew winced when he saw that the crew even included boys smaller than Pico scurrying to escape. A few ducked behind sacks while others leapt inside barrels. Two simply covered their heads.

But there was no place to hide.

"Plundering you wanted," Redbeard bent down close to his ear. "Plundering you have."

Bartholomew shook at his chains. He'd been too late. Again.

As soon as the merchant ship was lashed to its side, the pirates poured over like ants to spilled honey.

Although they'd already lost, one sailor fought so valiantly Bartholomew was sure he'd escape. Hand over hand this valiant warrior climbed the rigging and then swung back and forth jabbing with his rapier. Holding off a quintet, he cut down three and then leapt onto the deck. He made a wide arc with his sword before facing the remaining two. He was just about to drop a fourth when Pedro tripped him with his peg-leg.

Stumbling, the sailor fell onto Pedro's dagger. He let out a surprised cry as his sword wobbled in the air and clattered onto the deck.

The brave sailor crumpled into a heap and was still.

This time Bartholomew couldn't stop the tears. They dripped down his face, seeped into the last dry corners of the gag, mixing bitter salt with the metallic blood already in his mouth.

The rest of the pirates charged forward, threatening to cut down any who dared fight them. But no one else did. Many tried to dart away from the curved blades. Some even covered themselves in sailcloth. And one by one they fell.

In a matter of minutes, it was all over.

Bartholomew shook his head. It was like the aftermath of a hurricane. The splintered ship bobbed sideways in the bay, its mainmast broken in two. Smoke twisted from every hatch. Misshapen bodies were strewn about on deck.

A small cluster of young boys cowered while jeering pirates poked them with pikes. Bartholomew wished he could plug his ears and block out their plaintive wails.

One group of pirates started to sing sea shanties as they hauled up sacks of silk and spices. Then came a heavy chest. Two sailors carried it on board and laid it at Redbeard's feet. The captain struck the padlock with an old sword repeatedly until it broke. When it opened, jewels of all colors shone from inside. Redbeard Barbarossa picked up handfuls and let them fall like rainwater over his body.

"Booty! Riches! Treasure!" he roared.

"Hooray!" the corsairs cheered.

"Who finds treasure for all to have?"

"Redbeard!"

"Who be cutting sailors to shreds?"

"Redbeard!"

"And who is the greatest pirate that ever lived?"

"Redbeard! Redbeard! Redbeard!" they chanted again. A few started to dance a jig. Pedro the Peg-leg pulled out a flask and tipped it backwards until some liquid dribbled down his bristly chin. Another pirate grabbed it from him and soon they both were arm and arm yowling an off key.

Captain Barbarossa lapped up the adoration like a fat dog at a banquet. With his fists on his hips, he bowed his head at the reveling crowd. Then his eyes fell on Bartholomew and the wide grin faded.

"Shh!"

Bartholomew wondered if he'd suddenly turned deaf because the entire ship immediately grew quiet. If he ever doubted Redbeard's power, it wasn't then.

"It seems we have a traitor here."

Absolute stillness filled the air. Not even the wind dared to blow.

"And what do we do with traitors?"

The pirates all stared at Bartholomew but said nothing. The young Borax broke out in a cold sweat.

"I know what to do," a sneering Hizir said striding up next to his brother.

Bartholomew heart quickened but he didn't move.

Redbeard nodded to a pirate who held the ring of metal keys for every door and chest aboard ship, and even, Bartholomew realized, the shackles on his wrists. The Keymaster bent down and unlocked the chain that bound Bartholomew to the bench. At the same time, a strange scraping sound came from somewhere behind him, like someone dragging a log over the ground. The ship tilted slightly to one side.

Should I try to make a run for it? He glanced over at Mona Lisa, who held out her hands, so someone would unlock her manacles too. When no one did, Bartholomew's chest tightened.

"Get up Photo," Redbeard grunted with a sharp yank of Bartholomew's chain.

The crew parted as Bartholomew stumbled along behind the captain. He soon discovered what that scraping sound had been.

It was the gangplank. And it was waiting for him.

Chapter 46

Sweat poured down Alex's face and ran into his eyes. The ship's galley was like an oven. He wiped his brow with the back of his hand envisioning a cool protective suit.

Until he could work.

"Toss the iron balls in the flames," Vulcan instructed between hammer beats on the anvil.

Alex followed each step carefully. When the metal inside the stove changed from black to red, he removed it with tongs and placed the crimson coals on Vulcan's anvil.

The smith-god demonstrated how to strike the anvil and then handed the hammer to Alex. Alex raised an arm and began. Clang. Iron met steel. Pound. Teeth and scales emerged. Bang. A body took shape.

Faster his arm fell as the creation force cursed through his veins. Lumber became flicking tongues and iron swaying heads. A long thin tail appeared.

"Thank you, Vulcan. Nearly–"

Smash! Snapping teeth crashed through the hull just inches above his head. Alex leapt back just inches from dripping jaws. Ducking down behind his incomplete snake, he attached the last green plates.

Its body grew as long as the ship and thicker than the mast. Cool scales shimmered, and the sculpture morphed into a two-headed cobra ready to do his bidding.

Alex cradled one face in his hands. "Wake up," he said.

Blue slits opened.

"Attack the Leviathan. Now!"

It swayed back and forth as both cobra heads rose, forked tongues flicking at the air. One head hissed.

In response, Leviathan gnashed its jaws. Double rows of sharp teeth tried to close in on Cobra, but the snake heads dodged in opposite directions.

Bellowing, Leviathan struck again. This time Cobra whipped around, each head sinking curved fangs into its neck.

Sickhert's monster thrashed and shook, but the snake held fast. Pupils dilating, it jerked to one side. Alex scrambled out of the way as its huge head smashed against the galley walls.

"The poker!" Vulcan cried pointing at the hot stove.

Alex leapt over a barrel and grabbed it from the fire. The end glowed red, a steel cigarette poised to strike. Alex jabbed but came up short.

Leviathan turned toward him. It jaws snapped like a thousand slamming doors. Alex felt a tug and clapped a hand to his head. His hair was wrapped in those teeth lifting toward that hole.

Gritting his teeth, he jerked. "Yow!" he cried gaping at the tufts of hair still in the Leviathan's mouth.

Dropping to one knee, Alex raised his firebrand and waited for the Leviathan to sway his way again. Counted. Four seconds. Five. At six he thrust, and the metal punctured the creature's jaw like a hot knife in wax. Slowly, Alex stood and drove the poker deeper into the creature's mouth.

The shrieking monster jerked its head throwing Alex backwards. He landed with a thud near Vulcan's barrel.

Cobra sunk its fangs in deeper as the monster retreated out of the crack in the hull. Then, with a sucking whoosh of air, both creatures disappeared into the sea.

Alex peered out the jagged hole in the wall. The setting crescent moon and the patchwork of stars barely illuminated the water. In the faint light, all he could make out was the splashing of dark waves against the ship.

Boom! The cannon shot again, lighting up the sea just enough to see the thrashing monsters. One snake still had its fangs in the Leviathan's neck. The other one was somewhere beneath the surface.

When they rushed up on deck to watch, Alex grasped the railing and stared out to sea. The water began to bubble and simmer in a tangle of twisting scales. In the lanterns light he could just make out Leviathan's scaly back, spiked wings, and clawed feet. With gnashing teeth, it rolled, pitched, and plunged until Cobra raised one head and jerked Leviathan below.

A few minutes later, the sun began to light up the sky turning the sea a steely grey. The reflecting moon looked like a snake's fang, one he hoped would strike any moment. He could make out the Italian coastline but no movement anywhere.

Gwen sidled up to his side. "See anything?" she asked.

"They disappeared," Alex replied continuing to scan the waves.

The Mediterranean was as smooth as Venus's skin. Then far off he saw the waters rise.

"Look." Alex pointed.

Like braiding seaweed, the monsters wove through the waves. Coiling and wreathing, they battled. He couldn't tell who was winning.

"Go on. Dig your fangs in." Alex said.

"Yeah, get him." Gwen punched at the air.

They were about fifty yards away when the battling monsters rose out of the water. The sea dripped off the Cobra's hooded heads. Their triangular faces hung suspended as if on invisible threads, but they didn't attack.

Alex raised his hands in exasperation wondering what they were waiting for. More seconds ticked by.

When Leviathan rolled over, both heads struck. Curved fangs sank into the tender flesh of its soft underbelly. Convulsing venom glands pumped poison through their teeth.

The weakened Leviathan slapped at Cobra with its tail. Thrashing from one side to the other, its jaws snapped open and closed three times. Then a lolling tongue drifted over jagged teeth.

Alex's two-headed snake edged closer to the ship, the limp Leviathan in tow. At the port bow Cobra unhinged both mouths.

It floated on the sea.

"Whoa," Gwen said.

"Well done, Deliverer." Vulcan reached out to shake Alex's hand.

"Thanks, it–" Alex started to reply. Then Leviathan raised its horned head. "Cobra, watch out!"

Leviathan's tail smashed against the hull. Almost losing his footing, Alex grabbed the gunnels.

The monster leaned back, head poised to crash into their boat. Then two snakes rose, dripping water like gaping wounds and coiled around the monster's neck. Once. Twice. Three times.

The Leviathan threw its horned head back with a guttural bellow that drowned out all sound. Tighter Cobra constricted, twining round a fourth and a fifth time. The great beast thrashed wildly in their coils trumpeting its protest.

Bloody tears began to weep from its eyes, but the snake squeezed more, muscles rippling as it twisted and tightened.

The Leviathan opened and closed its jaw in silent protest. It raised its head toward the sky as if imploring the clouds for help. With a final convulsion, it withered in the snake's coils.

And moved no more.

Only now did Cobra release it. Leviathan's body bobbed on the surface before shrinking back into the sea.

"Yes!" Alex cried taking Gwen in his arms. He swung her around and around laughing hysterically. Until he realized that he was hugging a girl. Then he set her down abruptly and stepped back, blushing.

Did she notice? He quickly turned to shake Leonardo's outstretched hand, hoping that no one had seen the red creeping up his cheeks.

Suddenly Michelangelo, Leonardo, and the crew were all on deck applauding and congratulating him. The Three Graces joined hands, hummed in harmony, and began dancing in a circle. Meanwhile, Alex's snake crisscrossed from bow to stern their gentle splashes lapping off the hull in time to the music.

"Our world was born from the magic of two, magic of two, magic of two," their tinkling voices sang.

But many will perish before they are through. Alex thought as he stared at the Leviathan's watery grave.

Chapter 47

When Bartholomew shuffled past the jeering pirates, Redbeard gave his chains a vicious tug. The handcuffs dug into his skin, but for Mona Lisa's sake, he made no noise.

He wished he could utter reassuring words, but his mouth was still gagged. Still, he would hold his head high. He owed her that much.

"Now true pirates never made prisoners walk the plank," Redbeard said. "Real corsairs be using them for target practice." He leered at Bartholomew waiting for the boy to flinch.

Bartholomew caught himself before cringing. *Don't give him the satisfaction.* He thought jerking back on the chain.

"Yes, I be wondering if me crew needs some sharpening of their shooting skills." Redbeard turned to Hizir. "What think you, brother?"

"I wouldn't waste good musket balls," Hizir said.

Redbeard threw his head back and laughed. "Just what I thought you'd be replying."

"Let's get this over with."

"Aye, brother." But Captain Barbarossa didn't give the order, instead he waved little Pico over. "You, Ship's Boy. Come here."

Pico's eyes grew wide. He pointed at himself. "M-Me?"

"I not be seein' any other ship's boys."

"Y-y-yes sir." Pico stumbled forward.

"Now my brother be thinkin' that target practice on this Photo is a waste of shot. But I believe some of the crew could-a done better in the plundering. What think you, boy?"

Bartholomew knew that the last thing Pico wanted was to be involved. He was the type to help people, not order their torture. Anyway, whatever his answer was, it wouldn't make any difference.

Pico tugged on his ragged tunic, his lower lip quivering.

"Answer me. Or is the name Stupido rightly chosen?"

Pico's eyes searched Bartholomew's. Bartholomew nodded a silent signal saying that it was all right. Pico stuck out his small jaw and crossed his arms.

"So Stupido it is," Redbeard chortled.

The pirates all burst out laughing. "Stupido!" they taunted.

Pico hung his head but didn't answer. Bartholomew had to hand it to him. He refused to play Redbeard's game.

"Brother," Hizir lowered his voice so only Redbeard and Bartholomew could hear. "We have an appointment with you-know-who. Let's get this over with."

Redbeard's demeanor suddenly changed. He went from throwing his head back in laughter to furtive glances, keeping one hand on the hilt of his sword. He shook the chains attached to Bartholomew's hands and ordered him to move.

Bartholomew felt the point of Hizir's blade press into his back.

This is it. He thought when Redbeard let go of the chain. *I'll never see my friends again.* He imagined his mother bathing in the dark seeing more things that weren't there. Throat dry from the gag, he swallowed hard.

When he turned back toward Mona Lisa, her tear-stained face almost made him lose his resolve. He teetered wishing he could comfort her, but all he could manage was a weak wave.

"Go Photo," Redbeard said.

Bartholomew nodded and considered closing his eyes. But then he decided that if these were his last moments he wanted to see everything; the deep blue of the Mediterranean, the violet sunset, the rising crescent moon.

The board creaked and bent beneath his feet. At the end, he waited two seconds. Four. Ten passed. What were they waiting for?

"My brother's right," Redbeard said guffawing. "We shouldn't waste good ammunition on a Photo. Now jump!"

Bartholomew didn't have to be told twice but leapt. Water splashed up, releasing the gag. It floated away, and the bottom of the ship passed from view.

He sank deeper.

He dropped past the rusty anchor chain as schools of fish darted out of his way. Light beams like sparkling vines twisted around him. If only a glittery tendril could wrap around his waist.

He hit bottom with a thunk, shoes sinking into the sand. He tried to lift his legs, but those heavy chains made it impossible. Leaning forward, he gave them a sharp yank. The metal clicked and clanged but Bartholomew couldn't budge.

His chest tightened. How long could he hold his breath? Five, six minutes?

One had already passed, and he was stuck. And even if he could move, he didn't know where to go.

He tried to remember where the sun was when he was on the ship. Port? No, it was on the starboard side, so he should walk from the light.

Fighting the dizziness that was threatening to overcome him, he heaped the metal links in his arms. Started to raise a leg. Tripped.

He dropped the chains. His chest spasmed as panic driven bubbles escaped his lips.

Images of his friends flashed in front of his eyes. A teasing Gwen tossing pizza pieces at him in the quad. Jose giving him a thumbs-up before a math test. Alex sculpting proud animals out of mud with him.

All those floating memories will be gone. He thought and before sending a silent prayer safeguarding Alex and Gwen.

Bartholomew opened his mouth to let the sea take him. Then as if someone had turned a radio on from a forgotten place inside his mind, he heard a voice.

You create whatever you want. He recalled the goddess Isis saying. *Imagine strength and you are muscled.*

Imagine strength. I am strong. I can pull these chains.

Slowly he shuffled forward. First two feet. Then three. Strong. Stronger than steel. Faster he hobbled. The ship no longer cast a shadow on him.

Move!

Battling to create a lungful of air, he clamped a hand over his mouth. His spasming chest relaxed a bit. *Go!* Soon he was trotting over the ocean floor.

He heard a clank and felt pebbles scatter beneath his feet. Bartholomew tripped. Bubbles sputtered from his mouth and new pains shot through his chest. He started to see spots and silvery fish in front of his eyes.

He forced himself to lean forward. Running now, rocks flew out on either side of him. They floated back down in a turbid cloud making it impossible to see.

He leapt twice more, and waves crashed over his head, knocking him to his knees. Then he found himself crawling and gasping sweet air.

Bartholomew crept three more feet. And collapsed on the shore.

Chapter 48

Sludge paced back and forth in the grotto as water lapped up the sides of the rocky walls like tongues tasting fear.

He clicked his clawed hands together. things were going well. The pirates had rounded the toe of Italy and now were sailing to Venice and the Portal. No sign of that other Deliverer. And as for Bartholomew. Well, he was in chains and no longer part of the equation.

The only thing he still was a little unsure about was that human, Gwen. Would she betray the others when the need arose? He had planted the seeds in her mind, but humans were so unpredictable.

The rush of water from another crashing wave grated at Sludge's bat-like ears. He raised his nose. Was that a pirate, or just the fishy smell of the sea?

"Where are those idiots? I told them just after sunset."

The sound of rapping oars answered his question. Sludge turned to see a rowing Hizir, with his brother, Redbeard, in the bow. The Barbarossa Brothers were the perfect pair to betray Artania. Painted as cruel pirates who fought for sultans, their very creation was based on treachery.

"You are late! What took you so long?" Sludge growled.

Redbeard gave him with that stupid grin he thought was so charming. Sludge rolled his yellow eyes. *Fool. He thinks he's going to have so much power after the Change. Ha! I wouldn't let him lead a youngling from Swallow Hole Swamp.*

"Well?" Sludge hissed.

"We be havin' a situation." Redbeard said as he got out of the boat.

"Not to do with her? She still is–"

"Don't be a worryin'–" Redbeard cut Sludge's words short. "She still sits chained."

Sludge wanted to slap that smile off Redbeard's face. And he would have if he didn't need him to transport Mona Lisa to the Portal.

"But she be a little more lonely, now." Redbeard jabbed his brother in the ribs. "Ain't she?"

"What do you mean, lonely?" Captain Sludge demanded.

"It be nothin' to worry you about. Just a Photo we had to deal with."

"What!"

"Some Photo became a problem. So, we dealt with him the pirates' way."

"Won't be bothering us no more." His brother nodded.

Sludge's mind raced. They'd freed the Deliverer? "Where is he?"

"Drowned." Hizir jerked his head toward the sea.

Could a Deliverer perish here? Sludge licked his lips. No, taste there. He sniffed. The faint odor of human was in the air but that could be from when the Barbarossa Brothers had him. There was only one way to know for sure.

"Where's the body?"

"He be at the bottom of the sea. Under heavy chains."

"You have no proof."

"Believe me." Hizir shook his head. "No Artanian could have survived."

Sludge almost corrected him by shouting that they were dealing with humans not Artanians. "You had better be right," he snarled.

"Now what be the plan?"

Sludge showed them the new map he'd drawn. This route would take them away from the watchful eyes on shore and any possible rescue. Then he would meet them in Venice and take them to the Portal.

Redbeard murmured about all the riches they'd have once they were turned into Mudlarks. They were so stupid that Captain Sludge would have felt sorry for them, if he knew how.

But Shadow Swine can't feel pity. Oh, they can sense fear and build on it to make nightmares and they didn't hurt each other, unless necessary. But there had never been a Swiney born that could put himself in the jackboots of another.

Sludge ran his tongue greedily over his teeth. *Yes! One Deliverer dead and the other lost. Lord Sickhert will be most pleased.*

But then he stopped. Something gnawed at the back of his mind like a rat chewing on the bars of its cage.

Something wasn't right. But try as he might, Sludge couldn't figure out what it was.

Chapter 49

Gwen leaned over the railing letting the sea spray her face. After the monster battle, they'd immediately set sail and now were heading northeast. Gwen didn't understand it, but every time Venus laid a hand on Alex's back to do her keep them on course thing, it irritated her. Whenever Venus put one of those too beautiful hands on Alex's shoulder, she wanted to slap it away.

Everyone else was grinning from ear to ear. The Graces sang, Leonardo brushed his long beard as if expecting to see Mona Lisa any minute now, and even Michelangelo strutted from side to side like some sort of crowing rooster.

Yeah it might have been a victory but not one she liked. That Leviathan almost sunk their ship. Even though the two-headed snake was still guarding them, she still couldn't shake that hunch-backed monster's warning.

"*There will come a time when your friends will ask you to act, you won't.*"

Yeah right, like she'd betray her buds. Loyalty was her middle name. Even when kids had laughed at Jose's ponytail she'd stood by him and threatened to sock the next one who said a word.

But *that* was just teasing.

Gwen made her way across the deck to Alex. "Dude, good job."

He turned toward her slowly, his face a stiff mask.

"Some job," he replied in a dull voice.

"Huh?"

"Death is a great thing," Alex's eyes looked right through her.

"What are you talking about?"

"Never mind. Just ranting." Alex shook his head.

"Dude, are you okay?"

"Never better." His voice about as convincing as a doctor saying this shot won't hurt a bit.

Gwen didn't like all this cryptic avoidance. If you have a problem, deal. Don't hide your feelings away like some model putting a fake face on for the camera. She started to argue when a cry came from the crow's nest.

"Vessel! Off the port bow!"

Gwen turned and gaped. A lifeless ship bobbed in the bay. It must have once been beautiful, but now its charred remains were gouged with jagged holes. A cracked mast hung from tangled lines and the boom swayed back and forth like a cemetery swing.

But what Gwen saw on deck made her turn away.

She glared at Alex. Why had he brought her along? She wasn't an artist. She couldn't create ship-sized snakes or axes from dirt. She couldn't paint organ players like Landini. She was just a skater girl. And she didn't belong inside this nightmare of Leviathans, pirates, and hunch-backed monsters.

"Ease the mainsail! Ready a starboard tack!" Michelangelo cried.

When their caravel turned toward the dead ship and Gwen's nose started to twitch. Heart racing, she almost dove into the sea. Swimming toward Dad's bear-like arms.

As if that was possible, trapped in this freaky place.

As soon as they dropped anchor, Alex dashed over to the rowboat tied to the gunnels and began undoing the knots. "Vulcan! Give me a hand." He cursed at each uncooperative knot while the god of the forge hobbled up to help with the opposite lines.

A few moments later, Michelangelo barked at the crew. "Now, lower it into the water. Easy."

Alex, Vulcan, and Leonardo followed three sailors into the rowboat before Michelangelo passed swords and muskets to them.

Gwen squeezed her arms tighter about her waist and whispered, "Be careful Alex."

The search party rowed toward the wrecked ship. Meanwhile, everyone on deck was as quiet as death. Even Michelangelo had stopped his usual bluster. Gwen hugged herself.

After long minutes, they docked and climbed aboard. Why did Alex have to go first? The sailor guys were used to this sort of stuff. Even their weapons didn't reassure her. Muskets seemed about as effective as toys against the power she'd seen in Artania.

Barely breathing, they watched Alex lead Vulcan and Leonardo across the ghost ship's deck. Behind them, the sailors' muskets swept the air. So far, the enemy was invisible.

When Alex reached the hatch, he waved them back. Without a heartbeat of hesitation, he descended into the dark hold. Alone.

Gwen held her breath, wanting to scream. *Don't go in there. You're just a kid.*

Forty-five, forty-six, forty-seven. She counted waiting for him to come back up. Finally, curls emerged, and Alex shook his head and Gwen sighed.

Mumbling, Alex paced back and forth over the deck. Gwen could tell he felt terrible and was probably cursing those monsters and everyone on their side. Then he gave an excited cry. Waving his arms, he pointed toward the beach. "Look!"

Gwen glanced over and saw the footprints on shore. For the first time in days, her heavy heart lightened.

Waving to the others, Alex sprung into the rowboat and plopped down on the seat. As soon as Vulcan, Leonardo, and the search party scrambled onto the wooden seats, Alex pushed off.

And on that breezy morning they rowed to shore.

Chapter 50

Bartholomew woke with a start. He'd heard gravely laughter. Or had that been a dream? He rolled over. Sand was everywhere. It covered his face and body, clung to his hair and grated against his teeth and tongue.

He spat but it didn't help much. His mouth was still full of grit and his throat ached. With an effort Bartholomew sat up.

He rubbed at the raw places where the shackles dug into his wrists and thought about the night before. Exhausted, he'd made his way into the forest to a broad-leaved tree covered in long banana-shaped pods. There he'd gathered up some of the fallen leaves and scooped them into a pile to use as a mattress. When his carob leaf bed was reasonably soft, he'd stretched out on top.

But didn't sleep.

When the moon set, strange shapes emerged from the forest. Bartholomew's imagination turned shadows into icy arms. Reaching out like claws. He'd pulled a carob leaf up to his chin as something howled in the distance. Squeezing his eyes shut and plugging his ears, he'd kept the cold chains across his face all night.

Bartholomew turned to one side and cringed. The manacles scraped his raw skin. He had to get them off.

He glanced around until he found a large boulder entwined in twisted roots. Gathering what little strength he had,

Bartholomew shuffled over, raised both hands, and brought the shackles down.

The iron just cut deeper.

He picked up a nearby rock, placed the chains back on the slab, and brought it down. Didn't even dent the metal. Breathing heavily, he stared at the stone in his hand.

"Useless, like me." He let the rock slip from his hand and fall. It hit the ground with a soft thud and Bartholomew crumpled alongside it, burying his face in the crook of his arms.

"Is that any way to greet a friend?" a voice from behind him teased.

Bartholomew looked up. There on the forest path stood a grinning Alex, hands firmly jammed onto his hips.

Bartholomew blinked. "Alex?"

"In the flesh. How ya doin', B-3?"

Not sure if he was dreaming or awake Bartholomew took a tentative step in his friend's direction. Stopped. Gaped. But in two leaps Alex closed the gap between them.

Alex shook Bartholomew's hand until he winced from the cutting pain. "You look like Rembrandt after a rainstorm." Then he asked what had happened.

Bartholomew just stared.

While Alex began to explain what had happened during their separation, Vulcan limped up. "We should return. There will be time for talk later."

Nodding, Alex took Bartholomew by the elbow and followed the hobbling god.

"And Cobra is still guarding us," Alex finished when they reached the beach where Leonardo waited with some sailors. He helped Bartholomew into the lifeboat and took a seat next to him.

After the sailors pushed off, Alex kept turning to Bartholomew as if waiting for him to say something. Then about twenty yards off shore, he blurted out, "What happened?"

But a numb Bartholomew just watched the oars dip in and out the water, lip quivering.

Leonardo laid a sympathetic hand on his shoulder. His ocher eyes searched for good news that Bartholomew couldn't give. "Easy, bambino. Take a deep breath and then tell us. How is my dear Mona Lisa?"

"Safe-for-now," Bartholomew said in a halting voice. He licked his chapped lips achingly dry mouth then slowly recounted what had happened. "We'd almost escaped when Redbeard rowed up. But Mona Lisa was so brave. You should have seen her."

He went on and told about the ship's boy, Pico, whose grapes were supposed to cure everything. Bartholomew paused when he got to how he'd complimented Redbeard. He wouldn't let them know how he had caused the pirate's attack. Fighting the nausea gripping his gut, Bartholomew skipped ahead to his warning shout during the pirate raid.

"But I was too late." He looked into Leonardo's tortured face. "And they still have her. I'm so sorry."

"We'll get her back. Don't worry." Alex nodded with confidence.

Alex. Always so strong.

Bartholomew glanced back at the forest of twisted pines and shivered, trying to forget the troubled night he'd spent there.

He rubbed at his wrists again.

Aboard ship Vulcan used an anvil and hammer to remove the chains, while everyone gave him sympathetic pats on the back and said how brave he'd been. Their kindness only made him feel worse. If only they knew the truth.

Unable to meet anyone's eyes, he kept his head down and stared at his now gray shoes. Then he saw Gwen who wanted so much to go home.

"Dude, good job."

She was just saying that. She obviously thought he was a wimp for getting himself stranded there. He could hear it in her voice. He didn't answer. Just rubbed at his finally free wrists.

"So, where's this Mona Lisa? Can we leave now?"

Bartholomew shook his head.

"No way."

He knew she was waiting to hear the whole story. He cleared his throat, but when those horrible images flashed in his brain, he couldn't speak.

There was an awkward pause. Bartholomew rubbed the deck with one toe.

"Hey, I bet you're tired," Gwen blurted out, finally filling the awkward silence. "Want to crash in Alex's bunk?"

Bartholomew let himself be led to the sailors' sleeping quarters below. Gwen pointed to a niche in the wall and handed him a blanket.

Mumbling his thanks, he lowered himself onto the bed.

But sleep didn't come. Instead everything replayed over and over in his mind. *If it hadn't been for me those little boys wouldn't be slaves right now.*

And the others wouldn't be....

He squeezed his eyes shut but it didn't help. He kept seeing those people trying to escape. With nowhere to hide. Daggers in their sides. Scimitars cutting them down. Gaping wounds bleeding onto the deck.

The blood. On his hands.

His chest ached but the salty tears brought no relief. They only pulled him further down, back to the ocean floor where the pirate ship sailed out of reach.

Then he decided. He was done. No more. They all were better off without him. Let Alex save them. Alex was the real hero.

And when he finally surrendered, when all confidence was lost, and he had given up hope, Bartholomew let the blackness of sleep cover him.

Sensing a Deliverer's defeat, Lord Sickhert rubbed his bone white hands together and smiled. Victory would soon be his.

Chapter 51

Lord Sickhert looked down upon his assembled army from the balcony of his stalagmite castle. The Great Window of Red outside wept lava that made his long white cloak and chalky hands the color of blood.

Down on their knees, row after row after row of his soldiers had gathered. The River of Lies next to them bubbled, filling Caustic Cavern with salmon-colored mist. He breathed in. Once. Twice. Three times.

"Servants, underlings, minions! The time of creation is nearing its end."

His subjects barred their jagged teeth, smacked their gums, and pounded clubs on the ground.

"We have bleached the desert of Egypt, and now we have their most beloved daughter."

"Mona Lisa," a few Shadow Swine grunted.

"I did not hear you."

"Mona Lisa," more cried.

"Not good enough. Who will become a Mudlark? Who will turn the Renaissance Nation to white?"

"MONA LISA! MONA LISA! MONA LISA!"

Lord Sickhert nodded appreciatively when he saw Captain Sludge slap a few of the whispering soldiers who weren't paying attention.

"Now listen!" he hissed. And then waited for every yellow eye to train in on his balcony before continuing. "Soon she arrives in Venice. All must be ready."

"But what of Deliverers?" an extremely fat Shadow Swine blurted out. "I hear they come."

The silence that followed this outburst was quieter than death. Lord Sickhert fixed his gaze upon the soldier, anger burning as hot as the lava flowing next to him. His bone white eyes rolled back in his head. Slowly, he brought his desiccated hands together in the shape of pyramid.

The fat Shadow Swine rose in the air and floated up the castle wall until he was directly in front of his master. The terrified face brought no sympathy. It only incensed Sickhert more.

"I s-sorry my lord. I not think." His piggish nostrils flared as viscous sweat dribbled down each swollen cheek.

"I have no place for disobedience."

"I obey, I promise."

Lord Sickhert unfolded an arm and pointed one of his bony fingers at the Great Window of Red.

"No, please. I sorry. Please. No!"

Sickhert snapped his fingers and an invisible cannon ball shot into the squealing soldier's gut, propelling him backwards. When his back hit the lava with a fiery splash, his clothes burst into flames.

The soldier screeched as molten rock covered his fat arms and hunched back. His round face sunk back into the burning liquid going from red to white and red again until it finally disappeared in a whorl of smoke.

Lord Sickhert flicked out his serpent like tongue tasting the death smog. He then raised a crooked finger over the remaining Shadow Swine.

"And any who dare say those names will follow! The Portal opens at the stroke of midnight. Ready yourselves." He raised his voice to a roar. "Now go."

Led by their captains, row after row filtered out of Caustic Cavern. Mudlark mutations of wolves, rats, and spiders scurried out the exit tunnel while snakes and legless lizards slithered behind them. Whale-like creatures with bent fins and flukes backed into the waters. Finally, the Shadow Swine raised their battle axes and marched toward the Portal.

The rhythmic pounding of jackboots throbbed reminding Lord Sickhert of Mona Lisa's beating heart. He smiled imagining Mudlark Maker squeezing all that sickening kindness from it as he transformed her into a slave.

And then the Renaissance Nation would fall.

Chapter 52

Alex was worried. Bartholomew refused to get out of bed. Three days had passed and no matter how much he wheedled, goaded, or yelled Bartholomew still muttered, "I'm done. I'm done."

The only thing Alex could coax out of his friend was more information. He discovered that Redbeard was supposed to deliver Mona Lisa to Venice, but it was a secret. Only the ship's boy, Pico, knew the plan.

Alex might be able to use this info to get Pico to help them.

Of course, finding them was another thing. Although they knew what the *Red Raven* looked like, it was a common design. And Alex knew that Venice was a city of waterways and canals, so finding it would be like trying to find a single brush stroke in one of Michelangelo's huge murals.

From his bench in the captain's cabin, Alex rifled through the sketches that he and Leonardo had been working on. Crossbow machines, a catapult, and even an armored chariot drawing littered the roughhewn tabletop. The real Leonardo de Vinci had drafted them hundreds of years before and although most were too heavy or complicated to work on Earth, that was no problem in Artania. Here, when a Deliverer gave it form, the creation became real.

"I just don't see how this armored car works under water," Alex said, holding up one of the sketches.

"The original design may not function, but you can modify it."

"I would if I could read it. But that's one strange alphabet. I never saw anything like it."

"Really?" Leonardo's mouth twitched with a half giggle. "It's a secret code. See if you can unlock it."

"It's code?"

"Yes. Tee hee."

Alex smoothed the armored car diagram out on the table and leaned closer. At first it looked like Arabic, with the paragraphs indented at the right and the swooping letters backwards. But for him it made sense. Being left-handed, he'd always thought that starting from the left and going to the right was stupid. He had to twist his arm around in an awkward position to keep from smudging his letters. If writing were reversed he wouldn't have to do that.

"It's all backwards!" Alex cried, slapping his hand on the table. "Every single letter." He held up the parchment and his mind immediately began reversing the letters. Although it was in Italian, he could read it perfectly.

"My creator wrote backwards because he was afraid others would steal his ideas. Most need a mirror to read my writing." Leonardo grinned.

"Aww." Alex blushed slightly. "It's just because I'm a lefty."

"As am I. Well in actuality, I'm ambidextrous. When you can draw with both hands it opens up so many possibilities."

Just then, Gwen burst into the room. "Venice. Right ahead!"

Knocking over the bench, Alex sprung up and dashed to the ship's bow. He grabbed the railing as the front of their caravel rose and fell toward two small islands skirted in stone walls. Within them, bell towers jut out from like dual torches.

After passing through the narrow strait, they sailed into a large bay filled with all kinds of boats. Hansa cogs, Venetian galleys, merchant ships, and even a few caravels, like theirs, bobbed in the bay. Some sails flapped like unfurled flags while others stayed tied to masts. But rowboats and dinghies ferried people to and fro everywhere.

"It's beautiful," Gwen said.

For the first time during this trip Alex completely forgot everything. He didn't think about designing weapons. Or about how to protect Gwen and Bartholomew. Even his guilt over making Mom cry evaporated with the morning haze.

Across the water was a floating city. Amazing. Canals crisscrossed with stone bridges. Lanterns, buildings, and ships reflected in the rippling waters. And what colors! There were burnt orange tile roofs, feathery yellow houses, and white window casings. Carnation red and summer peach brick walls mingled with water-stained buildings. A bell tower painted duskyrose stood over them all while several silvery domes bowed reverently at its side.

As they sailed closer, more details came into view. The domes were attached to a Gothic palace with a pink and white checked wall.

"Look at all those arches," Alex gasped, staring at the bottom two floors of the palace.

"I think those are cool," Gwen said, lifting her chin toward the inverted smile windows.

Alex agreed.

The statue of a woman sword in hand stood on the center balcony. She lifted her blade skyward. "Just and strong, I am enthroned!"

"That's Justice, one of the Venetian symbols," Leonardo said as he strolled up.

"Maybe she can help us find the pirates," Alex replied, his thoughts returning to their work.

"I don't see how." Gwen crossed her arms. "Half of the boats look just like the pirate ship. We'll have to search hundreds to find the right one."

Alex almost told her his thoughts. *You won't have to worry about that since you aren't going anywhere near them.*

"She's right," he said to Leonardo. "How will we find the Barbarossa Brothers in all that?"

"Many will be needed. We must-" Leonardo's words were cut short by a blustering Michelangelo.

"Does no one pay attention to the captain? I said drop anchor!"

Everyone got to work. Some lowered sails or rolled them up. Others dropped anchor. Alex helped tie down the canvas with the knots he was proud to have mastered these past few days, using the half-hitch, a few bowlines, and a square knot or two to secure the rigging.

Once done, Alex trotted up to the captain's cabin to gather the sketches he'd been working on. When he opened the door, he was surprised to see the aged Leonardo there.

"How did you get-?" he asked the bearded artist.

"It was needed," Leonardo said as if that explained everything.

Deciding that this must be an Artanian quirk, Alex shrugged. Anyhow he had a more pressing question to ask.

"Leonardo?" he began.

"Yes?"

"Do you know of a jail-like place?" He held his breath.

"Why?"

"I-I-" His tight chest made it hard to speak.

"What is it?"

"I-I- need to lock Gwen and Bartholomew up for a while," he finally blurted out.

"But they are your friends."

"Exactly. And I need to keep them safe."

Leonardo looked at him quizzically. "Have you thought this through? You know the prophecy. *Hope will lie in the hands of twins.* You must work with the other to undo the evil."

"But we've already done that. And Bartholomew–" No words came to describe his tortured friend.

"The other Deliverer remains in bed?"

"He hasn't moved since we rescued him."

"I see. But the girl, she is strong," Leonardo argued. "I have seen her in battle."

"She's not an artist. She's here by mistake."

"I will see what I can do. But remember, an artist needs to be part of humanity to create. Detachment is not true art."

Alex didn't know what Leonardo was talking about. He wasn't detached at all. His problem was he cared too much. He couldn't stand to see his friends face another battle.

No, he'd find a safe place for them both and go on alone. It was time to drop into the half-pipe. And he'd ride it without the constant distraction of having to worry about his buds.

It was the only way.

But first he had to get Bartholomew out of bed.

Chapter 53

Gwen tapped her foot on the wooden floor of the rowboat. All this silence was making her jumpy. Reminding her of how she'd felt at Speedy Mart a few weeks back. One minute she'd been teasing Zach about too much hair gel, and the next she was as unsteady as a newbie skater because splashed across from the cover of *Fashion* was Rochelle. The jade green eyes Gwen'd inherited winked playfully from the magazine rack. Which made no sense since Mom was about as playful as a robot.

Making some excuse, Gwen had sent Zach ahead before buying the magazine for the secret scrapbook she kept under her bed. Later, as she thumbed through the pages Gwen imagined what it would have been like if she'd been with Mom during the Italian shoot. They could have fed the pigeons in St. Mark's Square, eaten frozen gelato, and maybe even gone on a gondola ride.

Gwen's nose twitched. *As if that would ever happen.*

She looked at Alex and then Bartholomew. These quiet koalas could at least pretend. Gwen pointed. "Check out the bridges! I bet you could totally get air skating over those."

She waited for Alex to reply but he was strangely silent. What was up with him? Not that he was a chatterbox, more the strong-keep-your-mouth-closed-until-you-have-something-to-say type. But he usually responded if she spoke to him.

Michelangelo grumbled something about a child's place as he tied the bobbing boat to a post. Turning away, Gwen made a face before glancing up at two freestanding columns.

Each was about fifty feet tall with a different statue on top. The man on a crocodile bowed reverently at them while the winged lion on the other raised a stone paw.

At least somebody appreciates my being here. Gwen thought waving back.

She glanced through the goalpost-like columns into St. Mark's Square. All kinds of people were cruising around. Dark-skinned men in turbans, blonde ladies in long gowns, and teenagers in hose and tunics. She started to imagine how funny Zack would look in one of those outfits. Mr.GQ in tights? Yeah right.

"Venice, or *Venezia* as we call it, is a cosmopolitan city," said Michelangelo, volunteering information for once. "With traders and immigrants from all over the Renaissance Nation, it is a hub for the exchange of goods. Here we have spices, gems and carpets from the exotic east, wool, silver, and tin from Northern Europe, along with fur, grains, and workers from the Black Sea. Venice is the pride of our nation, a city to admire and respect." He gave Gwen a long stare. "Not babble on about."

Gwen rolled her eyes. Arghh! Even when he was being a tour guide Michelangelo had to be a jerk. How she wanted to tell him off! But he was such a grump that he might dump her in the lagoon if she said anything.

Alex glanced right and left, his shoulders twitching as if he expected a hive of bees to attack at any minute. Only after turning each direction four times did he finally put out a hand to help Gwen and Bartholomew out of the rowboat.

"You okay?" Gwen asked, wondering if those monsters were nearby.

But Alex just turned away and followed Michelangelo toward the brick tower at the far end of the piazza. A shuffling Bartholomew followed along in a daze behind the rest of them.

"I could shake them both," Gwen muttered under her breath as the gods and goddesses they'd met on Mt. Olympus shouted hello.

Most seemed friendly enough but a wary Hera, with her peacock under one arm, stood to the side glaring at her husband. Gwen could see why. Zeus had already strolled over to a pretty Italian woman and was smiling broadly as he showed her his pet eagle.

Gwen shook her head. Poor Hera. At least her Dad wasn't like that. She remembered back when her parents were still married, Dad only had eyes for Rochelle. Not that it made any difference. Mom's were focused on stardom.

Everyone from the ship was milling about too. Venus and the Muses twittered away with an armor-clad god about their adventures on the ship. Leonardo was deep in conversation with a young god who wore a winged hat and sandals. What was his name? Oh yeah, Hermes.

She expected Alex to join in with the friendly reunion, but her bud stood apart. Body tense, he surveyed the group as if sizing each person up. But when Alex's gaze fell upon Mr. Clean standing zombie-like in the middle of the crowd, his expression softened.

"This way!" Zeus waved them toward Doge's Palace.

Everyone followed Zeus toward a great door topped with another winged lion. The cat flapped its wings and the dark doors opened as if by magic. Their party then passed through a series of vast halls, and up a richly decorated staircase that made Bartholomew's mansion look like a shack.

They finally entered a room with rows of chairs facing two of the hugest globes Gwen had ever seen. The rotating spheres with tan maps were twice her height and looked like something you'd see in an antique store.

When everyone took their seats, Zeus strode to the front of the room and gave the giant globes a spin. As they whirled, each began to glow. One gyrating sphere projected a starry sky on the ceiling while the other flashed multiple views of Italian looking cities.

"Friends." Zeus's voice was rich and deep as he pointed at the twinkly display. "As you know, the Barbarossa Brothers have kidnapped Mona Lisa and are planning to hand her over to the Shadow Swine."

"Beasts!" Michelangelo stomped of his foot.

"Of the worst kind." Zeus gave a curt nod of his head. "But the time for words is over. What we need now is a strategy. They obviously plan to open some sort of portal to Subterranea below. We need to stop them before that happens."

"Or the Smiling One will become a Mudlark," Michelangelo added.

There were scattered murmurs and gasps. Gwen shuddered, imagining how horrible it would be become one of those zombies.

"And if she falls so does this land," Hera said, giving the peacock in her lap a quick hug. "This land will be bled white. Never again to shine with the glory of paint, fresco, or mosaic."

Fearful whispers filled the room. Gwen glanced around. She hadn't realized how important rescuing Mona Lisa was until then. It wouldn't just break Leonardo's heart. But this beautiful place would disappear. Man. She could see why everyone wanted to find her so badly.

"Fear not, brethren." Venus said. "She still is one of us. I can sense her nearness."

"She's here?" Leonardo's eyes brightened.

"Within two miles," Venus replied. "But her exact location eludes me."

Zeus placed a hand atop one globe and a funnel of light cast a hologram of Venice in front of the god.

Zeus held out both hands as if cradling the hologram, then lifted the flickering image higher. The 3-d movie stretched. "Apollo, take your chariot over the city. Fly over every waterway, canal, and bridge." Zeus pointed at places on the spectral film then turned back to the assembled company. "Hermes, Venus, and Mars, go with him."

A god with a winged hat and sandals and another steel-helmeted one with chest armor immediately stood up. They marched to the back of the room followed by Apollo and Venus, and all four exited.

Zeus snapped his fingers and the projection disappeared. He waved Leonardo and Michelangelo forward. The two older men elbowed each other in a race to the front of the room. Michelangelo started to speak but Leonardo cut him off.

With a triumphant look Leonardo pulled out a thick roll of parchment from the folds of his robe. "The young Deliverer and I have designed new weapons. We will begin building them immediately."

Michelangelo sighed and rolled his eyes. "You should inventory what we have first before wasting time making new ones."

Gwen was sure that Leonardo'd tell him where to stick his ideas; they had some sort of crazy competition going. But she was surprised to see him put his feelings aside.

"Fine," Leonardo threw his shoulders back haughtily. "Then I shall inspect the armory."

"No, I will. It must be done correctly," Michelangelo said with a sly grin. "But you may accompany me if you wish."

"Accompany you? Ha. I think I can manage."

"Oh, you've managed things well up till now. Haven't you?" Michelangelo accused.

Leonardo flipped his long beard back and forth in one hand, reminding Gwen of her cat, Humphrey, flicking his tail. "What are you saying?"

"If I'd been in charge, we wouldn't be here in the first place." Michelangelo crossed his arms and gave Leonardo a condescending look.

"It seems to me that you helped design the Fortress," Leonardo retorted. "If you are so perfect, then why was she captured, mmm?"

"No, it was because *you* let her go for a walk."

Leonardo stepped closer to Michelangelo and slapped him with his beard. "I should throttle you–you- arrogant–"

Zeus stepped between the arguing men and pushed them apart. "We have no time for petty rivalries. You two, take the humans. Everyone else, search the canals. Beware. Spies are everywhere."

"If any of you see the *Red Raven*, send out the alarm," Hera added. "Ring the Campanile bell thirteen times and all will gather there."

Zeus nodded and clapped his hands once. "Now go."

People scattered in all directions leaving Gwen and Bartholomew with Alex, Leonardo, and Michelangelo.

"To the Armory. Come." Without waiting for a reply Michelangelo marched into the passageway.

When they reached a storeroom filled with weapons, Gwen saw a suit of armor she'd love to try on, swords, battle axes, a few bayonets, and crossbows like the one she'd used to hit the fish.

Without a word, Leonardo and a frowning Alex strolled headed straight for an old table. Then they started whispering and shooting glances back at Gwen.

What were they whispering about? She tried to get Bartholomew's attention but Mr. Clean just kept staring off into space.

"Okay then. Umm. Well. Let's get going," Alex said with atypical nervousness. "We need to go to the shipyard. Right Leonardo?"

"Yes. The shortest way is across the Bridge of Sighs." Leonardo laid a gnarled hand on Alex's arm. "Are you *sure* you want to take that route?"

"You *know* I have to." Alex nodded sadly.

As soon as she took a step after them, Gwen got a tingly feeling on the back of her neck. Pins and needles prickled down her spine but still she followed along.

Later, she'd regret it. Because if she'd known where they were going, she would have run as fast as she could.

In the opposite direction.

Chapter 54

A miserable Alex followed Leonardo down toward the Bridge of Sighs. And almost stopped at the exit.

Afraid his guilty face would betray him; he pretended to be interested in the covered bridge. He started pointing out the lattice windows until he noticed how their shadows resembled a tic tac toe game.

Alex always lost at tic tac toe.

A wailing wind severed the silence. For centuries condemned men and women had walked over this Bridge. Alex halted mid-step imagining their mournful cries.

"Not exactly the Ritz, huh?" Gwen remarked.

"No," came Leonardo's stiff reply. "This place has another purpose."

Alex shot Gwen a quick glance; afraid Leonardo would make her suspicious. But she seemed oblivious.

"So, what do you want me to do while you build all this stuff?" Gwen asked stepping down onto a sunny courtyard. "You know I'm not an artist."

"Worry not, young one. We have hands enough."

"You know I'm pretty good with a crossbow."

Alex squinted in the harsh sunlight. *She really is.* But then he remembered her wide eyes during the Leviathan attack. He never wanted to see that terrified look again.

They passed a rosy colored wellhead where the wooden door loomed. The white sun beat down upon him like an accusing eye. Should he turn back?

"Look there are bars on all those windows. I thought this was a good neighborhood." Gwen chuckled at her own joke.

They are going to hate me for this.

"This is the quickest way." Leonardo turned to Alex. "But we still can take the longer more difficult route, if you prefer."

Alex almost said yes, but then Bartholomew shuffled past, eyes glassy and distant, hunched over like a war refugee.

Alex's throat tightened. "No, this way is the best."

"So be it." With a sad nod Leonardo led them up two narrow flights of stairs and stopped in front of a half-sized door. He tilted his head toward something behind Gwen.

Alex saw the large key hanging on a hook above her head and clenched his fists. Then he gave Leonardo a curt nod.

Leonardo slid the bars back and opened the iron door. "Here is a shortcut."

Bartholomew bent down and scuffed inside. Gwen gave them a puzzled look but still followed.

"Now!" Alex shouted.

Leonardo slammed the door shut and slid the bolts into place while Alex grabbed the keys and tried to insert one in the lock. It didn't fit.

"Alex, what are you doing?" Gwen demanded.

Trying to steady his shaking hands Alex tried another. No dice.

"Are you crazy? Let me out of here."

Fumbling for a third, Alex dropped the whole ring.

"Bartholomew, tell him."

Bartholomew pulled out hand sanitizer and shrugged.

"Leonardo, come on," Gwen argued.

"I am but a creation."

She gave Alex a puppy look. Batted those beautiful green eyes.

Alex looked down and bent over for the keys. Bumped his head. *Ow.*

"Ha. Serves you right. Now open the door."

"Nope. Gotta keep you safe," Alex said.

Gwen shook the bars. ""No way! you better let me out of here, or so help me."

"Can't. But I'll send food and water later."

"I don't want snacks. I want out of here! NOW!" Gwen shook the barred window and kicked the door.

Alex finally fumbled the key in the lock and turned it. With a sigh, he whispered, "Someday I hope you'll understand."

"Understand? No way," Gwen growled, glared at him through the window.

Alex turned away and forced his feet forward.

"I'll never forgive you, Jerkwad!"

"I'm sorry," Alex whispered.

"I hate you! I hate you!" her voice echoed through the dark halls.

Yeah, Alex always lost at tic tac toe.

Chapter 55

"I thought he was my friend!" Gwen cried.

Bartholomew mumbled something from his crouched place in the corner.

"Oh, finally the zombie speaks. Heck of a lot of good you were when Alex locked us in here!" She crossed her skinny arms and shot him a dirty look. "What did you say?"

Bartholomew cleared his throat.

"Speak already!" Her freckled nose flared.

"I said Alex still is your friend."

"Yeah right. You are just as exasperating as he is!" She threw her hands in the air and groaned.

Just then she heard tinkling voices coming down the corridor.

"Eat, drink, and be merry. Drink, be merry, and eat."

"The Graces! We're free." She waved out the small barred window. "Over here. Come let us out."

"Eat, drink, and be merry. –be merry. –be merry," Splendor, Festivity, and Rejoicing trilled. They stood in the hallway, wooden trays in hand. One held a couple of goblets. The other had some sort of fruit. The third lady carried bread and cheese.

"Umm, hello Rejoicing? Could you open the door?" Gwen asked.

Rejoicing warbled a no.

"Festivity?" Gwen raised her eyebrows. "Come on."

"Nay," she sang with a giggle.

"Now Splendor. I know you'd love to unlock this door."

Splendor only smiled.

Gwen turned to Bartholomew. "Is everyone absolutely nuts in this place?"

Bartholomew shrugged but didn't reply.

When Festivity passed a goblet through the bars and sang, "Water," Gwen was tempted to slap it away, but she was so thirsty she snatched it and drank greedily. She was surprised to see the cup immediately refill itself; no matter how much she drank the goblet always ended up filled to the brim.

"Eat," Splendor warbled. She wrapped the bread and cheese in a scarf and held it out to Gwen who grabbed it out of her hands and began nibbling away. Splendor filled a second scarf for Bartholomew who took it with a polite thank you.

"Drink and be merry. Merry." Rejoicing twirled around in a circle.

"Okay," Gwen mumbled with her mouth still full of bread. "We're watered and fed. Now let us out."

"We can-not," They all sang.

"Sure, you can. Just get the keys and unlock the door."

"Only the Deliverers can decide," Splendor said.

"But Bartholomew is a Deliverer too, isn't he?" She turned to him. "Bartholomew, tell them."

Bartholomew shook his head.

"Please. I have to get out of here."

"No."

"But I'll go nuts in this place."

"Alex is right. We're safer here."

"No way!" She grabbed the bars and shook them. The door rattled on its hinges. "Let me out!"

Festivity cocked an ear to one side. "Time to go." She joined hands with the other Graces and they all skipped down the corridor singing.

Gwen spun on her heel. "Stupid wuss!" she fumed, shoving his right shoulder. "You blew our one chance to escape. How could you?"

Gwen pulled her fist back all ready to sock that stupid Richie in the face when a bell tolled off in the distance. She paused with her arm mid-air and counted; ten, twelve, thirteen rings.

"They've found her. And I'm stuck here with you!" she cried, punching Bartholomew in the stomach.

He doubled over clutching his gut. Sputtering and coughing.

Cheeks red, Gwen looked down at the wilted guy and immediately wished she could turn back time. She felt like a total tool.

Oh man. She'd really knocked the wind out of him. Plus, his lily-white pants were smeared with dirt, his dress shirt was rumpled, and that silly tie he still had on was all askew. She was just as bad as those bullies Ty and Con.

"Hey dude," she began.

Bartholomew was gasping to get air. Or was he crying?

"B-3?"

He *was*. God. She hated to see people cry. Gwen reached out and gave him an awkward pat on the back.

Bartholomew jerked away and plopped down on the wooden bench. "Leave me alone," he sniffed.

"Dude. I'm sorry. It's just-I don't know."

"At least here we're safe," Bartholomew retorted.

"But what about Alex?" Gwen asked. She thought if she reminded Mr. Clean about their friend he might suck it up and cool the waterworks. Have you thought about him?"

"He has the gods to help him. He'll be fine."

Bartholomew started to go off again about how the amazing Alex was better off without his blundering, but Gwen wasn't convinced. It all sounded too much like a pity party.

"This sucks." Gwen drew her leg back and kicked the bench. It didn't make a solid thud but rattled as if something were inside. Intrigued, she kicked it again.

Bartholomew gave her an incredulous stare. "It's bad enough you sucker punch me, you don't have to–"

"Get up," she ordered. When he stood, Gwen tapped on the edges of the bench. At the far-right corner it rattled like a loose door.

Gwen felt around underneath the top until her fingers caught on something flat. She wrapped her hand around it and pulled. Slowly a bit of dark metal appeared. She yanked harder and soon was holding an iron bar about half as long as her arm.

"What was that doing there?" Bartholomew asked.

"I don't care, but I'm gonna use it to escape. And you better not try and stop me," she warned. Gwen shook the bar at him before getting up on her tippy-toes to tap the ceiling.

"Gwen, I don't think–" his words were cut short by some falling splinters.

They both glanced up. Light streamed through a small hole.

"Now we are getting somewhere." Gwen began hammering away. As the hole grew, she pried pieces of wood away until there was an opening large enough to fit through. She turned to Bartholomew. "Are you coming?"

He didn't answer.

"Well I'm not waiting around while you decide." Using her feet to shimmy up the wall, she pulled herself up.

"Hey B-3. It's easy. And there's a big window down at the end." Gwen called. She removed one long splinter from her arm. "Come on."

Silence.

"Fine. Have it your way."

Holding the tool in one hand, Gwen began a shuffling crawl toward the window. The metal went scrape-clang with each scuttling step. *This isn't so bad.* She thought feeling confident, until she reached the end and realized what kind of window she'd have to deal with.

A skylight. On a steep roof.

Now Gwen was not a wimp. She could skateboard up the sides of an empty swimming pool with her eyes wide open. But she wasn't stupid. She knew which situations were risky. And climbing on a roof four stories high was one of them.

Gwen poked her head up through the open skylight. About ten feet away was a second skylight with a third further down. If one of them were open, it might lead to an exit.

The heat waves rising on the leaded roof told her that this not only was going to be dangerous, it would be hot as hell. But if she stuck the iron bar between the gaps in the roof tiles while she climbed, she might be okay. And it'd keep her hands from being burned.

The smell of hot metal and summer dust made Gwen's nose twitch. She rubbed it with the back of her hand before tucking the piece of iron into the belt loop of her torn jeans.

Gwen brought her other knee up on the window sill. Here, the noonday sun assaulted her face. Heart pounding, she pivoted around on the windowsill and stretched her legs out. When she let her feet dangle below, her knee grazed a roof tile. Ow hot!

Holding the window frame with one hand, she reached down and extracted the iron bar from her belt loops.

"Easy Gwen. Don't drop it."

Gwen slowly tested her foothold. Then grasping the metal bolt in both hands, she inserted it between the lead shingles. Now fixed firmly, she pulled herself over to the next section. Then, repeating the process, she crawled and scooted from roof tile to roof tile.

The sun beat down burning the exposed back of her neck. Freaky how real everything was even though it was made of art. Far below the city chattered and twittered but no one pointed, shouted, or, thank God, shot arrows in her direction. Not a single

Artanian seemed to notice a skinny redhead creeping across the prison roof.

The heat soon had her drenched in sweat, hair plastered to her head. It dripped in her eyes and off the tip of her nose. The iron bar grew heavier in her rubbery arms until she could barely lift it.

She aimed at a place between the shingles but missed. Gwen blinked. Lifted it again.

Her feet slipped and started to slide downward.

Toward that sheer drop.

Her free hand shot out, but her reflexes brought it back again, rasping against the hot metal. Her other gripped the iron bar and plunged it between two tiles. The edge cut her palm, but it stopped her.

Gwen hung there, heart pounding like an alien bursting from a chest in that scary movie she'd watched with Zach and Jose. Panting, she looked down, praying no one had noticed her.

A little boy glanced up shielding his eyes from the sun. Trying to think as thin as a model, Gwen flattened her body against the metal roof. Waited. One second. Two. Five.

When all remained quiet, she took a deep breath and placed another hand on the bar. *Pull yourself upward, Girl. Dig your toes in. Careful now.*

Taking careful aim, she inserted the bar between two roof tiles and tensed her muscles. Gwen pulled up two feet, stopped, and caught her breath. Then she repeated the process.

Slowly she climbed.

After what seemed like forever she reached the second skylight. She heaved a sigh of relief when she peered into the space below where a narrow staircase led to freedom.

Gwen wriggled through the opening, dropped onto the landing, and dashed down a couple flights of stairs. Barreling through a long corridor, she found the great doors they had come through earlier.

Pressing up against the wall, Gwen got a quick lay of the land. She would have to hide. If Alex found out about her escape, he'd probably tell those Artanians creatures to capture her again.

She glanced down at her clothes. Shoot! Tennies, torn jeans and skater logo t-shirt didn't exactly fit in with all these ladies in long gowns.

She'd have to find a way to camouflage herself.

But what Gwen didn't know was that she'd already been spotted. And it wasn't the painted eyes of a kind Creation that saw her. It was the glowing yellow orbs of the enemy.

An enemy ready to use her against her friends.

Chapter 56

Sludge smiled when he saw Gwen. Everything was going according to plan. The Barbarossa Brothers were anchored in the Lagoon. One Deliverer had drowned, and the human girl was creeping along with no idea he was following her. Now all he needed was to wait for midnight when the Portal opened to transport Leonardo's precious Mona Lisa to Subterranea.

Fresh slime tingled on his face as he imagined the destruction to come.

Long shadows crept up the weathered stone buildings. It was time to send his warriors forth.

He bent down on one knee and tapped the cobblestones with the butt end of his battle axe. The pavement groaned and sighed. When it parted, a hole appeared just large enough for a hunchbacked soldier to pass through. Sludge raised the axe skyward.

"Shadow, muck, and whither wall. Listen servants to my call. A waging war is ours to win. I call for help from my minions."

The ground rumbled with the sound of marching jackboots. Soldiers emerged from the opening and lined up in formation. When thirty dark heads were bowed in front of him, Sludge pounded his chest once.

"Corporals, take your squads to theses marked places," the captain ordered while passing out rolls of parchment. He waited for the soldiers to open them before continuing. "Memorize the maps. Then destroy these scrolls."

"How?" a soldier with twisted lips asked.

The captain glared at him but ignored the question. "When you hear Mudlark Elephant bellowing, you will strike. By midnight I expect no Artanians to be left in the streets."

"What if are?"

"There won't be."

"But they fight good." The soldier's misshapen lips began to quiver.

"Idiot." Sludge stepped closer to the corporal. "That is why we attack now."

"And Deliverer be on their side."

Sludge wondered how this soldier ever made it to corporal. But he was not about to face the Correction Chamber for some slimeless coward.

Grabbing him by the collar, Sludge shoved the stupid idiot up against a building. He pulled a dagger from the folds of his dark cloak and held it to the soldier's throat. "Failure is not an option. Understand, soldier?"

"Y-yes sir."

Sludge turned back to the rest of the corporals. "That goes for the rest of you. With one Deliverer dead, this should be as easy as bathing in Swallow Hole Swamp." He paused, making sure every yellow eye was focused on him. "But no mistakes will be tolerated. Are we clear?"

"Yes sir," they all mumbled.

"I said, are we clear?"

"YES SIR!"

"Stench and I will follow the human. The rest of you gather your squads, now!"

One by one they trooped double quick through the streets. To Sludge the sounds of their thundering feet were glorious.

Almost as beautiful as the whimpers of a nightmare-invaded child.

He could hardly wait for darkness to fall. And watch that Deliverer, Alexander, experience real nightmares.

Revenge would soon be his.

Sludge flared his piggish nostrils and grinned. Yes, everything was going according to plan.

Chapter 57

Head in hands, Bartholomew swayed back and forth. Even though the shadows were getting longer, this cell was still oppressively hot. He doused his head with the water goblet from the Muses. It washed away some of the grime but did little to cool the sweltering heat.

He was in the middle of combing his hair back with his fingers when he heard the rasping. Unsure sure if it were voices or hissing snakes, Bartholomew cupped an ear.

"The Deliverers-s-s' friend. Ha!"

Shadow Swine? Here?

"Yes-s. She so easy to deceive. Nightmares in her mind."

Gwen never mentioned that Shadow Swine had invaded her dreams. Bartholomew knew all too well what those nightmares were like. And what they could do to a person.

This was a disaster.

"Soon the Captain will make her betray the remaining Deliverer."

So, they thought that Bartholomew had drowned. Good. But the Swineys still might trick Gwen into laying a trap.

Gurgling sounds like dogs tracking a scent joined the growing voices.

Bartholomew squirted some hand sanitizer into his hand. *I should go. Now.*

But outside were a thousand ways he could mess up. Just one wrong turn, and more people could die.

"Up this-s hallway. I smell human."

With no choice, Bartholomew leapt onto the bench and pulled himself up through the hole that Gwen had made. Wriggling over the jagged edges, he paused when the kicked-up dust tickled his nose hairs.

Bartholomew pinched his nose.

He could hear the Shadow Swine jiggling the cell door and cursing its lock. His chest spasmed as he fought the sneeze.

Scuffling boots retreated down the hallway. There was a jangle of keys.

Now Bartholomew began to crawl. He moved slowly praying that the monsters' fumbling would cover any noise he made.

At the end of the shaft, he realized that the only way out was over a pitched roof.

Bartholomew hated heights. And this skylight was four stories up at least.

What a choice. Face Shadow Swine or scale a slippery roof? God, he wished Alex were there.

Bartholomew lay stomach down on the window frame. With a gulp, he forced himself through the opening and swung his legs around. Then he looked down. Big mistake.

The courtyard tiles blurred like a camera lens going in and out of focus. He started to see odd colors; red and green spots eclipsing his vision.

His head spun in nauseating spirals. He tasted cheesy bile in his throat. Why had he eaten that pasta?

His heart was beating too fast, a thousand hammers in his chest. Starting to retch, Bartholomew covered his mouth.

And began to slide.

He reached out, but it was too late. Both hands clutched at air. Down, down he went until his body met stone.

And everything went black.

Chapter 58

Shots? Gwen flinched.

It was beginning, and Alex was alone. Superman might think he could do everything by himself, but she knew better.

She had to get to him.

Gwen blinked, imagining Mr. Hero flat on his back, a monster standing over him, leaning right just before the axe fell. He'd look around for help but there'd be none.

She clenched her fists and headed toward the booming sounds. Keeping to narrow alleys and doorways, she mapped her route twenty feet at a time. With each step, the clanging of metal grew louder.

Gwen turned a corner and froze. Scores of those hunch-backed creatures were battling Italians straight ahead. Axe blades flashed. Backs heaved. A condotierri dude raised his sword and fell.

Gwen looked away, clamped her jaw.

Swallowing hard, Gwen shot forward. *Stupid Alex, why'd you have to be such a martyr?* She thought. Her tennies slapped against the stone pavers as she willed her legs faster through streets, over bridges, and alongside canals.

Gwen glanced over her shoulder. So far so good. Speeding up, she leapt over an upturned cart.

And skidded to a halt.

"Hello human," the monster sneered.

"You!" she gasped, covering her mouth with one hand.

His yellow eyes glowed like hellfire. "I told you we would meet again. Remember?"

Her eyes grew wide. How could she forget the nightmares? And what he said.

"I see you do," Captain Sludge said.

"I told you before," Gwen said crossing her arms defiantly across her chest. "I'll never sell out my buds."

The monster bared shark teeth in a sick smile. "Oh, that won't be necessary."

Was Alex hurt? Or worse? Gwen didn't dare ask.

A pig-nosed creature marched up and saluted. "Captain, the Deliverer fades."

"Good job, Corporal. Now on to their precious daughter." Sludge turned to Gwen. "It seems we didn't need you after all. Your idiot friend stood right in front of our arrows."

"What do you mean?" Gwen's stomach turned.

"His armor thin. He falls-s. Blood." the second Swiney licked his bulbous lips.

Alex wounded? No! Gwen felt her face blanch.

"Where is he?" she demanded.

"In the Arsenale," Captain Sludge replied. "But don't go there. It's guarded by hundreds of *Condottieri*. You'll never get past them."

"They'll let me in. I'm Alex's friend."

"Good luck, human. I'm off to celebrate." The hunch-backed creature turned to go.

She had to get to Alex. She doubted that even the gods knew how to help him. But she did. After Mom left, Dad got so paranoid about emergencies he made her take advanced first aid classes.

"Captain, the troops are waiting."

Sludge nodded and took a few slow steps down the alley.

She could save him, she knew it. But where was this Arsenale? Venice was such a confusing maze of canals and streets she'd never find it on her own. Couldn't ask an Artanian, they probably had orders to capture her.

She stared at Sludge's retreating back. He took two more steps, then stopped to adjust his long black cloak.

"Umm, sir."

"Yes?" He cocked his head to one side but didn't turn back.

"Do you know which way, that this, umm, Arsenale is?"

"Perhaps." The sharp spikes on his head bobbed slightly as he spoke. "But what would you give me for this information?"

What did she have? No weapons. No jewels. Even her pockets were empty.

She shrugged.

Sludge did an about face and in three strides was in her face, rotten egg breath blowing down her neck. His clawed hand reached out. Gwen recoiled.

"You have this," he said rubbing a slimy hand over her hair.

"My head?" Gwen gulped.

"No," Sludge guffawed. "Braids. My Lord would be most pleased to have your red locks on his wall."

That was easy. Gwen didn't care about her hair. She only braided it to keep it out of her face.

"Take 'em."

Sludge pulled something from the folds of his cloak. A glint of steel appeared, and Gwen's throat tightened. What had she just agreed to?

The dagger drew near. Gwen felt her jugular vein pulse. Held her breath.

Slice. One pigtail floated to the ground. Slash. The other landed at its side.

Captain Sludge picked them up and fingered them lovingly. He flattened a few stray hairs with the slime coating on his skin, and then tucked them in his cloak pocket.

"It is this way. Come."

Keeping her gaze fixed on Sludge's dark back. Gwen followed.

But never saw the pack of Swineys that shadowed her along the way.

Chapter 59

When Bartholomew ran a hand over his head, he recoiled. Ouch. His throbbing head felt like it was in a vice with the slightest movement clamping it down tighter. Probing around gently, he discovered a long gash oozing blood.

He blinked. How did he end up in this blistering hot place?

It slowly came back to him. *Venice. The Doge's Palace Prison. Shadow Swine in the corridor.*

Gwen! She was in danger.

He started to rise but then the doubts began.

It hurts. And you'll just mess up again.

"No, you are a Creator. There is no blood. No gash.," he said.

The dirt. The filth. Just like when Bartholomew Junior... Mother's words flashed in his mind. He started to imagine his head rotting from gangrene.

"No, healing."

Filth! Germs! Infections!

"No. Health and strength."

Stop. Lie down or you'll need a scalpectomy.

"No!" Bartholomew cried. "I am a creator, like my father and grandfather before me. And I can do this." He blinked to force Mother's words from his mind and imagined himself healed and whole.

And his head was just like before the fall. No blood. No gash. No pain. His hair could have used a comb, but aside from that, it was clean.

He glanced around.

The entire courtyard was now in shadow, so he'd have to act fast. Who could he trust? Not Leonardo.

Michelangelo?

Of course! He wouldn't know about the imprisonment. He argued with just about everything Leonardo did.

Figuring that Michelangelo must be inside the armory, Bartholomew dashed over there.

Sure enough, the old grouch was still passing out crossbows, muskets, and two-handed swords to the Condotierri.

"Be careful with that one. Hold it high. Think, soldier, think." Michelangelo grumbled. He glanced Bartholomew's way and got a quizzical look.

"Hello Mr. Michelangelo." Bartholomew waved weakly.

"Why are you here boy? The battle rages."

"Well, I kinda need your help."

"Of course, you do." Michelangelo said. "You are but a child."

Bartholomew tried to ignore these comments as he explained what the Shadow Swine said, how Gwen was off alone in the city while an ignorant Alex helped Leonardo.

The lines in Michelangelo's forehead deepened. "There are many ways a Shadow Swine could use a human."

"I know."

"But why haven't you sent the other Deliverer a message?"

"I-I." Bartholomew didn't know what to say.

"What is it? Speak child."

Bartholomew looked into those dark eyes. There he saw impatience, but he also detected a hint of kindness. Could he trust him? This man had lovingly sculpted the David and built a fortress to protect Mona Lisa.

"Bah! Time is wasted with children." He turned away and told a *Condotierri* to call the messenger god Hermes.

Bartholomew's voice was barely a whisper. "Alex didn't believe in me." He stared at his stained shoes.

"Of course, he didn't. You are but a bambino." Michelangelo didn't turn around, but Bartholomew thought he noticed his posture softening.

"Well I might be young, but I can sculpt."

"Can you?"

"And fight. I am a Deliverer you know!"

"Really? I thought you were a whining babe."

"You don't understand."

"Then tell me." Michelangelo kept his back turned, making it easier for Bartholomew to speak.

"They all died, because of me." Hot tears rolled down his cheeks as the whole story poured out. How first his hesitation lead to capture, and he'd joined the noble Mona Lisa as a prisoner. They spent several days tethered to the mast before he finally came up with a plan to flatter Redbeard. But it backfired because he was too stupid to consider the consequences of praising a big-headed pirate.

"He raided the ship, killing the adults, enslaving the boys. And none of it saved Mona Lisa. She is still in chains," he finished with a sniffle.

"As long as shame and dishonor may last. It is my pleasure to sleep and even more to be stone." Michelangelo waited several moments before finally turning around.

Wiping a tear away with the back of his hand, Bartholomew peered into the older man's face. Michelangelo was right. That was just what he'd tried to do. Sleep the pain away. Become stone, forget his shame. But it didn't do any good.

"I am so sorry." His lips quivered.

"Tell me all."

Bartholomew explained about Alex's mistrust, the prison, Gwen's escape, and finally his. And soon the shame wasn't so crippling.

With that release, he even felt empowered. He *could* help his friends.

If only he acted in time.

Chapter 60

Musket balls sizzled over the Arsenale walls. "We're low on shot here," a *Condottieri* cried.

Alex sprinted over to the hot forge where he and Vulcan had been making weapons and ammunition for the face-off with Shadow Swine and pirates. "More heat for musket balls!" he shouted tossing handfuls of old nails into the spoon-shaped molds.

Vulcan stoked the fire with his bellows while Alex closed the hinged bullet makers. They reminded him of Mom's waffle iron except here you put in something hard, like nails, and it turned soft. He shoved both forms into the furnace and waited for the lead to melt.

In real life, this process would have taken close to an hour, but in Artania the musket balls were ready in a matter of seconds. Then, the young gunners, called Powder Monkeys, scooped up handfuls from the knee-high pile to deliver to the fort's soldiers.

"Where are they all coming from?" Alex asked throwing more scrap metal in the forms.

"I don't understand it." Vulcan shook his head. "A Shadow Swine has never been seen in, much less attacked, Venice."

Leonardo looked up from the giant catapult he was inspecting. "People on Earth doubt us. Many have turned away."

"But isn't that the way it's always been?" Alex dumped another bunch of musket balls onto the pile then set to making cannon shot.

"Yes," Leonardo agreed. "Earth has always had those who deny their creativity. But perhaps this wasn't caused by people in that realm." He opened his mouth as if to say more but stopped.

"What?" Alex demanded.

"Events in Artania can also give Swineys power. Since the Deliverers are like two sides of a circle, if one mistrusts the other, their ripples of doubt can open cracks in our world."

"You aren't telling me that that what I did to Bartholomew caused more Swineys to come in?"

"I have seen it before," Leonardo said. "Back in the nineteenth century. Monet was full of doubt and we lost a whole village in the Alps."

"I had to keep them safe." Alex set his jaw firmly. He turned his back on Leonardo but still he felt the man's eyes boring into him.

Walking stiffly, he headed for one of the ladders to the ramparts and climbed. Alex paced back and forth over the brick parapet, muttering, "What does he know? Has he seen someone almost die?"

The battle was raging as far as the eye could see. Duels. Sword fights. Hand to hand combat. The flash of musket and cannon filled the darkening streets. The Shadow Swine's hunched backs looked even more grotesque under this eerie firework show.

In Saint Mark's Canal, the god Poseidon straddled two dolphins and raised his three-pronged trident to spurt triple waterspouts at the *Red Raven*. "Let Mona Lisa go!" his voice boomed.

Alex held his breath and waited. Would the pirates give up now? One minute passed then two.

The explosion of cannon from the pirate's bow answered his question. "That's where I should be," he muttered.

He thought he'd planned it so well; Apollo and Venus in the sky, Poseidon in the water, Leonardo and the other gods with him in the Arsenale. But never in a million years had Alex imagined so many Shadow Swine.

For hours, they'd tried to drive them back. But as soon as a few would fall, ten more would take their place. Where were they all coming from?

Alex's mind raced. Swineys waited at every street and canal. There was no way to get near the *Red Raven*.

He glanced at what was supposed to be their secret weapon. Heck of a lot of good it was doing them just sitting in the courtyard.

Alex and Leonardo had molded it from the real da Vinci's design. The metal submarine-tank was about the size of Volkswagen Bug, with a glass top and four iron wheels attached to cranks. These worked like bicycle pedals with a rider cycling from the center seat.

Alex banged his forehead on the hull. Resting it there, he noticed the giant crossbow to his right. It was big enough to launch a car.

And it shot straight.

Turning on his heel, Alex put two fingers between his lips and let out a loud whistle. "Leonardo, Vulcan, bring the crossbow. Quickly," he called, not stopping to explain.

When the gigantic arrow was under the submarine, Alex gathered a few gods, some *Condotierri* and Leonardo together. "If this works like I hope, it should land just short of the *Red Raven*. Once I splash down, cover me."

Mars pounded his breastplate. "I will guard you myself."

"While I fly to deliver messages," Hermes said, a serious look replacing his usual smirk.

Alex pondered a moment, wondering if he was forgetting anything. He nodded three times. "Okay. Let's do it," he said.

When the *Condotierri* soldiers lifted the tank's glass lid, Alex scrambled up the curved sides. He lowered himself through the opening onto the hot metal floor and cringed. He took a long breath, trying not to imagine that he was one of Mom's pancakes on the griddle.

Barely worked.

After the soldiers bolted the top back into place, Alex gave his friends a shaky thumbs-up. In a minute they were going to launch him into the air, but if their aim was off by even a couple of inches, he'd crash into the Arsenale wall.

Alex hesitated and glanced out the domed window. There Leonardo was using his beard to double-check the giant arrow's aim. The old man pointed it toward the lagoon then drew a line through the air back toward the tank.

Not very exact science. Alex thought, clenching his fists, almost shouting for them to let him out. Then he remembered that dead ship and all those bodies on deck. He saw Bartholomew's hollow eyes reliving the horrors and Gwen's panicked face. Those pirates had to be stopped.

Placing his feet on the pedals, Alex leaned back to brace himself before making megaphone hands. "Ready!" he cried.

The crossbow trigger released the bolt with a loud twang, and his tank-sub climbed. The increasing g-force pressed against Alex's body and drove his head backwards. When his chest tightened, he sucked at air, but it felt like a giant hand was crushing it into the wall and no oxygen reached his lungs.

He gripped his throat and watched the moon appear through the domed window above. Unable to breathe, he squeezed tighter, began to see flashes and colors. A haze descended but still he climbed. Barely on the edge of consciousness, he saw the inevitable crash into the brick wall.

He was going to fail.

Just before blacking out, everything stopped and for a moment, the tank was suspended in air. Alex coughed as some mist cleared from his mind. Then his stomach lurched, and he was plummeting.

Down he went until the tank hit the water with a splash. Banging his head against the wall, he finally came around. Alex watched the sea rise over him, pooling around his feet. With an open floor, how high would the water go? Leonardo had said that the domed top would make a pocket of air.

If it worked.

Soon his shoes and the back of his pants were soaked. Water splashed on the walls and trickled down the metal sides. Alex looked up at the fading stars as he descended further. Then a soft thud told him that he'd hit the sea floor.

The darkening sky cast long blue shadows and a bright yellow moon rippling through the sea. Leonardo was right. There was air inside.

Alex decided to use the moon as a navigation marker. Since it rose in the east like the sun, he knew to keep it on his right and hopefully head off Barbarossa's ship before they escaped.

But first he had to get this tank moving.

His feet splashed on the pedals, but it didn't move. Alex strained, pressing harder until he finally crept a few feet forward.

"Yes," he cried feeling new energy course through his legs.

Then a spike shaped shadow fell across the moon and the dome darkened.

Alex blinked.

The pirate ship was heading his way.

Chapter 61

Gwen ran her fingers through her now short hair wondering why Sludge was keeping his end of the bargain. From the center of the stone street he pointed at the Arsenale. Following his slimy finger's imaginary line, Gwen saw high walls and two square guard towers. A huge arched gateway with a roaring lion on top loomed between them.

At the notched battlements, Italian soldiers called out and scrambled into position, crossbows and long pistols aimed at the advancing Shadow Swine. To Gwen, the monsters firing muskets and launching boulders from wooden catapults looked like a cockroach horde infesting this cool city.

No wonder Alex was hurt. The battle was full on gnarly, but she had to give those *Condotierri* props; they returned musket ball for musket ball.

Suddenly, a flash lit up the evening sky. There was a boom and a fiery ball shot over the ramparts. It leveled six Shadow Swine like a bocce ball over pins.

Gwen started to raise a triumphant fist but quickly lowered it. Didn't want to tick off that cruel captain. But when she glanced back, Captain Sludge was nowhere in sight. He had suddenly disappeared. Strange.

An oil lantern flickered to life above her. Gwen flinched. Then another.

She'd have to be careful.

Ducking down on all fours she crab-crawled to a doorway. When there was enough musket smoke to cloud the street, she darted behind an overturned cart.

The winged lion roared again. Then a yowling horn bugled. Gwen peered between the cart's wooden slats.

She immediately wished she hadn't. For in the center of the street was a trumpeting elephant. But this didn't look like any of the sweet ones she'd seen at the Santa Barbara Zoo. It had a ridged back, sharp pointed tusks that dripped mud, and fiery red eyes. Its ears were off balance as if someone had yanked its left ear through its skull. This left a tiny flap of skin on one side, but a curtain of meat on the other.

Every Shadow Swine halted. As if hypnotized, they turned on their heels and marched off. Soon, their boots crunching sound receded.

Above the Italian *Condotierri* exchanged confused glances. Gwen was just as bewildered. Then a horrible thought came to her.

She was too late.

She didn't think. Just started running, tears streaming down her face. "Let me in! Let me in!" Gwen banged on the huge wooden door.

"Who goes there?" an Italian soldier called from the parapet above.

"I'm Alex's friend." Gwen glanced up. "Open the door!"

"*Perche*?"

"I don't have time to explain. He needs me. Hurry!"

The soldier conferred with someone behind him for a moment. Gwen's leg twitched nervously. *Please let him be okay.*

"We-a let you in," the soldier shouted down. "But be-a quick."

Like a racer waiting for the starting gun, Gwen leaned back. When the great door creaked open just enough for her to squeeze through, she vaulted forward.

She had just crossed the threshold when something hit the back of her knees. Her legs crumpled beneath her. Gwen fell against the door.

"Idiot human," a cloaked shadow hissed as it slipped past her.

"What?" Gwen muttered.

More dark legs poured past. They flooded the Arsenal with a single cry. "Destroy! Destroy! Destroy!"

Out front, Sludge pointed where to attack, his clawed fingertips glinting in the torchlight. Noble *Condotierri* fell right and left. Shadow Swine surrounded Leonardo and Vulcan. The god lifted a fiery brand and jabbed at the Swineys but even he couldn't hold back the dark warriors.

Gwen sunk down against the door. "Oh my God. What have I done?"

Chapter 62

Even from inside the Doge's Palace, Bartholomew could hear the cries. And they terrified him.

"What was that?" he asked Michelangelo, pulling out his hand sanitizer.

"It does not sound good. Come," the sculptor replied.

When Michelangelo headed for the exit. Bartholomew shoved the bottle back in his pocket and followed him up some stairs to a bank of windows on the third floor. It was too dark to make out what was happening, but Bartholomew thought he saw brown floodwaters surging into the fort.

Squinting, he soon realized that it wasn't mud flooding the Arsenal but Shadow Swine. Somehow, they had gotten past the gates.

Bartholomew gasped. "There're hundreds, maybe thousands. We have to do something."

"Too late." Michelangelo shook his head sadly.

"No. You can't say that."

"It is as futile as carving in brittle stone."

"I don't believe this. Just a while ago you were telling *me* to fight."

"We are too few." Michelangelo pointed at the city below. "There are ten of them to every one of us."

"I didn't come this far to give up now." Bartholomew was about to launch into an angry speech when Hermes flew in the window.

The tiny wings on his helmet and sandals fluttered. "I bear sad news! The Arsenal has been overrun."

"We saw." Bartholomew jerked his head toward the window. "What happened?"

"The girl, Gwen, asked them to open the gates and the Shadow Swine forced their way in," Hermes explained.

"And Alex?"

"He was elsewhere."

Bartholomew felt a pit in the bottom of his stomach. "Where?"

"He paddles a machine in the Northern Canal." Hermes quickly described how Alex was using a submarine-tank to rescue Mona Lisa before adding angrily. "He risks himself while the girl betrays us all!"

So, that was what the Shadow Swine had meant when they said they'd trick Gwen.

"It may look that way but believe me Gwen would never betray us on purpose." He paused, stared off into space. The idea of tricking them sparked a sudden plan.

"Deliverer?" Hermes asked waving a hand in front of Bartholomew's face.

"Okay, here's what we're going to do..." Using his hands like air sculptures Bartholomew outlined his idea. As he spoke, twinkles of hope sparkled in Michelangelo's eyes.

"–then we approach undetected," the boy finished with a proud grin.

"I shall bring them in all haste." Hermes's winged hat and sandals buzzed as he hovered in front of the window. He fluttered for a moment then shot out the opening like a hummingbird.

Bartholomew didn't waste time watching him go. It was time to get to work. He had some sculpting to do.

Chapter 63

Alex stopped pedaling. It was time. He got down on all fours next to the seat, took a deep breath, and dove down. He pushed past the wheels and glided into open water before kicking toward the pirate ship above.

When he surfaced, he saw the pirates on deck rushing back and forth in the moonlight. They lit several lanterns, but none revealed Mona Lisa's face. Trying to be as silent as a bull shark, Alex paddled toward a ladder at the stern and began creeping upward.

He flinched. Were those footsteps?

The sounds drew closer. He pressed up against the ladder.

"We should tell the crew."

"That be too risky," a different voice hissed. "Even with their belief in my greatness."

"But when it opens–" the first began.

"Bah. You and I can row one lady into place."

There was a pause as if one of the pair was thinking. "I hope you're right, brother."

"I always be right. Put your mind at ease, Hizir. Go now, busy the crew."

The Barbarossa Brothers! Alex thought, almost leaping up to punch them both in the face.

"Aye Aruj. Until it's time."

"Then we'll be the most powerful corsairs in all of Artania."

Chucking like snuffling bears, their voices retreated. *Twenty-seven. Twenty-eight. Twenty-nine.* Alex cocked an ear before scrambling up the final rungs and stealing into the space behind the captain's cabin. From here he could see turbaned men checking lines and polishing swords.

And the shackled Mona Lisa.

Her sad face made him suck in a quick breath. Her famous smile was gone, replaced with a thin line. Still she held herself high, like a noble princess.

What spirit! Alex thought. *I can see why she holds the Renaissance Nation together.*

Surveying the ship, Alex realized that he couldn't just rush headlong across deck. There were at least twenty pirates between him and her. He could swing down the lines attached to the mast. But Mona Lisa was handcuffed, and he didn't have the key.

Alex chewed on his lip. How about coming from below? No way. Too many oarsmen to get past.

When he started to get a cramp in his leg from crouching for so long, he stood and twisted his torso to one side. That helped.

But when he turned back, Alex froze. Staring at two round eyes widening from an elfin face.

"A-another ph-photo?" the small boy stammered.

Alex almost clamped a hand over the kid's mouth until he remembered Bartholomew's story.

"Pico, right?" he whispered.

The little guy gave a quick nod and started to fidget with one of the frayed edges on his stained tunic.

"You know my friend?" Even in this dim light Alex could see the boy's face blanch. He tugged harder on the loose threads of his shirt.

Pico had a guilty look. Reminding Alex of how he'd felt after Mom had her heart attack.

The child's voice was barely audible. "I s-sorry."

"Sorry? About what?"

"I n-no save him. He g-g-g-. He d-d-." Pico clamped his mouth shut.

Then Alex realized that the poor kid saw Bartholomew walk the plank. He must think he drowned.

"Hey, don't worry. He is okay."

Pico raised his puppy eyes. "R-really?"

"Yeah. I just saw him. He's safe."

Pico threw his arms around Alex's waist. "I like Photo but feel bad. He so sick." He started to tell a story when Alex raised a shushing finger.

"S-sorry," he said again, lowering his voice to a whisper.

"It's okay. But Pico," Alex began. "I need your help."

"A-anything."

"We have to free the lady."

"I kn-now. R-redbeard be in with…S-s-s-s," he stuttered but couldn't seem to get the word out.

"Sickhert," Alex finished.

Pico clutched at Alex's t-shirt as if that word could knock him off the deck.

Alex patted the boy's head. And started to outline his plan.

Chapter 64

Gwen couldn't believe she'd been so stupid. Even Mr. Clean wasn't that dumb. He'd stayed in the cell, sure, but that was because after consideration he thought it was safer. She hadn't even been suspicious when that monster offered to help her.

And Alex! He was hurt and maybe dying.

The half-light made it hard to see much of anything; a relief since Gwen didn't want to see the horrors all around. Moaning people writhing. Crumpled remains. God, she prayed Alex wasn't one of them.

"Leonardo? Vulcan?" she whispered as she made her way inside.

She clicked her tongue. *Yeah right. Like anyone is going to hear you with all this sword clanging.*

She tried calling out louder. "Leonardo?"

The only response was another falling body. Gwen leapt back as a huge Shadow Swine collapsed right in front of her.

"Take that, beast!" a man said.

"Vulcan?" Gwen ventured, hoping that the new figure was an Artanian, not a slime monster.

When he didn't answer, Gwen flattened herself up against the wall. A long lance pointed her way. Gwen ducked and threw her hands over her head. But instead of a jab, she heard a sound like a shovel digging into sand.

Trembling, Gwen peered through her fingers. A monster with a lance in his back crumpled right next to her. Then it shuddered once and turned to dust.

Painted hands pulled the lance back. A helmet bobbed. "Ha! Try cornering Mars, will you?"

Sighing, Gwen stood up and cleared her throat. "Mr. God dude, do you know where–"

In a flash, she was up against the bricks, something sharp pressed into her throat.

"You betrayed us all!" the war god accused pressing his lance deeper into her skin.

"No-I..."

"I should skewer you right now." Mars said.

"I didn't know they were behind me...." Gwen's lower lip begin to quiver. "But I have to find Alex. He's hurt."

"The Deliverer?" The armored god narrowed his fiery eyes. "He is fine."

Gwen shook her head. "No. That monster said he's wounded. I need to get to him. Now."

"He isn't here. He rides in a machine. Seeking Mona Lisa." Mars pressed the triangular tip a little deeper into her throat. "Are these lies? More deception?"

Gwen felt the blade dig into her Adam's apple and swallowed. "No, I swear. That slime thing told me Alex was hurt. I didn't know the way, so he said he'd lead me here if I gave him my pigtails." She tugged on her short hair for proof. "He disappeared when I was about a block away. I thought I was alone when they opened the gates. Honest."

"You were deceived?" Mars eased up on the lance.

Gwen nodded. "Now take me to Alex. I know first aid."

"Human. You were lied to. As I said, the Deliverer is safe."

"You mean he's not hurt?" Then her stupidity really hit her. "No way!"

She barely had time deal with how dumb she'd been before five Shadow Swine approached. "Easy pickins," the largest one grunted.

"You will soon see just how easy!" Mars cried with a jab of his lance. He swiped at the closest Swiney, but Mr. Slime dodged to the left. Mars swung again and grazed a second's cloak.

But the next few thrusts weren't so easy. Mars charged three, four times. Missed. And to add insult to injury, the Shadow Swine slapped each other on the back every time he missed.

Jerks.

An angry Mars glared at the group while Gwen raised her fists and took a step forward. Mars pushed her out of the way and swept his lance right. A long gaping scratch started to ooze brownish blood from the tallest one's cheek. The monster clutched his face and roared.

The others bellowed with rage. And closed in on them.

Chapter 65

Alex crept out from under the captain's cabin and raised a finger. Then two. When he held up three, a loud boom exploded from the starboard bow.

"Good job, Pico," Alex whispered as he dashed out from his hiding place and began climbing the main mast toward the empty crow's nest.

There were scattered cries as the pirates ran in circles trying to figure out what had happened. More oil lamps flickered to life.

"New attacks?" a voice called.

"The canal were empty, weren't it?"

While the confused pirates tried to figure out what was happening, little Pico slipped away from the cannon. In a fake walk any actor would be embarrassed by, he strolled past a few corsairs toward one with a rope keyring hanging from his belt. The ship's boy reached a tiny hand toward it, but when a glance came his way, snatched it back.

"Careful now, Pico," Alex whispered, crossing his fingers.

The Keymaster turned just as Pico was extending his hand again. Alex tensed.

With a plaintive wail, Pico wrapped his arms around the Keymaster's waist. "S-s-save me!"

"Get off Stupido," The pirate snarled trying to push Pico away.

The boy clung tighter. Whimpering, he weaseled his legs around the Keymaster's ankles while sliding one hand toward the ring. Alex held his breath as Pico untied the knot and slipped off a key.

Pico dropped it down his shirt scarcely a second before the Keymaster grabbed him by the hair. "Stop!"

The little guy fumbled to retie the ring but when the Keymaster yanked him upward, it was out of reach. The rope dangled ever looser. Sagging with the weight of all those keys.

Alex could just hear them clattering as they fell. Ruining their plan. He began to climb out of the crow's nest.

The Keymaster yanked Pico's head back. "Get off I say!"

Pico tightened the knot and let go. "S-sorry," he said hanging his curly-topped head as if terribly ashamed.

"Bah!" The pirate stormed away.

Lifting his head, Pico gave Alex a thumbs-up. Then with a quick glance over his shoulder, he stole over to Mona Lisa and started to unlock her handcuffs.

Meanwhile Alex looped some line around his hand by using his arm as a measuring stick. Once he'd unraveled enough, he glanced down, praying that Pico followed the plan.

"Don't completely remove her handcuffs," he had said. "Just unlock them. We don't want anyone to notice she's free until the last possible second."

Pico gave Mona Lisa a hug goodbye and crept off toward the stern just before a turbaned man with a reddish beard emerged from the hold.

"What be this?" he cried. "Hizir!"

A man with one hand on the hilt of his sword shimmied up the ladder and slowly surveyed the surrounding scene.

Alex figured that those must be the Barbarossa Brothers B-3 had told him about. He could easily tell Redbeard from his brother; strutting across the deck like a show-off. But

Bartholomew said the other one, Hizir, was smart. He would figure out what was going on if they didn't act soon.

"Were that the blast of cannon?" Hizir asked. "I see no ship."

"Aye, Brother. It appears that the canal is not as empty as we were led to believe. "But they not know who they be dealing with." He gave his velvet cloak a dramatic snap as he stepped closer to Mona Lisa.

Alex felt the seconds ticking.

A shadow fell across the mast. Movement in the corner of his vision. Alex gave a start, threw up a fist.

Heart pounding, he turned his head. A white gull had landed on some nearby rigging behind him. Alex blinked.

Then the bird cocked its head and winked one dark eye. "Time," it cawed.

Alex didn't think but leapt. The line unraveled above him like a spider's silk in free fall.

The rope grew taut. He swooped down and drew his legs up kicking the sword from Redbeard's hands. "Ha!" he cried sailing over the gawking pirate.

Swinging back, Alex reached an arm towards Mona Lisa who had just undone her shackles. With a whoop, he grabbed her around the waist.

"What the blazes?" Redbeard sputtered.

Grimy hands snatched at them, but Alex kept his legs up, and their weathered paws met only air. Mona Lisa covered her mouth and giggled as they flew over the railing.

Beneath them the dark black canal reflected their gliding figures. For a moment, Alex thought of Mom before the heart attack. She had been so vibrant and strong, racing Dad on long runs every morning. Most days, she'd come in snorting her victory while Dad insisted that she'd cheated, waiting until he tied his shoe. "Still, I won," she'd say with a gentle smile, turning her cheek upward for his reluctant kiss.

When the swing hit its apex, Alex told Mona Lisa to get ready. "Take a deep breath. Three, two, now!"

He released the rope and they plummeted toward the canal, hitting feet first. Now submerged, he grabbed Mona Lisa's hand and kicked towards the bottom. The growing darkness made it impossible to see more than a few feet ahead, disorienting him. Swimming with one hand, he pulled her through the water toward where he thought his sub waited.

A few moments later, he felt soft mud between his fingers and began groping along the canal bottom. He tried to think, remembering that he snuck aboard at the stern, so it made sense that the sub-tank would be behind the ship.

Tugging on his arm, Mona Lisa signaled her lack of air. Alex gave her hand a squeeze, placing it on the back of his t-shirt for her to grab. Little bubbles escaped his nose as he tilted is head back. He could barely make out the dim light of the ship's lanterns through the murky water.

With the ship as a point of reference, he got down on all fours, and started crawling forward.

Lungs aching, he tried to remember Isis's words. "Do not forget that you are a Creator. Air, water, food, is all at your command. You have only to dream it," the goddess had said during his first trip to Artania.

He imagined he was home, sitting at the kitchen table breathing in the sweet aroma of Mom's blueberry muffins. And suddenly it was true. He had all the oxygen he needed.

But next to him Mona Lisa had no such power. Close-mouthed screams pulsed in her throat as she dug her fingernails into his back. Then she began making gurgling noises, and Alex knew that she beginning to drown.

He pressed his knees deeper into the soft mud, willing his body to go faster. But the submarine was nowhere to be found.

Had it moved?

Wailing bubbles blasted from her mouth as Mona Lisa's tugged on his shirt making his collar a noose. Swallowing hard, Alex scuttled forward. Groped. Mud and more mud.

Then her grasp grew slack.

He grabbed her hand and bounded forward. She spasmed. Once, twice.

Just as Mona Lisa began to float upward, he felt smooth metal. But before she slipped from his grasp, he placed both hands on her waist and shoved her under the tank. Circling around he used one foot to drive her under the wheels. Then he dove under and lifted her towards the little pocket of oxygen inside the sub's dome.

Clinging to the metal ribbing of the domed walls, Mona Lisa threw her head back and swallowed mouthful after mouthful of air.

"Are- you- okay?" Alex asked when he popped up beside her.

Even in this dim light Alex could see how pale her face was. She placed a hand on her chest and nodded.

"Good. Then let's get out of here." Alex sat down, put his feet on the pedals, and started to maneuver the vehicle towards where he figured shore was.

He had gone about ten feet when there was a violent rumbling and the sub began to shake. They both stood up and peered through the glass dome. The sea floor was giving way. Crimson light rose from to a gaping hole as the entire canal filled with a red glow.

Alex gasped.

The doorway to Subterranea was opening right in front of him.

Chapter 66

When Mars brandished his spear, Gwen dove between the closest Swiney's legs. Half-scooting, half crawling, she'd almost wriggled through when cut-cheek squeezed his jackboots together like a lion's jaws.

Gwen pounded on his feet with her fists, but he tightened his legs even more.

The monster raised his club. "I get you now, human."

"Oh no you don't," Gwen said coiling around his legs like a snake. "I happen to like my brains inside my skull, thank you very much." Gwen held her breath hoping he was smart enough to realize that he'd hit himself if he hit her.

But she overestimated his intelligence and the club came down. Smacking her butt with such force Gwen's jaw snapped shut, almost breaking her braces. Man, that hurt!

Then she heard whimpering. Gwen touched her voice box to see if maybe she'd moaned involuntarily.

But it was the Swiney. He'd whacked himself when he hit her, and now brownish blood dribbled from his knee.

"Owie! Ow! Ow!" he blubbered, dropping his club on the cobblestones.

Seizing the moment, Gwen started to wriggle away. Would have made it too if that creature hadn't bent down to clutch his knee just then. He saw her escaping and grabbed her by the collar.

His sharp nails were like thorns in her back as he raised her over his head. "You pay for pain."

Tensing every muscle, Gwen gathered her strength into a single kick. Her foot didn't even come close. She lashed out with the other leg. No dice. Nose twitching, Gwen slapped and punched his gorilla arms.

The snorting creature just lifted her higher.

Shielding her face, Gwen tried not to imagine what her bones would sound like when they crunched on the ground.

Moments passed, but no blow. Instead she felt soft hands under her arms.

"What the–?" Gwen started to ask. Then she looked up and saw Hera floating overhead.

"Fear not, young one. We have come," Hera said tilting a head toward the peacock's talons around her shoulders.

Their climb was a bizarre sight. Above the goddess, the peacock flapped its iridescent blue and green wings. Its feathers filtered the moonlight in a kaleidoscope dream. Crazy.

Gwen ventured a peek at the raging battle below. That club-wielding monster was now bearing down on Mars. She drew a sharp breath.

Then out of nowhere, Bartholomew appeared, swinging a curved sword.

"Get him, B-3," Gwen urged.

Bartholomew leaned back and thrust. There was a cry of surprise and the Swiney crumbled like brittle leaves.

"Whoa," Gwen gasped.

"The Deliverer battles well. And true," Hera said.

"I wouldn't have guessed," Gwen murmured, surprised by Bartholomew's new-found strength.

"He is a Chosen One," Hera replied as if she expected no less. Then the goddess called up to the peacock and pointed a sandaled foot at a quiet place near the fortress walls. "Set us down. Over there."

The bird descended and landed near the wall some twenty yards from Bartholomew and Mars. The peacock hopped in front of them before fanning out its feathers in a multi-eyed shield.

"We are safe," Hera cooed as she pet her peacock's shining green head. "You may relax."

As the bird lowered its multi-colored feathers, Bartholomew turned toward Gwen and waved.

"Hey B-3!" Gwen called out. "Looks like you escaped after all."

Bartholomew walked up and gave her a sheepish grin. "It was about time."

"I'll say." Gwen cleared her throat. "Umm, you know dude, like thanks for coming up when you did. That Swiney thing had me to rights."

"No problem. I was glad to do it." Bartholomew shrugged. "But what's happening? Have you heard from Alex?"

Gwen shook her head before explaining how Captain Sludge had tricked her into letting the whole Shadow Swine army in.

"-and then I discovered that Alex wasn't hurt at all. Man, I should have known better," she finished.

"Shadow Swine are stupid, but they are still good liars," Bartholomew said. "They have to be, to turn our dreams against us."

Gwen stared at him. So, he knew about the nightmares? Mr. Clean was full of surprises.

Michelangelo came up leading David by the hand as if he were a toddler. Since the giant was still naked, Gwen turned her focus toward a strong-looking lady holding a shield. She remembered meeting her on Mount Olympus, but the name escaped her.

Athens? No. Then she remembered. Athena, goddess of wisdom.

Mars beckoned everyone closer to tell how he'd helped Alex launch before dropping a few Swineys. "They thought they could win. But few defeat a battle king." He said polishing his knuckles on his tunic.

Gwen had to fight to keep from rolling her eyes. Mars might be a war god but if B-3 had come any later, he'd be Mt. Olympus toast. She was about to put him in his place, when she heard a trumpeting voice that turned her stomach.

Captain Sludge.

"The Portal opens. Come, it is time to take her home!" his distant voice ordered as a red glow filled the canal.

Gwen's eyes grew wide. The doorway to the monster's home was opening.

Gwen could only hope that Alex had got there in time.

Chapter 67

The red crater kept widening. Drawing closer to Alex's sub. Brackish water sloshed under his feet.

Alex stared.

"Move bambino!" Mona Lisa urged peering through the glass dome.

He started pedaling backwards. Moving the tank-sub a few centimeters. But then it sunk into the mud and stopped. Alex pressed harder against the stubborn crank. His legs strained as sweat trickled off his chin like a ticking bomb.

Still, it wouldn't budge.

"Try changing direction," Mona Lisa suggested.

Alex pedaled forward, closer to the glowing void in front of them. Stopped, then reversed, but the wheels sunk in, deeper this time.

They were stuck.

"Stupid thing!" Alex drew both legs up and kicked one pedal.

The tank wobbled.

"Go right!" he cried. "If we shift our weight, maybe it'll move."

Mona Lisa stood and leaned over while Alex pressed against one pedal.

The sub nudged forward two inches. Maybe they would escape. Then it moved a few more feet. Alex turned to give Mona Lisa a reassuring smile when and a deep rumbling came from below vibrating the walls so hard it knocked his foot off the pedal.

The tank lurched to one side dropping Mona Lisa in his lap.

"Get back up there!" he cried pressing against her shoulders.

She tried grabbing a hold of the metal ribbing, molding her body into the curved wall. Alex leaned too. But they only they slid closer to that growing crevice.

As the sub began to fill with water.

Alex stared out the now sideways window. Rosy bubbles simmered from the ever-widening crater.

"We'll have to swim for it!" Alex yelled over the sound of rushing water.

Mona Lisa's calm expression had vanished, replaced by a look of absolute terror. Alex wondered if she could keep it together long enough to make it to the surface.

At that moment, he noticed a new sight. Just as terrifying. A whirlpool had formed at the surface and was spiraling down into the crater.

From above, a Shadow Swine corkscrewed past. Then another. One by one they leaped onto the whirling vortex to ride the spiraling waters toward their underground home.

"We gotta go!" Alex cried grabbing Mona Lisa's hand. "Get a breath. Now!"

Still holding Mona Lisa's hand, he plunged into the water and began swimming away from the red tornado.

After a few feverish kicks, he thought they were going to make it, but then the vortex grew by a third. Alex felt a tug on his feet. He fought but the current was too strong. He doubted even Poseidon could swim against it.

They were trapped. Revolving, spinning, and spiraling, Alex felt as powerless as a leaf in a river.

He thought about his friends. That could be helping him right now *if* he hadn't locked them up in the prison.

And when the vortex sucked him down he groaned. *Why did I decide to do this alone?*

Chapter 68

Bartholomew felt the air grow suddenly quiet as every Shadow Swine stopped fighting mid-stroke. Next, they all pivoted on heavy heels and began a crunching march toward the water. In the distance, the red canal fizzed and churned. Row after row of the hunch-backed monsters lined up at the edge of the canal and waded out a few feet, before disappeared beneath the water.

At first, he thought they might be headed towards the *Red Raven* to escape. But then he realized that was impossible. There was no way that even a fraction of them could fit on Redbeard's ship.

"What are they doing?" Gwen asked.

"I think they're going home. That must be their doorway," Bartholomew replied. "That is one strange sight, even for Artania."

"Cha," Gwen agreed with a quick nod. "But what about Mr. Hero? Could his tank thing get past all of them?" She pointed out at the glowing canal that was now full of floating and wading creatures.

Bartholomew shrugged and glanced around. The growing pit in the bottom of his stomach made him wish he had a helicopter. The he'd buzz over the canal, find Alex, and bring him back. But the wings on Hermes's sandals and helmet were only powerful enough to lift one person and Apollo's flying chariot was nowhere in sight.

For some reason, he thought about Leonardo's notebooks. Something in one of them kept itching at his brain.

"What machines were in Leonardo's workshop? That he said needed better propulsion?" he muttered tapping on his forehead.

Gwen shoved him. "Dude, who are you talking to? It's time for action; Alex could be like in a gnarly half pipe right now."

Skateboarding. That seemed to be all those guys ever talked about. They loved rolling up and down concrete ramps and slanted curbs. He remembered standing on the pier in Santa Barbara watching them all sail through the sky. And sometimes falling, like Alex could be right then.

Suddenly it hit him like a skater on pavement.

"Of course. Why didn't I think of it earlier?" He shook his head and started barking orders. "Leonardo, Gwen, get that bench. Michelangelo, bring those crossbows. And Soldier, I need your shield, over here."

The older men gave him a long stare while Gwen just stood there. Well, he didn't have time to explain.

"Move!" he shouted.

A few minutes later, the final bundle of wood and iron was at his feet. Bartholomew touched it lightly to get a feel for the material. Each had a distinct property. He'd mold the bench into a frame and the shield would become the lightest of feathers.

He closed his eyes and went to that place in his mind. Time suspended as he envisioned the sculpture, bending wood, molding metal, and etching steel. Everyone around him slowed to a snail's pace, but he moved at light speed, hands flying at 186,000 miles a second.

A second blink and it was done. He smiled at a long-wheeled board and wings just his size.

"What the–?" Gwen's mouth hung open. "How did? You were just… but now you are-"

"It's how we create here."

Gwen shook her head like a freshly washed dog.

"Can you help me launch this?" Bartholomew asked.

Narrowing her green eyes, Gwen placed a foot on the skateboard and rolled it back and forth. "No problem."

Praying he wasn't already too late, Bartholomew waved Leonardo over, so the bearded man could help him into the harness. He was proud of how he'd altered the original design by attaching the wings with rope. Once Leonardo cinched it tight, Bartholomew slipped his arms through the straps and flapped the wings a few times. His feet lifted off the ground, but he'd need more than that to take off. He looked to Gwen.

"Okay I need at least twenty feet to launch." She glanced around and pointed at the parapet walk below them. "If we lean the ramp up against that low wall over there, it'll give me enough space for some bucco speed."

They didn't have to ask. Leonardo and Michelangelo were already carrying the ramp below. When Gwen lifted the long skateboard up onto her head and fell in behind them, Bartholomew tucked in the fragile wings and made his way down the winding stairs.

Once there, Gwen rolled a few feet on the brick walk before flip-turning back. "Not bad, Mr. Clean," she beamed, skidding to a stop in front of him.

Just then the sky reddened even more. "We better hurry," Bartholomew said. "The doorway is widening by the second."

"Kay." Gwen set the board down in front of Bartholomew.

"Ready?" he asked, placing one foot into the strap he'd designed at the front of the skateboard.

"Always. Now, keep your weight low with your torso lowered. It'll stabilize you," she pushed down on his shoulders and rocked him back and forth to demonstrate.

"A lower center of gravity to help with balance. Got it," Bartholomew said crouching down on the skateboard.

"Stay in that position until we launch," Gwen said. She kicked a few times and soon they were racing towards the ramp.

Bartholomew clenched his jaw as they picked up speed.

"Hold on. Almost there!!" Gwen cried, leaning into the turn.

When they shot up the ramp, Bartholomew slipped his foot out of the strap.

And was airborne.

"Yes!" Gwen cried as she rolled back down.

Higher he soared, the wind whooshing past his face. Fighting the urge to cover his eyes, he kept his focus on the distant Portal. He figured if he didn't look straight down he wouldn't get dizzy and fain like when he fell from the prison roof.

Moments later, he was almost about the vortex. He leaned back to get a better view but didn't see anything that looked like a tank or a submarine. Just Swineys bobbing in the sea.

He circled the canal three, four times and was about to give up when a flash of color caught his eye. Rotating his arms, he homed in on the red whirlpool. Still unable to make out whatever it was, he descended a few feet. Then he saw what looked like a pair of mice being flushed down a toilet. Bartholomew tucked in his wings and dove down for a closer look.

His heart nearly stopped at the sight of Alex and Mona Lisa. Stuck in the vortex's current, his best friend about to drown. Or worse yet, end up in Subterranea a slave of those monsters.

Bartholomew hollered.

Alex looked up. His curls were flattened against his head and his usual tan face was as pale as paper. "Huh?"

"Grab my legs!" Bartholomew cried over the roaring wind.

Bartholomew hovered over them, while Alex and Mona Lisa each grabbed a knee. Tilting the wings upward, he flapped his arms again and again. His shoulders ached but he didn't climb a bit.

"We're too heavy!" Alex shouted.

"No, you're not," Bartholomew grit his teeth and pumped harder. They ascended three inches. Then a glorious yard, rising slowly.

They just might make it.

The swirling vortex sprayed his face. The sound was deafening; a giant vacuum with growling monsters. Spiraling Shadow Swine slid by so quickly they didn't notice what was in the center of their water slide.

Bartholomew prayed that wouldn't change.

About halfway up, a single yellow eye zeroed in on them. Its owner unleashed a howl and slammed his fist into Alex's back throwing Bartholomew off balance and into a downward spiral.

Hitting a fat Shadow Swine square in the gut, they bounced off his huge stomach. Bartholomew clutched at the misty air, forgetting all about the wings attached to his arms.

They plummeted downward. Deeper into the vortex.

"Bartholomew," Alex cried. "Your wings!"

Three confused seconds passed before Bartholomew extended his arms. It stopped their descent, but now they were at the bottom of the whirlpool. Here the funnel-shaped opening was so narrow it soaked Mona Lisa's gown. The added weight forced him to flap twice as hard to stay aloft.

"Alex, Swiney behind you!"

He held his breath as Alex drew up his legs and kicked it away. Only to face a second lunging creature. And a third.

Bartholomew felt like a cork stuck in the neck of a bottle. But this had no sweet juice; but monsters bent on drowning them. He pumped his arms but stayed stuck.

Mona Lisa's hands started to slip down his leg.

Another passing Swiney swung its fist, connecting with a wing. Bartholomew jerked backwards. Flailing, he barely he managing to hold his position.

"Pump harder!" Alex cried.

"I'm trying," he said watching a few silvery feathers flutter into the vortex. His arms strained with each stroke.

Mona Lisa slid to his calf. "I can't hold on much longer," she said, her voice weaker with each syllable.

A Swiney corkscrewed past swinging an axe. Another threw a club, missed and swiped with its jackboots.

"We're too heavy. It's no use."

"No, Alex." The wind whipped at Bartholomew's wings and they descended six more inches.

"Save Mona Lisa. I'll be okay."

Thrashing his arms, Bartholomew pointed his chin at the growling monsters. "In Subterranea? With them?"

Mona Lisa slipped down around Bartholomew's ankle, her grip loosening.

Alex looked up and shook his head. "It's not working."

Bartholomew fought against the sucking air. A vacuum of water and Swineys. "No please," he whispered.

Alex started to release one hand from his knee. "You have to let me go."

His friend's words filled his mind. '*Come on, B-3 you can do it... That's it, we're done. Just one breath, Bartholomew... you're safe.*' Taking care of everybody was Alex in spades. Always ready with some noble sacrifice.

But not this time. This time Bartholomew would be the one helping him.

"Oh no you don't, Alex." Imagining that he was a great eagle, Bartholomew lifted his arms overhead.

Before Alex could let go, he thrust the wings downward, straining against the weight. The howling winds swirled around, beating him back.

He drove his winged arms faster, pushing against the currents. And began to rise.

He remembered every smile his friend had given him. All those thumbs-up and high fives.

Suddenly, he shot upward. Past the groping Shadow Swine. Through the swirling water. Higher and higher. Cresting over the crimson vortex.

And they were free.

"Yes!" he cried.

With another whooping cheer, he turned toward the city, Venice's crisscrossing canals reflecting soft yellow lanterns. Feeling as light as the clouds above, he darted in and out of painted stars.

Giggling, he started shooting for the moon when a tug on his pant leg brought him back to reality.

"Umm, Bartholomew? Do you think you could set us down now?" Alex smirked.

"Oh, yeah." He started a sheepish apology, but then realized he had nothing to apologize for.

Bartholomew cleared his throat and, in a voice stronger than all that swirling water cried, "You got it, Bud!"

Chapter 69

Gwen paced back and forth, her nose twitching. The Arsenal was so quiet now. People spoke in low voices as they tended to the wounded or carried away those that didn't make it.

"Fear not, the Deliverer is strong," Leonardo said when he came up beside her. "He will rescue them."

Gwen wished she shared Mr. da Vinci's faith. But she'd seen Mr. Clean screw up too many times. Of course, she had to give him credit. He had rescued Mars from with those Swiney things. And that skateboard launch was awesome.

"I hope so," she said.

The Venetians below suddenly began jumping up and down and pointing skyward. Gwen looked up and saw what looked like a stork carrying two babies.

"Daughter!" Leonardo cried.

Sure enough, there was Mona Lisa gown billowing behind her. It curled around Alex's waist who wore a grin as wide as the canal.

The trio swooped over the fortress walls toward the gathering crowd below. When Bartholomew hovered a few feet above the courtyard, Alex and Mona Lisa let go, descending like fluttering leaves.

Hand in hand, they landed on the cobblestones before turning to face the crowd. Then the pair raised their arms high, and a loud cheer arose.

Bartholomew leaned back, flapped his wings, and climbed until he was barely a dot among the stars. Just when he seemed to have disappeared, Gwen heard a whoop before his growing figure dropped into a spinning dive.

Gwen leaned out over the battlements. He was going too fast!

After a crazy turn, Bartholomew headed straight towards her. Gwen ducked down and held her breath.

But there was no booming crash.

"Hi Gwen!" he shouted pulling up at the last second.

"Show off," she mumbled.

That stinker rocketed over the parapet and did a wide loop over the Arsenal that turned into a barrel roll, landing safely in the center of the crowd.

Fuming, Gwen scrambled down the stairs, pushed her way through the Artanians who were helping Bartholomew take off his wings. She called out, "Hey B-3!"

"Yes?" Bartholomew asked as innocent as you please.

"You are–" Gwen put her fists on her hips for a scolding. But then she smirked. "Not bad." She extended her hand for a fist bump.

"Thanks," he replied tapping his knuckles on hers. A little hard too. She shook out her hand. Payback for punching him in the cell?

Alex chuckled. Gwen turned to give him a hug until she remembered how he'd put her in jail. She slapped his arm instead. "Dummy!" she cried with a stomp of her foot.

"What?" Alex shrugged.

Gwen raised a hand to hit him again but wagged a finger instead. "You locked us in a cell!"

"I was keeping you safe. In case you hadn't noticed, there are some pretty gnarly creatures around here."

"Worked great didn't it?"

Alex started to reply but Gwen cut him off.

"Do you know what I've been through? I thought you were dying, or worse. Those, those, monsters, they tricked me. And I let them in… Dumb-butt!"

"Sorry."

"If it hadn't been for B-3, I might be–" Gwen couldn't finish the sentence. She cleared her throat and went on. "We should work together."

Alex clenched his jaw and looked her square in the face. "I realize that. Now."

Gwen could see the regret in his soft brown eyes. He really did feel bad. Her voice softened. "It's all right. But next time…"

"I'll tell you what, next time you can lead."

Imagining marching with a battalion of soldiers made Gwen grin. "So, it's over. That Mona Lisa dudette is saved. We can go home. Right?"

"But what of the bambino, Pico?" Mona Lisa asked, stepping between them. "He is still Redbeard's slave."

"Poor guy," Bartholomew said. "Those pirates are so cruel. Running him ragged. Calling him names. Jeering at him. They even made him watch while I walked the plank."

"Then we rescue him," Alex said as if it were the simplest thing in the world.

"Of course. We must." Bartholomew agreed with a nonchalant nod.

Gwen stared at them both incredulously. She couldn't believe what she was hearing.

"But didn't you just escape from them?" she asked. "Wasn't that like, the point? And wasn't it wicked hard?"

"But then I didn't have my friends at my side." Alex replied as he arched an eyebrow at Bartholomew.

"We are the twins." Bartholomew added.

"Born on the cusp of the second millennium," Alex finished with an impish smile. He turned to Gwen. "And with a third that makes us triplets. What do you say? Ready to kick some pirate butt?"

"I get to fight?"

Gwen could see Alex's playfulness turn to fear. He hated putting anyone in harm's way. But at the same time, she knew he would be good to his word.

"You got it." He nodded.

Chapter 70

From the rowboat, Captain Sludge scanned the dark water. Something was wrong. The last of his soldiers had all dove into the swirling opening, yet still there was no sign of Redbeard's ship. Had those idiot Creations forgotten the delivery time?

If he'd had a watch he would have checked it. But Shadow Swine don't wear watches. They would just slip off their slimy wrists. Lord Sickhert kept time for all, letting them know when to dream drain, replenish their energies, or when it was time for war.

Sludge secured the oar, crept up to the bow, and scrutinized the edges of the vortex. The strong current did not dare tug at his ship; as captain, even the waters feared him. Surely the Barbarossa Brothers shared this fright, knowing full well the consequences of being late. Ruthless corsairs should know enough to fear the most powerful captain in all Subterranea.

Although the night was warm, Sludge shivered, his hunched back crinkling as if his body knew something his mind did not. Finally, Captain Sludge couldn't take it anymore. The moon was dipping deeper by the minute and the Portal would only be open until sunrise. He slid to the back of the boat, picked up the long oar, and began rowing toward the *Red Raven*.

As he drew closer he could hear the strained voice of Redbeard shouting orders at the crew.

"Raise the anchors. Hoist the sails. Be quick with you!"

Barbarossa leaving? Sludge's yellow eyes narrowed. Those pirates were running away. He ran his hand over the hilt of the dagger inside his long black coat.

"Fools! They'll soon know better than to betray me!"

Chapter 71

Bartholomew peered over the port side of the *Vento Buono* to get his bearings. Now that they'd doused the lanterns, the only light came from stars twinkling above.

He wondered if the *Red Raven* was still following them. Probably. Those Barbarossa Brothers were so greedy that even now they'd seek riches. And Redbeard was arrogant enough to think that he could capture any ship. Even one so dark it appeared invisible.

Bartholomew cocked an ear to listen. Just the wind snapping the main sail above their creaking ship. He patted the quiver of arrows slung across his back and double checked the crank on the crossbow at his feet.

But where was the pirate ship?

Crack! A flash of lightning lit up the sky, revealing their location. Bartholomew groaned.

"We overshot Saint Mark's!" Bartholomew called through cupped hands. "We have to go back!"

"*Si* Deliverer, I tell Michelangelo," an Italian accented sailor said with a quick salute.

Bartholomew wrung his linen tunic in his hands. Instead of turning, their ship kept sailing west, away from Redbeard.

"Did someone tell Michelangelo?" he asked.

"*Si.*" The Italian sailor's voice came out of the darkness.

Chewing his lower lip, Bartholomew twisted his shirt more. When they didn't change course, he shimmied down the ladder and made his way toward steerage where Michelangelo was bent over a table muttering to himself.

"North by northeast. Come about. Tack south." Michelangelo held a compass up to the small oil lantern swinging from a peg, then scratched a note with his quill pen on the map spread out on the table.

Bartholomew cleared his throat.

"No. Tack south first, then go northeast," he mumbled.

"Umm, Mr. Michelangelo?"

"What!" The older man turned and threw his quill down. "Can't you see that I am working?"

"Well yes, but did you hear? We overshot Saint Mark's.

"Of course I heard. What do you think I'm working on?"

"Well can't you just turn around and go back?"

"Children!" Michelangelo threw his hands into the air. "This ship is forty-two feet long. And powered by sails. Do you think I just give the tiller a shove and it turns around like a toy in a stream?"

"Well, uh, yes?"

Michelangelo started to go into a tirade about ridiculous children, but Bartholomew didn't stick around to listen. He had to do something. Fast.

If he was a giant, he would just push the ship in the right direction. But he was a kid, and a grubby one at this point. Bartholomew shrugged to loosen the dress shirt that clung to his skin and glanced down at his grimy sleeves. They were as grey as stone.

"I'd flip us around, if I was big," he said. Shaking his head, he realized that he might not be, but somebody was. "David? Where are you?" he shouted, dashing up and down the deck. "David!"

A marble hand on his shoulder made him jump. "Is it time to attack?"

"No, something else." Bartholomew outlined his plan before scurrying below deck to tell Michelangelo to release the tiller.

"And then?"

"Leave the rest to me," Bartholomew told him as he plucked a candle from its holder. Cupping the flame, he hurried up the ladder and shouted, "All hands. Lower the sails! Quickly. Weapons and lanterns at the ready!"

A few of the sailors just stood there looking at him dumbfounded. Was this the same boy who had laid in bed for days not speaking to anyone?

"But this no wasa the plan," the heavily accented one protested.

Bartholomew didn't have time to explain. "I said move. Now!"

The Italians stopped grumbling and scrambled to their places while Bartholomew spent a few seconds conferring with David.

"Ready?" he asked.

"As easy as annoying Father." The handsome giant smirked and lowered himself into the water.

Bartholomew guffawed. That was an understatement. Michelangelo got peeved if you glanced his way.

"Now push!" he called down to the wading giant.

The great statue put his shoulder against the stern and leaned forward. The ship lurched to one side before beginning a turn. Meanwhile the sailors relit the lanterns. Bartholomew knew that this would make them an easy target but that was what he wanted.

He had to draw Redbeard's fire away from Gwen and the others.

Meanwhile the sailors aboard his ship gathered weapons. Bartholomew nodded approvingly until he saw a few pour gunpowder down musket barrels. His face blanched. Bullets could hit Pico or the young slaves on board.

"There are hostages on that ship," Bartholomew reminded them. "Arrows or hand to hand combat only."

"Non problema." The Italian sailor held up a long sword. "We give-a them a shave, eh?"

Bartholomew was in the middle of a nod when a cannonball's boom told him that the *Red Raven* had seen them. He sighed as the ball splashed fifty yards short of them, relieved to draw their fire away from Gwen.

Gauging the distance by the size of the pirate ship's lanterns, he figured they must be about a quarter mile away. With David keeping this nice pace they'd soon be within reach.

Then he could rescue Pico.

There was a sudden jerk halting the ship. Confused, Bartholomew glanced around and then rushed back to the stern.

"We're almost there, David," Bartholomew shouted down. "Keep pushing."

"Just repositioning myself for the turn," The statue said stretching his muscular arms over his head.

"'kay, but hurry."

David nodded and put his shoulder back against the ship's hull. It listed to one side. Bartholomew held out his arms for balance. David righted the ship and began kicking along behind. They picked up speed.

"And stay back there, okay? I don't want you to become a target."

The lanterns on the pirate ship grew larger. Now Bartholomew could make out the screeching Redbeard on deck who was cursing everyone around him. Bartholomew couldn't help but smile.

When the two ships were about to converge, Bartholomew picked up his crossbow and notched an arrow in the wooden groove. He thought he had a tight grip, but one hand slipped, and the reel started to unwind.

About the same time, he heard the *Red Raven* crash into the stone wharf, he reached for the rotating crank. It rapped on his knuckles and smacked his palm. Ignoring the pain, he leaned in and grabbed. This time his grip was firm. Muscles twitching, Bartholomew continued to pedal with his hands.

Finally, the arrow was in place.

Bump. Their ship docked behind the two tall columns of Saint Mark's Square.

Just yards away the crippled *Red Raven* bobbed ever lower in the water. Bartholomew quickly scanned the deck. There beneath a turban, Redbeard's astonished face gaped at him.

Bartholomew winked at him as he raised the cross bow to his shoulder. And let the arrow fly.

Chapter 72

Boom! Gwen covered her head as another cannon whistled her way. Two seconds later the ball splashed down in the canal, drenching her back.

She poked her head out from under the *Paglia* Bridge. "That was too close for comfort," she muttered flicking some water off her shoulders.

Squinting, she tried to check on everyone's progress, but when Venice had doused all lanterns, it plunged the city into total darkness.

But Bartholomew's ship shone in the distance. They'd planned to lure the *Red Raven* in, and then have that Pico kid mess with the rudder when the pirates turned toward their ship. As soon as the *Red Raven* ran aground Gwen was supposed to attack with Mars, Athena, and the *Condotierri*.

But nobody said anything about cannons.

The two war gods were hiding behind some columns about fifty yards away. That seemed a lot safer than a bridge right next to the water. Gwen considered making a run for it. Or maybe not. *Great, dudette. You can't even decide what to do.*

She would have sat there arguing with herself until the sun rose, but a sudden jolt shuddered from underneath. She thrust out an arm to keep the shock from knocking her over.

Earthquake! Duck and cover!

She started to get into the crouch position she'd learned in school when the sound of splintering wood told her that this was no earthquake. The *Red Raven* had finally run aground and was splitting apart.

Loud curses filled the air with language that would have made most kids blush. But Gwen was used to it. Mom cussed a lot before she left.

"Me ship's breaking up!" a pirate's shouted.

Gwen stared at the eerie silhouette of sail and hull. "Now we have you," she said.

"Rowers, reverse!"

The ship creaked and groaned as the oars splashed wildly. "Don't move, please," Gwen prayed crossing her fingers.

"I said reverse! Or feel me brother's lash!"

More scraping and crunching sounds came from the shadowy outline of the lantern-lit ship.

"Row slaves, row!" a pirate bellowed. When after a few moments the ship still didn't budge, he cried, "Hizir! The whip,"

Gwen cringed when she heard the men's agonizing cries, feeling each lash as if it were her own. Like the time just before Mom took off.

Gwen shook her head trying not to remember the day Mom left.

"*Gwen! Get in here!*"

She ran in to her mother's bedroom as quick as her legs would carry her, Mom had been so angry recently. Even raised her hand twice but had stopped short of slapping her.

"*What Mom?*"

"*Did you talk to my agent yesterday?" Rochelle asked pointing at the land line.*

Gwen clamped her mouth shut. She didn't want to answer.

"*Did you tell him that I was sick and couldn't do the Paris shoot?*"

"*No." Gwen rubbed one skater shoe over the other.*

"Liar. I just spoke to him." Mom took a step closer.

Gwen started to back away. "I didn't. I swear."

"Don't lie to me. You've been trying to ruin my career."

Then, instead of being afraid, Gwen got mad. She stopped and stood her ground.

"Well it's a stupid job anyhow. You're always gone. And my–" No she wouldn't remind Mom about her upcoming birthday. Moms were supposed to know about that stuff on their own. She crossed her arms defiantly. "You're getting too old for modeling anyhow."

"Old? I'll show you old, you spoiled little brat." Rochelle picked up a hairbrush and threw it. Gwen ducked but it still hit her leg and a hot welt immediately rose. Mom reached for a perfume bottle next. But Gwen didn't stick around. She ran. Down the stairs. Out the front door. All the way to Dad's gym.

She didn't tell Dad about the mark on her leg. Only that Mom was freaking out. By the time they got home, the bedroom was in a shamble. Broken glass on the floor. Clothes strewn everywhere. And Mom was gone. No note. No message. Nothing.

Snap! The whip cracked again.

"Please, Cap'n. Mercy. Stop."

"Row!"

"It won't move. We're stuck!"

Gwen couldn't take it any more. Signal or no signal she had to something. Trying to remember the exact path over the bridge she threw her skateboard down and kicked off into the darkness.

Right toward the waiting pirate ship.

Chapter 73

The flickering lights of the *Red Raven* above reminded Alex of a dying fire. One he planned to put out once and for all.

"Come on Roberto. Just a little closer. Quietly now," he whispered to the rowing soldier. Next to Roberto, Vulcan nodded.

They approached the back of the beached ship, where Alex could see some pirates scrambling to push it back into the water. Others loaded muskets and cannon or held scimitars and daggers at the ready. Bartholomew and Gwen were keeping them busy. Good. Now it was his turn.

This time Alex wouldn't just swing from the sail lines. This time he'd sneak aboard and blend in with his disguise; a linen tunic, some loose-fitting striped pants, and tasseled cap.

Vulcan tossed a rope over the pirate ship's railing above and tied it off while Alex crawled toward the bow. Grabbing the gunnels, he looked back at Vulcan holding the line taut in his strong hands.

"We could change the plan," the fire god suggested.

"I'm in costume," Alex said, waving a hand over his loose tunic. "Anyhow, you guys have my back, right?"

Vulcan held up his hammer. "I'd pound any to powder who dared harm the Deliverer."

"We will be watching, and ready," Roberto added.

"See you back at the palace." Tightening his sword belt, Alex grabbed the rope with both hands. He made sure his grip was bucko tight before worming around the rough cable, to inch upward, ever closer to the chaotic deck above. One foot. Three. Almost there.

When he reached the top, he heard a loud sigh from Vulcan. He arched an eyebrow at the god of fire and then peered through the wooden rails. No pirates yet. Next, he began to swing his legs back and forth, each pass higher until he'd cleared the railing to land with a dull thud. Keeping low, he checked to make sure the coast was clear before tossing the rope back to Vulcan.

Alex watched them row to safety and crept forward.

When he reached the entry to the raised captain's cabin he stood up, blinking at the empty room. On the rough-hewn table, half-finished meals waited to be eaten while wine spilled from overturned pewter mugs. A treasure chest stood in one corner, padlock still firmly in place.

He turned back.

On the deck below, pirates ran in all directions. Turbans askew and loosely clenched knives in their teeth, they tried to follow Redbeard's chaotic orders but tangled pikes and tripped over each other instead.

Alex scooted a little closer to scan the shadowy deck. No ship's boy. Since Pico's job was to carry munitions for the battling pirates, Alex figured he was probably below gathering powder or grapeshot.

Arrows whizzed from Bartholomew's ship. *Atta boy Richie. You show him.*

Then the ship lurched to one side.

"Cap'n we're takin' on water!" a voice cried.

Cursing, Redbeard twisted his long mustache in one hand. "Then patch the hole! Quickly!"

"We be tryin'."

"Must I do everything myself?" Redbeard cried ducking below with a wave of his velvet cape.

Alex could see the remaining pirates exchange nervous glances on deck. A few whispered amongst themselves as they tiptoed toward the starboard side of the ship. A shirtless man stared at the dark water, his back bleeding from a recent whipping. With a backward glance, he leapt over the side into the canal.

I'd do the same.

Another was right on his tail when a sopping wet Redbeard appeared. With a groan, the fleeing sailor lowered his leg and stood at attention.

"Prepare for a takeover. On my signal!" Captain Barbarossa cried pointing at Bartholomew's ship.

"Gather the cannons and treasure chests," his brother said. "Shields at the ready. We'll commandeer the caravel from that-" Hizir paused and spat. "-*dead Deliverer.*"

"But Cap'n. That not be a fast galley. How are we supposed to-?"

Redbeard roared and raised his saber. He struck, and the arguing man spoke no more. Pointing at the crumpled heap on deck, he snarled at the crew. "Any more of ya landlubbers have questions?"

When no one replied, he jabbed the air with his sword. "Then attack!"

Still ducking from the arrows that continued to fly from Bartholomew's ship, the corsairs immediately unbolted the cannon, tucked daggers in their belts, and filled their pouches with musket balls.

When Redbeard turned, one pirate lifted a finger to his lips and pointed into the distance. His partner nodded.

"You are *so* going to lose," Alex said under his breath.

The galley lurched again. Alex clutched the railing to keep from sliding onto the pirates below.

Boom! A ball flew toward the Column of Saint Mark and crashed into the square. Using this cannon and musket fire as cover, the pirate crew gathered at the bow. Then in one great rush the capped and turbaned heads spilled over the side.

Alex spied one smaller head among the others. Could it be? Wide eyes turned upward as if begging the sky for help. Poor Pico was shivering in the middle of all that chaos.

Hurdling down the wooden steps, Alex leapt into the fray, coming up right behind Pico. When he grabbed him by the shoulder, the small boy cringed as if expecting a beating.

When none came, he looked up. "You?"

Alex put a finger to his lips and nodded. Next, he pointed to the bell tower across the square. Nodding in understanding, Pico grabbed a hold of Alex's rope belt. Keeping the smaller boy in tow, Alex rushed over the forecastle with the rest of the crew.

The whooping pirates shook their swords as they charged toward Bartholomew's ship. The next few moments were critical. Alex would need to turn at the last second and keep low to escape.

"Argh!" Alex cried trying to sound like a mean pirate. Next, he grabbed Pico's hand and began counting off several storming sailors. "Seventeen, eighteen, nineteen..." When he got to twenty, he turned away, towing Pico behind.

Swallowing hard, Alex pulled his sword from its sheath. No one was going to hurt Pico. He would strike anyone even daring to try.

Then Alex saw the strangest sight. A huge skateboard with a rider that would have looked epic at the Volcom Games. The skinny redhead kicking furiously held a Medusa-etched shield while tic-tacking back and forth. Mars jogged beside her, lance at the ready while row after row of Italian *Condotierri* took up the rear.

He almost called out but then the pirates at his back would realize who he was. So instead he waved his sword.

The snake-headed Medusa on the shield opened her mouth in a grating screech.

Alex skidded to a halt. "Hey, it's me. Stop!" he cried.

The gorgon's eyes began to glow, ready to turn him to stone.

Alex turned Pico's head away and pivoted ninety degrees. "No!"

Meanwhile Mars drew closer. His lance pointed straight at Alex's chest.

Chapter 74

"Mars, Medusa, no!" Gwen cried, skidding to a halt. "It's Alex!"

Medusa closed her eyes while the war god wrenched his spear upwards, stopping just millimeters in front of Alex's ribcage. He froze staring at the quivering blade.

"Hey, I thought we were on the same side," he accused wrapping a protective arm around the small boy beside him.

"Well maybe if you weren't so ugly we'd know that." Gwen stepped off her skateboard and cuffed him gently on the shoulder.

Alex removed his tasseled cap and chuckled. "Better?"

Gwen nodded appreciatively. "Still revolting, but better." She glanced down at the trembling boy at his side. He looked like a mini-Alex with the same dark curly hair and wide brown eyes. But he had a mousy nervousness that was totally unlike her bud.

"Oh, Gwen, meet Pico. He's the one that helped rescue Mona Lisa."

"Hey," Gwen said.

The pitiful thing shifted nervously from one foot to the next. "*Buongiorno.*"

"Yeah, and hola to you."

"That's Spanish, Gwen not Italian," Alex corrected.

"Whatever."

When Mars cleared his throat, the three of them turned toward him. "Are we here to converse or fight?"

"Fight Redbeard," Alex said.

"Yeah well then come on. Let's get to it," Gwen said, rolling her skateboard back and forth with one foot. "Mr. Clean can't fight all of them alone."

Alex looked down at little Pico then exchanged a glance with Gwen. "First gotta get this guy to safety."

"But I can help," Pico protested.

"Oh no," Alex said. "We went through too much to rescue you."

Pico's face scrunched up and he looked back and forth from Gwen to Alex. "You mean, all this was for me?"

"Sure." Gwen shrugged. "Who else?"

Pico gave a long sniff and wiped his eyes with the back of his filthy sleeve and Gwen's heart went out to him. His oversized clothes were tattered and stained. Grime streaked his cheeks. And he was so thin, the wind could have blown him over.

"So, you see why we gotta tuck you away. Right?" Gwen asked.

"Yes." Pico snuffled. Then he leapt at Gwen and threw his arms around her waist.

With Pico still hugging her tightly Gwen waved a few *Condotierri* over and asked them to take him inside the Doge's Palace with Mona Lisa for safety.

"We'll see you when this is over, okay?" She removed his arms from her waist.

Pico grinned and gave a quick wave as the Italian soldiers escorted him into the palace. Next, Alex called over the *Condotierri.*

"Lines One through Six, circle around behind these columns with me. Everyone else block the palace entrance with Gwen. Let's go."

With Athena in place back on the long skateboard, Gwen gave a quick salute to the already running Alex and kicked off.

The sun was just beginning to light up the night sky making it easy to see most of the pirates now. The plan was to herd them into Saint Mark's Square with two groups of Italian soldiers fanning out on either side of Mars and Athena. That way the corsairs would have nowhere to turn but the plaza where the rest of the Artanian army was waiting.

Gwen rolled over to the same corner of the palace she'd hidden in just a little while ago and watched the pirates scramble for the ship. An early morning breeze picked up and whipped through Gwen's ragged hair.

She couldn't help but smile.

Chapter 75

Captain Sludge adjusted his long cloak and grimaced, remembering how the Correction Chamber spray had scalded his back. Remembering Lord Sickhert's piercing eyes adding disgrace to his pain. Remembering how he'd been ready for revenge.

"Mona Lisa may be lost. But I will not return to my Lord empty-handed," Sludge muttered before turning to his second in command. "Mudlark-Maker is hungry," he said in a louder voice.

"For pirates?" Stench asked, raising one eyebrow.

"Redbeard and his scheming brother will be a nice little snack for our morphing comrade."

"Yum!" Stench chuckled.

"Lie to me, will he?" Sludge sneered. "That Deliverer wasn't dead. He probably escaped."

"We get em, yeah?" Stench asked, his dark mud eyes turning to quicksand grey.

"Yes, and reward them for their *excellent* service. Idiots! I can't wait to see them in Mudlark-Maker's arms."

"They scared tell you, boss."

"Rightly so. If I had known…" Sludge flared his piggish nostrils. "Come, let us make a *new door*. A trap door."

Using scent to guide them, Captain Sludge led the way through the labyrinth of Subterranean tunnels. All the while, Stench joked about how terrified the Barbarossa Brothers would look when captured. But even the cruelest joke didn't change the hard line of Sludge's lips. He had failed.

Every jack-booted step through the lava tube tunnel felt as heavy as lead. The torches in the smooth obsidian walls flickered their disapproval. Like Sickhert's eyes. Burning into him.

Sludge came to a halt and blew out an angry breath. "Redbeard will pay." He pointed at the cavern ceiling just inches above his slimy head. "Make the opening here."

Removing a long club from beneath his black cloak, Stench bent down on one knee. When he tapped the ground three times, a hole opened in the floor. Next, he drew a square shape in the air and a wooden trap door appeared overhead.

Sludge slipped a black-bladed dagger from the top of his boot. Using one arm to steady the other, he scratched the ancient symbol into the wood. He stood back and watched the etching swell until a world covered in mud took form.

"It is just as in the beginning," Captain Sludge said reverently, reciting the story all Shadow Swine knew. "Like that glorious time when Kandart smeared water and ash over the cave painting of the first artists."

This act had birthed his race. Now Sludge used this symbol to lay a trap.

And capture two betraying pirates.

Chapter 76

Alex glanced at the rising sun. He suddenly felt terribly tired. And old for his twelve years. With a heavy sigh, he squared his shoulders and sprinted to catch up with the others.

Gwen rolled just a few feet ahead Medusa's shield in hand. Beside her Bartholomew wore that goofy puppy grin he wore whenever he was part of a team.

The two of them looked ridiculous; a Raggedy Anne holding a shield as big as she was, and a white-suited cowboy waving a scimitar in the air like a lasso.

"There they are!" Bartholomew cried pointing across the plaza.

Sure enough, the Barbarossa brothers were crouched behind a bell tower dodging flying arrows.

No more cocky sneers for Redbeard. Now, his mouth twitched as he clung to his brother. He whispered something in Hizir's ear and both made a dash for the nearest street.

Bartholomew gripped his sword tightly and turned to Alex. "Ready, buddy?"

"You know it," Alex replied. Gripping his lance tighter, he took his place on the other side of Gwen who had just hopped off her skateboard.

Gwen lifted her shield and the snake-headed Medusa in its center screeched.

Turning at the Gorgon's caterwaul, Redbeard, grabbed his brother's paisley sleeve and came to a dead stop. Lower lip quivering, his ruddy skin turned as pale as his victims' bones.

But his brother was not so easily frightened. His eyes narrowed. "So, the Deliverers try once again to defeat the Barbarossa Brothers."

"In case you hadn't noticed, we beat you hours ago," Alex said, relishing each word. "And with no ship, nowhere to go, and no help, you are triply beat."

"And now it's time for that shadowy walk over the Bridge of Sighs," Bartholomew said pointing past the Doge's Palace with his scimitar.

"To the *Piombi* Prison, where you'll spend the rest of your days." Gwen smiled, flashing her Halloween braces.

With a conspiratorial glance, the pirates took a step backwards.

"Now!" Redbeard cried. Brandishing a dagger, Hizir drew his arm back. There was an evil glint as the knife whizzed through the air.

Right at Gwen.

Alex tripped. Fell to his knees.

Time seemed to slow. But not like during the creation process. This was like a horror movie with the girl about to die. And all Alex could do was watch.

The blade drew closer.

Gwen raised her shield. There was a loud thwack and one of Medusa's snakes hissed in agony.

In the confusion, the brothers dashed toward Saint Mark's Basilica. Alex started to pursue them when suddenly the Barbarossa brothers disappeared. Headless turbans fluttered but both pirates were gone.

"What the-?" Alex gasped racing forward. But three seconds later skid to a halt just short of a swinging trap door. Alex immediately thrust out his lance to keep his friends from falling into the hole. He started to speak but what he saw next silenced them all.

Two deflated turbans lay on the cobblestones like skinned rabbits. Next to them a wooden door hung from a square hole creaking ever slower with each swing.

Alex bent down and peered below. A rotten egg smell wafted up from the hole. He wrinkled his nose as torch after torch flickered and died underground in the long winding tunnel. Then the screams began, turning Alex's blood to ice.

An eerie voice echoed. "I am Mudlark Maker," it said as Redbeard begged for mercy. "I devour creations."

Redbeard kept squealing, haggling, bargaining, bartering; anything to escape. But Alex knew that it was no good. In moments both brothers would be swallowed by that mud monster. And made into Mudlark zombies. He exchanged a glance with Bartholomew.

His friend shook his head. "They would have been better off in the Piombi Prison."

Alex nodded. Suddenly the shrieks stopped. The ground rumbled as hot gasses spewed from the hole. The trap door closed.

And the Renaissance Nation was safe again.

Chapter 77

Gwen cheered along with everyone else until her cry turned into a long yawn. Man, she was wiped. Not only had she stayed up all night but she hadn't sat down once, skateboarding and fighting the whole time.

She rubbed the cramp that was spasming down her calf.

Leonardo hobbled over to where Alex and Bartholomew were exchanging high-fives.

"You youngsters look like an old anatomy study left in my studio," he remarked with a giggle.

Gwen thrust her fists into her hips. "Is this how you repay us? With insults?"

"But he's right," Bartholomew argued. "You both look like some sort of taxidermy experiment gone wrong."

"Well you don't look like you're ready for the cover of *GQ*, Mr. Clean," Gwen shot back.

Bartholomew glanced down at his soiled and torn slacks and started to laugh. Then he pointed at Alex whose curly hair was sticking up in wild directions.

Gwen made twirling curls with her fingers and guffawed.

"It is time for rest." Leonardo put an arm around the boys' shoulders. "You deserve it. Come, rooms await us in the Doge's Palace."

"Sleeping in a castle doesn't sound too bad." Gwen bobbed her head up and down. "But I don't know, it *is* next to the prison. Alex?"

"What?"

"Can I trust you? Or will I wake up behind bars?"

"Only if you keep making fun of me." Alex hit her playfully with the back of his hand. "Because, in case you hadn't noticed, I am–" He rubbed his knuckles against his t-shirt as if polishing his fingernails. "–one amazing kid."

"Yeah right." Gwen rolled her green eyes and punched him back.

Chuckling, they entered the Doge's Palace for a long-deserved nap.

Chapter 78

The sounds of distant drums woke Bartholomew. Blinking repeatedly, he rolled over in the huge canopied bed and glanced at the checkered pattern on the marble floor. He'd just remembered where he was when scurrying feet and giggling joined the distant music.

Alex rushed into the room and with a flying leap onto Bartholomew's bed. "Get up!"

"Yeah," Gwen hooted, right on his heels. "Wake up sleepy head. It's time to celebrate!" She skipped across the room, vaulted up on the silk bedspread, and began hopping in a circle around him.

Pressing his palms into the mattress, Bartholomew tried to keep from bouncing. "Alright," he groaned. "I'm up. I'm up."

Both of his friends plopped down on either side of him.

"It's over B-3," Alex said. "We did it."

"Cha!" Gwen agreed holding up her hand for a high five.

Bartholomew started to slap her palm, but the redhead snatched it away. "Hey, you–" Bartholomew's words were cut short when they both started jumping up and down again.

He laughed, for the first time in months feeling free. The heavy burden of bad grades, getting caught cheating, and the pirate raid faded away. Dissipating into the rippling folds of the velvet bedspread. He hopped up, chasing his friends around the huge bed until an angry voice stopped him mid-jump.

"What are you doing?" Michelangelo demanded, both fists jammed into his hips.

The frozen trio just stared at first, but then Gwen piped up, "We are celebrating. We saved your land, you know."

"Mah! Perhaps." He glared at them and clucked his tongue. "But as such you could at least respect workmanship. That bed you are jumping on as if engaged in a leaping competition was designed for Doge Gritti hundreds of years ago."

"Umm, sorry sir. We didn't know." Bartholomew apologized scrambling down from the mattress.

"Humph. But, amazingly, you were correct. It is time for a celebration. Venice wishes to honor Mona Lisa's rescuers."

In that moment Leonardo entered. He had a dark robe draped over one arm and held a large bird-like mask with a long-curved nose. Pushing past his old rival, he made his way toward Alex.

"Here are your masks for the Carnivale. I think you will find an, um, hmm interesting, effect when you put them on." Leonardo suppressed a chuckle.

Michelangelo approached Bartholomew with a costume in his own hands. Bartholomew wondered where it had come from. He hadn't noticed it before. But he was too abashed to notice anything with that crotchety man bellowing.

"Don these Deliverer," Michelangelo said holding out a tall sugarloaf hat, a pair of loose pants, and a black mask with a hooked nose. "Quickly. The Renaissance Nation awaits."

Bartholomew took the clown-like pants from Michelangelo and slipped them over his stained slacks. He glanced down at the white fabric ballooning around each leg. Then he slipped his arms into the puffy sleeves and turned to Gwen. "How do I look?"

"Ridiculous. As usual." She lifted her eyebrows twice.

"Thanks."

"Don't mention it."

Alex put the hat on his head and tied the stays on the robe. He shook his head. "This is spooky. Like some sort of reaper."

"Just the opposite." Leonardo chuckled again. "But we will explain shortly. Michelangelo may be gruff, but he is correct when he says that people are waiting." He stroked his long gray beard and grinned broadly at Gwen. "Now for the human girl." Leonardo put two fingers in his mouth for a high-pitched whistle.

Immediately, two painted women in mouthless black masks appeared in the doorway holding some ribbons and a long-ruffled gown between them.

Gwen took one look at it and held up a hand. "No way. I don't do dresses."

"Humans!" Michelangelo raised his arms in exasperation. "Even when it is time to honor them, they argue. Now young lady, the customs of Venice dictate that girls must dress in female costume for Carnivale. Put those on and meet us outside for the celebration."

Bartholomew was surprised that Gwen didn't argue. He guessed that even she couldn't stand up to the old grouch. Instead of retorting, she snatched the dress from the closest woman and started to slip it over her head.

"Hey, it doesn't fit," a wriggling Gwen said when the dress got stuck at her shoulders.

"You might try removing that-," Michelangelo looked her up and down and cleared his throat. "-ensemble."

"But−" she began. But when Michelangelo took a warning step her way, Gwen threw her hands up, told no one to peek, and followed the two masked women behind the silk partition. Next, there was a rustling of cloth followed by the appearance of a t-shirt and some very stained athletic sox thrown over the top of the screen.

"If anybody laughs I'm going to punch him in the nose," Gwen said from behind the partition. A red-slippered toe appeared. "I mean it."

They didn't laugh; they gasped. In place of that scrape-kneed, chopped-hair tomboy stood an elegant young lady. She had on a floor length gown with a tight bodice and wore a lacy apron. Her red hair was tucked up under a floppy beret and a black mask covered the bridge of her nose.

The only thing that made it still look like Gwen was the cuff of her ragged jeans showing just above her slippers. When everyone stared she gave them a sheepish smile and bent over to roll up them up.

Bartholomew couldn't help but admire her perfectly formed chin and pouting lips. If he'd started thinking about girls, which he hadn't, he would have got a full-on crush right then.

"Gwen, you're beautiful," Alex gushed.

"Shut-up. You are making fun of me." She shook her fist.

"He's not," Bartholomew said. "You look like someone in a movie. Like a model or something."

Gwen's nose started its rabbit imitation making her mask twitch up and down. "But I'm not a girly-girl like my mom," she said. "I'm– different."

Leonardo walked up behind her and laid his hands on her shoulders. "Your differences are what saved us. Now, come." He pointed her toward the doorway and gave her a gentle push. Then he looked over his shoulder at Bartholomew and Alex. "Well what are you waiting for?"

The boys exchanged a glance and shrugged. After fitting his mask over his face, Bartholomew surveyed his friend's costume. Alex looked like a cross between a short monk and a vulture. The effect was kind of scary.

Bartholomew wished he had a mirror. He wondered if he looked like a clown. *Of course, they'd give me the goofiest costume. They think I'm a joke.*

Following Leonardo, the group went down the ornate staircase with the gold leaf and stucco figures in the ceiling. The sculptured people above bowed as they passed.

"Thank you, Deliverers," they trilled.

"You're welcome," mumbled Gwen adjusting her black mask for the seventeenth time.

Bartholomew smiled and waved while Alex just stared straight ahead.

Leonardo returned their bows before leading them through a labyrinth of passageways to a huge carved door. "Prepare yourselves," he said resting an ancient hand on the door jam. "Wonders await." He pulled on the iron handle and the door creaked open.

What an understatement. It was more than wonderful; it was a menagerie. White masked men in tricorn hats and black cloaks ate delicacies from silver trays. Ladies in harlequin dresses with variegated colors chatted while men in feathered caps and tights volleyed slingshots filled with perfumed eggs. And everywhere acrobats juggled, and magicians tricked amidst fire-eaters blowing flames overhead.

A chariot lead by clip-clopping stallions parted the crowd. At the reins Apollo wore his own Carnivale costume. He had leaves in his curly hair and his stone body was draped in rough patches of fur. Next to him stood the beautiful Mona Lisa, her gentle smile feeding the crowd.

Apollo turned his steeds toward them and threw his head back with a howl. "Owoo! I am the Wild Man."

"Owoo!" the revelers repeated.

"I represent the joy returning to our land."

"Owoo!" the crowd howled.

"The Deliverers have not only saved our dear Mona Lisa. They have also driven away that scourge on our seas, Redbeard."

The crowd hissed.

Two lightning bolts flashed from above revealing Zeus and Hera floating hand in hand on a fluffy cloud. As they waved, Hermes zipped around them, his winged sandals glowing like fireflies. All three glided to a landing in front of Apollo's chariot.

Now the crowd's cheers grew to a frenzy.

"Let the parade begin!" Zeus thrust a fist upward as Hera beckoned Bartholomew and his friends to join Mona Lisa in Apollo's chariot.

Alex hopped in quickly but Gwen, who usually was a lithe cheetah, stumbled. After tripping over her dress several times, the groaning girl gathered up the skirt and tiptoed into the carriage.

"Loving that dress, huh?" Alex gave her a shove.

Gwen lifted her chin and curled her hand into a fist. "Shut up or the only thing you'll be loving is your one good eye."

Bartholomew adjusted his hat before stepping onto the golden floor. He felt a little shy at first, but when he realized that no one could see him blushing behind his black mask, he puffed up his chest and waved his arms windmill fashion. He was surprised when the throngs threw their heads back in laughter.

Me, making people laugh?

"Apollo advance." Zeus's voice boomed through the crowd.

With a snap of the reins the stallions trotted forward. While the sun god maneuvered them past St. Mark's Square, a winged lion roared at them from his perch on the column above.

Mona Lisa waved, and Apollo howled. Feeling bold, Bartholomew raised an arm in a disco pose much to the delight of the Venetians waving from every window.

Next, more masked revelers joined in their parade while the horses quick-stepped over bridges, pranced across canals, and leaned into sideways gaits through streets. It felt like the entire Renaissance Nation was behind them.

Surprised by how much he enjoyed the attention, Bartholomew waved at the crowd and tipped his sugar loaf hat at the painted ladies in the windows.

"Ha! Take that," he cried tossing a perfumed egg at the *Mattacino* clown capering around them. Splat! It hit the guy's multi-colored tunic and the scent of rosewater filled the air.

Bartholomew breathed it all in with a smile.

Chapter 79

Alex wasn't enjoying leading a parade quite as much as Bartholomew seemed to be. The bird mask was hot and made his face slick with sweat while the wax-covered tunic that covered him from head to toe blocked any breeze. He wanted to rip the whole costume off. But he thought it might offend his Renaissance Nation friends.

And the beak! Ugh. It was filled with strong herbs. Every time he went to take a breath, pungent garlic and rosemary filled his nostrils like Mom's kitchen when she was experimenting with tribal recipes. He may have ribbed her a lot, but he really thought it was cool that his mom cooked up things like Ziggurat pancakes with grasshopper topping.

How was she? Was her heart worse because of what he'd said? Or did she know he had just been mad? Well soon he'd be home and then what? He had no clue what he'd say or do. It seemed that no matter how hard he tried his temper got in the way.

"Hey Alex! Watch this!" Bartholomew cried tossing a perfume-filled egg at the crowd. "What do you think? Should I try out for the baseball team?"

Alex snorted. He thought about teasing Bartholomew but then remembered how that Richie was being pulled out of school anyhow.

"Sure. Why not?"

"Hey, just because I have a dress on doesn't mean you can leave me out of the fun. Give me one of those." Gwen took an egg from Bartholomew, glanced around at the cheering people, and took aim at a fat captain. When it exploded on his big belly she raised a ruffled arm in victory.

* * *

After passing through what felt like every street in Venice, they returned to Saint Mark's Square where a platform had been set up in their absence.

Atop it were all the people they'd met on this journey. Venus stood one arm around Vulcan the other resting on Pico's head. Leonardo and Michelangelo were arguing again while the sculpted David tried to part them with his marble hands. Flanking them, Mars and Athena raised shields in salute. And in the center Zeus and Hera sat on golden thrones, their togas shining in the afternoon sun.

"Whoa, easy now," Apollo said. He pulled back on the reins and shook his wreath crowned head. A single laurel leaf came loose and flew off landing atop Bartholomew's ridiculous sugar loaf hat.

With atypical flair Bartholomew took off his cap and pretended to stare at the leaf. Then with exaggerated motions he jiggled the hat and the leaf fluttered down to his balloon pants. When he brushed it off, it landed on his oversized shoes and he kicked his clown-like feet in the air. As the crowd giggled, Bartholomew did a clumsy cartwheel right out of the chariot.

The crowd loved it; chortling and chuckling as Bartholomew tripped again and again. When the roar of laughter reached its peak, a bronze statue dressed as a peasant girl timidly stepped forward and offered to help him up. He leapt to his feet and bowed dramatically at her.

Alex couldn't believe his eyes. *Who was this stranger?*

Suddenly, Zeus snapped his fingers and the sound of thunder filled the air. "Let the dance begin!" he cried.

In a flash, the organ-playing Landini appeared. The bronze girl led Bartholomew into the square while Mona Lisa held out a finely painted hand for Alex to take. Alex shrugged. He'd never really danced with a girl before. But technically Mona Lisa was a painting, not a girl, so he guessed it didn't count.

He let her lead him out next to where Bartholomew and the peasant girl were waltzing over the tiles. Then awkwardly he grasped Mona Lisa's hands.

"One, two, three. Forward, side, together," Mona Lisa instructed as Alex tried not to step on her dark gown.

To his left Gwen swayed arm in arm with that handsome Apollo. Alex suddenly felt even hotter under his mask. Why did Gwen have that dreamy look in her eyes? Just because Apollo had big muscles?

He shook his head.

Landini's organ grew louder and others joined them in the square. Meanwhile delicious looking dishes were placed on tables at the outskirts of the piazza. Alex's mouth began to water at the sight of such a glorious feast.

"Umm, Mona Lisa?" he asked, slowing his waltz.

"Yes, young one?"

"Could we take a break?" He tilted his beak toward the tables.

"Of course." She gave him a tinkling laugh. "I think Father is waiting for a dance."

Sure enough, Leonardo was on the sidelines; a wide grin splitting his beard. He raised the half mask on a stick to his face and bowed when they glanced over.

Thanking Mona Lisa, Alex dashed over to the table and grabbed a plate. Mouth watering, he surveyed the feast in front of him before piling on the grub. First, he scooped up some translucent meats in salty slices and covered them with caramelized onion. Next, he got big helpings of guinea hen in black pepper sauce and something called *polenta*.

Sitting down at an empty table nearby, he cut off a piece of meat and started to raise the fork to his mouth. Then he realized. Oops. He still had his mask on. Carefully he untied the silk stays and placed it on the ground next to him. The breeze cooled his sweaty face.

Alex hadn't realized how hungry he was until he dug in. Oh yum! He stuffed one bite after another into his mouth, shoveling the food in until his plate was as clean as one of Mrs. Borax's floors. Then he dashed over to the banquet table and piled it high again.

When he returned, Gwen and Bartholomew were opposite each other munching away. Both faced dishes that matched their personalities. Gwen, ever the health nut, had a plate of arugula and radicchio salad topped with olives and raisins. Bartholomew's plate was arranged neatly with bite-sized morsels of stir-fried fegato and zucchini flowers which Alex knew he'd chosen to keep from spilling anything on his clothes.

"Hey Alex, you have to try this," Gwen said holding up a spoonful of whipped fig pudding.

Alex started to lean in for a bite. But when he saw how Gwen's eyes sparkled like sea glass, he froze.

She was beautiful. Unmoving, he gaped at this stranger sitting across the table.

"Earth calling Alex." Bartholomew gave him a shove.

"Huh?" Alex blinked.

Gwen giggled.

"Hello? Are you going to try the *zambaglione* or not? It's a traditional Venetian dish made with egg yolks, cream, and figs. It was often–"

"Okay, okay. I don't need a history lesson." Alex grabbed the spoon from Gwen and gulped it down in a noisy slurp.

"Ooo gross Alex. You'd think you'd have a little more class at a place like this." Gwen wrinkled up her nose.

"You want to see class?"

"Yeah."

"You're sure?"

"Bring it on."

"Alright. You asked for it." Alex sprinted over to the banquet table and scooped up a bowl full of zabaglione. As he strolled back to his friends he slowly stirred the pudding. "Now class, I want you to listen carefully. Whenever you're at a fancy party the first lesson you must learn is *not* to play with your food." He flicked a spoonful at Gwen.

Buttery yellow pudding splattered her face and dress.

"Hey!" Gwen cried wiping the cream from her eyes. She glared at Alex and chucked a fig at him. It bounced right off his wax-covered tunic.

Alex wiggled his ears at her.

Bartholomew leaned forward and gave her a conspiratorial glance. "I do not think he has learned his lesson yet. Perhaps some tutoring?"

Grinning, Gwen pushed away from the table and came around to Alex's side. She stood over him lifting her bowl up and down as if testing its weight. Meanwhile Bartholomew held Alex's arms behind his back.

"Now guys. Think about it. You don't want to do this. We're at a party. Not the beach."

"We don't?" Gwen batted her light green eyes. "Bartholomew?"

"Maybe we shouldn't." Bartholomew smirked.

Alex heaved a sigh of relief.

"Not!" Gwen cried and dumped the entire bowl onto his head.

Alex shook his head to splatter both his friends. At the same time, he scooped up a handful of polenta and ground it into Bartholomew's tie. B-3 cried out and immediately mashed a zucchini flower into Alex's hair. Soon all three were lobbing grapes, pasta, and spinach pie at each other.

Alex had just picked up another handful of rice, when he felt a long stream of water showering down on him.

"What the?" he sputtered, looked up.

Towering over him, the eighteen-foot David, held a bucket in one huge hand. Shaking his head, he poured the rest on Bartholomew and Gwen.

Bellows in hand, a tongue-clicking Vulcan shuffled over and pumped a few puffs of air at them. In a matter of seconds, they were perfectly dry, their costumes as clean as before.

"There," Vulcan said. "Now you are presentable. Follow me."

"Well Bartholomew and I might be, but I don't know about you, Alex," Gwen teased as they climbed the stairs toward Zeus and Hera's thrones.

Alex opened his mouth in retort when a hush fell over in the crowd. The dancers parted for a stooped man.

The dark bronze statue hobbled through Saint Mark's Square as if the weight of the world rested on his shoulders. Every Artanian took off their mask and bowed reverently as he passed.

"Who is that?" Gwen whispered.

"The Thinker, their leader" Alex replied. "He knows everything. All about Bartholomew and me. Why we're here. That we have to complete seven tasks to save Artania."

"Seven?" Gwen raised her eyebrows.

Alex sighed and nodded.

When the Thinker reached them, he extended his bronze hand toward Alex. As he shook it, the boy noticed how soothing the metal was against his skin. Switching Alex's hand to his left, the Thinker grasped Bartholomew's in his right before lifting both in the air.

A resounding cheer rose from the audience.

"Give thanks, Renaissance Nation," The Thinker said in the gravelly voice that Alex always thought had a twinge of sadness.

"The Deliverers have completed the second task. The prophecy is being fulfilled."

"Soothsayer Stone. Soothsayer Stone!" The crowd chanted as one.

Keeping Alex and Bartholomew's arms raised, his noble speech continued. "Yes, as it was foretold:

Our world was born from the magic of two.
The smiling twins whose creations grew.
They painted walls with ideas anew.
Until the dark day we came to rue.
When one jealous hand used mud to undo.
And the life of many too soon was through."

When the Thinker released his hand, Alex bent closer and whispered to Gwen. "He's telling the story of how Artania and the Shadow Swine were born."

The Thinker continued, "*But listen to this prophecy with open ears.*
To know what happens every 2,000 years.
The Shadow Swine will make you live in fear.
Bringing death to those whom you hold so dear."

"We have avenged those lost in battle!" Mars cried raising his spear.

The bronze man nodded then kept speaking.

"*For they will open the doorway so wide.*
That none of you will find a place to hide.
And the creators will stop
As their dreams are drained
Before 12 moons wax and wane."

He placed his steely hands on Alex and Bartholomew's shoulders.

"But hope will lie in the hands of twins
Born near the cusp of the second millennium.
On the eleventh year of their lives.
They will join together like single forged knives.
Their battle will be long with 7 evils to undo.
Scattered around will be 7 clues.
And many will perish before they are through.
But our world will be saved if their art is true."

"Their art was true!" the costumed revelers cried.

"Yes. And now we honor them." The Thinker turned to the gathered gods behind him. "Venus?"

While doves dropped fluttering rose petals, the goddess of love made her way towards them. Then, she gently removed the Gwen's cap.

"Thank you human for your excellence with a crossbow, agility on the rolling chariot, and strength in battle."

"No problem," Gwen said.

"But do not forget your own beauty or that of the Renaissance Nation. Keep this beret as a reminder that you were both brave *and beautiful* in Artania."

Alex was sure Gwen would burst out laughing at this; she hated to be thought of as a girly-girl. But she didn't. Instead her nose twitched, and green eyes grew misty.

Venus blew on the velvet cap which began to shrink until it was small enough to for a mouse. Placing it in Gwen's hand, she curled her fingers around the girl's. "Love and beauty are yours, child."

Gwen curtsied awkwardly.

"Hermes?" The Thinker said after giving them a slight smile. "Come forth."

Ever the showman, the god extended his arms and tilted his head back. The wings on his sandals and helmet fluttered wildly as he rose into the air. Hermes did a loop the loop and landed in front of Bartholomew. While the crowd was still chuckling, he grabbed Bartholomew's mask by the hooked nose and gave it a tug.

It snapped Bartholomew in the face.

"Hey! What did you do that for?" Bartholomew cried.

"Tee hee! To remind you, Deliverer, that playfulness will lighten your load."

Not seeming to know what he was talking about, Bartholomew shrugged.

"Remove your mask and give it to me."

Bartholomew did so.

"This is Pulcinella," Hermes said. "The melancholic dreamer. He coasts through life's problems, a simple poet." Hermes held up the mask with the ridiculously long nose and wrinkled face.

"So, he's nothing like me."

Hermes lifted his chin and his helmet wings fluttered faster. The breeze they made blew back the mask's strings and then, just like Gwen's beret, the Pulcinella began to shrink until it was small enough to fit in Bartholomew's palm. Hermes placed the tip of the mask on one finger and gave it a spin. Twirling and twisting, it rose into the air, flew over their heads, and landed in Bartholomew's open hands.

"When burdens seem too heavy, pull out this clown mask and recall that you once brought laughter and lightness."

The sides of Bartholomew's mouth turned up to a wide grin. He took off his sugarloaf hat and made a sweeping bow for the crowd.

"Pulcinella. Pulcinella," the crowd chanted.

The Thinker held up a bronze hand for silence. "The father of our dear Mona Lisa has his own words."

Leonardo released his arm from around Mona Lisa's shoulders and climbed the stairs of the platform. Stroking his long beard, he smiled down at Alex.

Alex didn't want this. Even though they'd saved her, it had been such great cost. His friends' trust. His belief in himself.

Leonardo's kind smile was almost more than he could bear.

"Pico," He called down and pointed where Alex had been sitting.

The ship's boy scampered over to the table where Alex had left his mask and picked it up in his small painted hands. He scrambled up the stairs and handed it to Leonardo.

"Thanks Pico." Alex grinned at the little curly top.

Pico backed away bowing again and again.

Leonardo turned the mask over in his hands and held it out toward Alex. "Young Deliverer, what did you notice when you donned this costume?"

"It was hot. And stuffy."

"Now that is obvious, tell me more."

"It frightened people. And it smelled."

"Yes. There is good reason we chose such a mask for you. Yours was the Plague Doctor costume. It was a disguise doctors wore when visiting people afflicted with disease. The strong herbs were to overpower any dangerous fumes while its ugliness kept others away."

Alex had no idea where Leonardo was going with this. He was certainly no doctor.

"We give it to you as reminder." He stroked his beard three times and the vulture-like face began to shrink. "As much as you may try to keep others at arm's length and be the lone hero, it is but a mask. Not your true face."

Alex shifted uncomfortably. He knew he shouldn't have locked up Gwen and Bartholomew. But he was trying to protect them! He opened his mouth to protest. "But–"

"Remember," Leonardo cut him off. "You are true when you stand shoulder to shoulder with your celestial twin."

Alex glanced over at Bartholomew who was nodding in agreement.

"And the herbs are a second reminder. That although loved ones may seem to inhale poison, you have the power to fill your lungs with healing perfumes to ease and calm each breath."

Alex thought of Mom and how he worried so much about her that he tensed up every time she was near. Maybe that was why he kept losing his temper. He took the small mask from Leonardo and held it up to his nose, imagining Mom as he took a long fragrant breath. And in his mind's eye she became healthy and whole. He gave a long sigh before looking into Leonardo's soft eyes.

"Thanks."

"No, thank you, young one." Leonardo gave his shoulder a squeeze. "Because of you, my daughter dances in my arms again."

In the square below Mona Lisa gave a twirl and waved.

"Remember your gifts Deliverers," The Thinker said. "You are still needed."

"We'll do our best, won't we, twin?" Bartholomew puffed out his cheeks in a goofy face only Alex could see.

Alex gave him a playful shove. "You know it B-3."

"Find your wonder. Create." The Thinker turned away from them and bowed to the crowd. The Venetians below donned their masks again. "Apollo!" the bronze leader called.

The sun-god threw his head back. "Owoo!" he cried.

"Owoo!" the Venetians repeated.

"Art was true!"

"True!" they echoed.

Apollo was right. When he'd worked side by side with his friends, at long last his art had been true. Alex draped an arm over Gwen and Bartholomew.

"Ready to go home?" he asked.

Bartholomew grinned and said, "Right on dude!"

"Finally," Gwen chimed in.

Alex shook his head and chuckled as they stepped into Apollo's chariot. The handsome god snapped the reins and the fiery stallions began trotting across the square. They rose into the air. Above the waving crowd. Higher and higher. Between the Bell Tower and the Doge's Palace. Over the Venetian canals.

"Goodbye!" they called, as Saint Mark's became a model town below and their friends like toys peppering its streets.

A rainbow shot out of the east, arcing under them. All three of their costumes flew off and fluttered back to Venice. Gwen's hair grew back, and her red slippers were replaced with marked up skater shoes. Bartholomew's white suit brightened until it was just as clean as before.

"Owoo! Keep your art true!" Apollo hooted as both he and the chariot faded away.

"Oh, we will," Alex said, stroking the Plague Doctor mask with an index finger.

"You know it twin." Bartholomew pointed to their feet.

Three pairs of legs were draped in color. Riding faster and faster over that shining rainbow.

That carried them back.

To the real world.

THE END

Dear reader,

We hope you enjoyed reading *Artania - The Kidnapped Smile*. Please take a moment to leave a review in Amazon, even if it's a short one. Your opinion is important to us.

Discover more books by Laurie Woodward at https://www.nextchapter.pub/authors/laurie-woodward-childrens-fiction-author

Want to know when one of our books is free or discounted for Kindle? Join the newsletter at http://eepurl.com/bqqB3H

Best regards,
Laurie Woodward and the Next Chapter Team

The story continues in:

Artania - Dragon Sky by Laurie Woodward

To read the first chapter for free, head to:
https://www.nextchapter.pub/books/dragon-sky-fantasy-adventure

About the Author

Laurie Woodward is a school teacher and the author of the fantasy books: *The Artania Chronicles*. Her *Artania: The Pharaohs' Cry* is the first children's book in the series. Laurie is also a collaborator on the award-winning Dean and JoJo anti-bullying DVD *Resolutions*. The European published version of Dean and JoJo for which she was the ghost writer was translated by Jochen Lehner who has also translated books for the Dalai Lama and Deepak Chopra, In addition to writing, Ms. Woodward is an award winning peace consultant who helps other educators teach children how to stop bullying, avoid arguments, and maintain healthy friendships. Laurie writes her novels in the coastal towns of California.

Why do I write? I get to be a kid again. And this time the bully loses while the quiet kid wins. Also, I get to have awesome battles with wings and swords, while riding a skateboard.

Why did I write Artania? Several years ago when education changed to stress test score results over everything else, I began to think of art as a living part of children that was being crushed. But I have watched children create and discover the wonder inside. To me, Shadow Swine represent bullies who subdue that most beautiful part of children.

"Our world will be saved when their art is true," the Artanian Prophecy says. Every year I tell my students how every sketch, painting, or sculpture instantaneously becomes a living being in

Artania. Then I stand back as they hurriedly scribble a creature, hold it up, and ask, "Was this just born?"

"It sure was," I reply with a smile. "You just made magic."

And for that cool moment, they believe.

Books by the Author

Artania: The Pharaohs' Cry
Artania II: The Kidnapped Smile
Artania III: Dragon Sky

Lightning Source UK Ltd.
Milton Keynes UK
UKHW021056021120
372650UK00004B/856